Once a Princess

Look for these titles by
Sherwood Smith

Now Available:

The Trouble With Kings

Sasharia en Garde! Series
Once a Princess (Book 1)
Twice a Prince (Book 2)

Once a Princess

Sherwood Smith

A Samhain Publishing, Ltd. publication.

Samhain Publishing, Ltd.
577 Mulberry Street, Suite 1520
Macon, GA 31201
www.samhainpublishing.com

Once a Princess
Copyright © 2009 by Sherwood Smith
Print ISBN: 978-1-60504-170-4
Digital ISBN: 978-1-60504-048-6

Editing by Anne Scott
Cover by Anne Cain

First Samhain Publishing, Ltd. electronic publication: June 2008
First Samhain Publishing, Ltd. print publication: April 2009

Dedication

To M. She knows why.

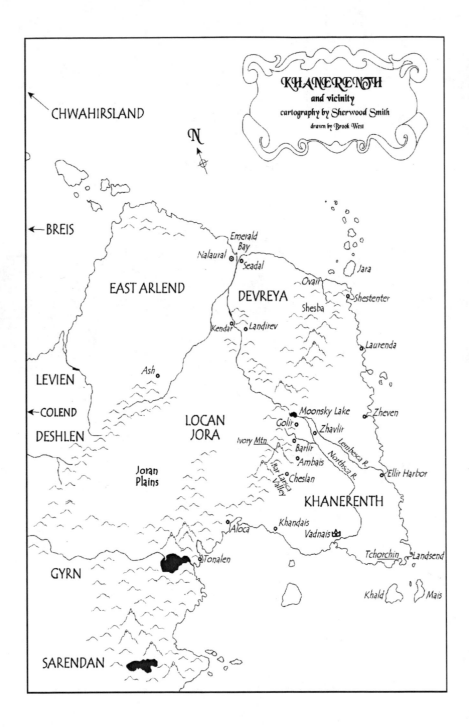

Chapter One

The rap, rap, rap at the front door beat a counter-rhythm to the rapping in my skull.

I sighed, sat up and realized I didn't have anything on as the typical January Los Angeles heat wave had given us a ninety-degree morning. Rap-rap-RAP! They weren't going to go away. So I pulled my bedspread around me, and my hair swung down over it like a neo-pre-Raphaelite cloak as I lurched out of my bedroom, kicking aside a train of gold silk fringe at each step.

Mentally preparing some sizzling remarks, I yanked open the front door. Instead of somebody begging money for some weird cult or a door-to-door sales scammer, a pair of older men faced me expectantly, one short and stocky, one tall and lean. Not American men, oh no. Their clothes didn't fit them right, they didn't stand with the slump-shouldered bend I was used to in L.A. guys, and their eyes were pinkish at the rims in reaction to the smog. I knew that because once, years ago, I had come from pure, clean air to the smog-clogged heat of Los Angeles, though that had not been the sole reason my eyes had been red.

"What," I snapped, my body tensing. I almost lost my grip on the brocade coverlet, and shoved my hair behind me.

Both of them stared at the coverlet. The one's eyes widened, the other's jaw slackened. They were not staring at me in it, they were looking at the pattern of firebirds chasing up and down intertwined vines with little white flowers—queensblossom, it was called.

And it doesn't grow anywhere on Earth.

One of the men exclaimed, "Sasharia Zhavalieshin?"

I hadn't heard my real name for many years. "Wrong house."

"You have a look of your father," the other man promptly replied in a very strong accent—one I had worked hard to get rid of all those years ago.

Again an exchange of glances, and one of them said, with a furtive air, "We come with an offer."

"A fabulous offer." The other peeked furtively left and right as though spies lurked in the palm trees and parked cars. "One might say, of magical proportion..."

"Wait a minute, wait a minute," I cut in. "So you're trying to tell me that there's tremendous treasure waiting for me?"

Both heads nodded.

"If I take up a cause, one that includes deep magic?"

Vehement nodding.

"And perhaps an ancient castle full of sinister secrets?"

"Yes!"

"And all for truth, justice and honor?"

"Yes, yes!"

My anxiety flared into anger.

"Oh no you don't," I snarled. "I've been there, done that, and they don't even give you T-shirts."

"Tee—"

"Shirts?"

10

"Let me make it plain. N-O, which in English—the language you are using now—means no mystery offers, no fantastic treasure, no magic and especially no causes. They hurt too much!"

And I slammed the door.

That is, I tried. One put his foot out, and the door thumped into it. He gave a muffled "ooof", his eyes watering, and the tall gray one glanced back over his shoulder yet again. Still no one there, if you didn't count the string of tightly parked cars belonging to the other tenants of the apartment buildings on my street, and their roommates, boyfriends, girlfriends and whoever else could crowd in.

He turned back to me. "We must discuss your father. May we enter?" Now he didn't even speak English.

And though I hadn't heard *that* language since I was a child, I understood it. Its cadences, the clear, almost singsong vowels after the flat affect of American English evoked so powerful a memory my arm tightened to slam the door in their faces. My throat hurt. "Is he dead? Just tell me. Yes or no."

"Please." The tall one held out his hands. "We must discuss your—your inheritance."

My heart gave one of those knocks against the ribs that echoes through body and soul with fear confirmed. With the pain of regret.

The younger one said quickly, "That is, we do not know for certain that he is dead, and that is why we—"

So they don't know either. I pointed past their shoulders. "Whoa, the Winged Victory of Samothrace!"

As they hadn't read *Bored of the Rings*, they peered skyward, shifting their weight as they did so.

This time I got the door to slam.

11

They pounded, of course, and I half expected them to blast it inward with magic—then realized that if they could have, they already would have. Magic, so untrustworthy on Earth, was on the ebb. They probably had just enough access to whatever magical energy was floating over L.A. to return through the World Gate.

So I hotfooted back to my room and slammed that door too.

I flung myself onto my bed, which sloshed and undulated, but even pulling the pillow over my head didn't shut out the fact that at last, at last, after all these years, what my mother had warned me about had come true.

They'd found me. Had they found Mom?

"Argh," I croaked, my sleep-deprived brain finally catching up, and I sat up again, so sharply my head swam in a different direction than the water bed undulated. "Oooogh." My insides lurched along with the sloshing water.

But I ignored that too and reached for my cell phone, which I'd turned off before work the night before, and hadn't turned back on as my shift had ended at 3:30 a.m. I flipped it open, and saw about a hundred calls from Mom. Uh-oh.

She answered on the first ring. "Darling?"

"Mom?"

"Sash! Oh babe, I am so relieved," she exclaimed, as if a month hadn't gone by between our last fight and now. But then it was always that way. After we cooled off we were too glad to hear the other's voice to continue whatever fight had sent me stomping off—Mom's words usually echoing behind me, *You're too much like your father: stubborn, dream-driven, won't compromise—*

"Mom—"

"Sasha." I could hear her breathe. "*They found me.*"

"You too?"

"You—*you* too?" she said, her voice too high with anxiety for either of us to laugh at the echo.

"Two old guys. Something about Dad and an inheritance. I slammed the door in their faces. Mom, he isn't, like, dead, is he? They wouldn't tell me. Or is it the Merindars, and some sort of trick?"

She heaved a shuddering sigh. "I don't know, *chiquita.* The one I got was young, and he isn't any Merindar, unless Canary has mellowed in his old age. If he's aged."

Canary was our private name for Canardan Merindar, usurper to the throne of Khanerenth, on the world Sartorias-deles. It had once been a funny name, meant to ease my fears while we were on the run, back before we'd lost everything but one another.

Mom said urgently, "Look, I don't want to get into this stuff on the phone. It's way too heavy-duty, and I don't know what they can or can't do with magic and phones. Meet me...at the old place. Okay?"

"Why not at your house? You've got those security guards and everything—"

"And they got past. Roger's in the middle of getting our tickets, and we are gonna beat feet. But first I needed to talk to you." Her voice roughened, and I knew she'd been worried sick.

Filled with remorse, I nodded, remembered she couldn't see me, and said, "Give me five."

In about a minute and a half, I'd dressed, grabbed my travel bag and was out the door.

"Five" in L.A. traffic is likelier to mean five hours than minutes. An hour later, I'd inched my way across town through the morning commuter traffic to the street we'd first lived on when we blasted back through the World Gate with nothing more than the clothes we wore, a jumble of jewels and keepsakes wrapped in my firebird bedspread, and each other.

My mother drove up from the opposite direction seconds after I arrived in my battered old car. She had the door open almost before she'd turned the engine off. Heads turned on the street as we flung ourselves into the other's arms. Even in L.A. you don't often see a couple of women close to six feet tall hugging—one blond and elegant in hand-tailored haute couture clothes, the other in old jeans and a tee, a hawk's beak of a nose, and butt-length, wildly curly honey-colored hair.

"Sorry, sorry," I muttered into her linen-covered shoulder.

"Sorry, darling," she whispered into my hair.

We backed up to draw breath, caught some smiles and curious glances from people on the sidewalk watching, and remembered why we'd come—I could see it in her face as clearly as I was thinking it.

We looked around guiltily for lurking magical spies as we crossed the dusty L.A. street, Mom whirling to beep her car locked. I didn't bother. No one would want to steal mine, even if they could get it running.

Our "place" was an old fifties diner that miraculously hadn't been axed when the rest of the Bean Fields at the bottom of Sepulveda and Centinela had sprouted into the Hughes Center. We headed toward a corner table, settling our chairs so that our backs were to the wall and two exits in sight.

Mom hadn't forgotten Dad's training. She'd been on the run for several of my childhood years. What for me had been training had become habit for my mother, the idealist hippie "performance art" chick who met a prince from another world, crossed with him back to his world. Dad had never tried to fool her into thinking a "happily ever after" awaited them. There were problems at home, and one of the reasons Dad had left to visit Earth was to think about them, and perhaps to learn how to cope. But my mother had always believed in good causes— even if her prince looked a lot like Harpo Marx.

She said, "This kid came. Young. Your age, I'd think."

I nodded. Comparing in years was almost meaningless between a world with 365 days and one with 441 days.

"He told me your father had set something or other up, some spell. If he wasn't heard from in ten years, they were to activate this spell, and it eventually led to us."

She didn't say *I told you so.* She never did, and I had learned not to either. Our last fight had been over my reluctance to move yet again. We'd run every year since we'd first arrived, after Gramma died. We always returned to some part of L.A. School after school, town after town, getting used to new kids, new rules, new clothes and slang and styles— grammar school, middle school, high school, college. I'd finally rebelled, declaring I would stay in L.A. and go to graduate school. I'd been grimly slogging my way from work to school ever since, but I had yet to learn to make and keep friends. I got along with everyone I worked with. I just never got close.

She sighed. The waitperson behind the counter called out, "Moira."

Mom got up to fetch our drinks. When she sat, I hunched over my latte, stirring in sugar.

"Moira?" I asked.

"My latest name." She made a face. "And yes, they found me anyway."

I didn't say *Told you so* either.

She sighed. "Okay. Roger is getting you a ticket as well. I

kept hoping you'd call, and I was going to wait until the last minute."

"Where are you going?"

"New York." That had been our last destination. She added defensively, "Sash, we can get lost in New York City better than anywhere else."

"We can't in *L.A.*?" I waved a hand. "All right. Consider the argument already done, me saying how much I hate running, you with the anonymity, me hating fake names and faker people, you with safety, and me with the fact that we're probably never going to be safe. It looks like we're unfinished business for those guys, and when it comes to tech versus magic, guess who wins?"

"Over there? Magic. But here?" She shrugged. "We've got tech on our side."

"Tech wins only if there's an ebb in the magic. Or a cold spot, or whatever they'd call it. Anyway, they did find us. And even if we run again, those guys are smart enough to find their way to tech if they want us bad enough."

She pushed our cups aside and gripped my hands. Tears slipped down her cheeks as she studied my palms. "You've got strong hands. That was about all I could give you, when your father disappeared." She met my eyes. "But I am afraid. For us both. They can't be tracking us for anything good. If it was good news, your father would come himself. I would rather have you with me."

"Mom, I'd like to stay with you too. Nothing better. Heck, I even like Roger, even if he does tend to bore on about the stock market."

She smiled faintly, looking young and old at the same time. Vulnerable—though I loathe that word. Kittens are vulnerable. Orchids are vulnerable. When something wants to hurt me, I want to kick its butt from here to Mars.

"Mom, I'm going to stay. I don't see any difference between New York and L.A. for hiding in. Except I can hide better here since I know L.A. But really, I just don't want to run any more."

"We ran in fear fifteen years ago," Mom said. "Sasha, we're not running from shadows. They are *here*."

"Oh, I'll move. I'll go back to using Gramma's last name, but that's it. I have at least a semblance of a life for the first time. I like my studies, I like my sport. I think I might maybe even learn how to make friends. So I'm staying. If they try to come after me, I know this ground, I'm going to stand and fight."

She held my hands so hard that I had to flex them so her grip wouldn't hurt. Despite her tears, her elegant, poised appearance, it was obvious she'd stayed in shape too.

She sighed and wiped her eyes on the sleeve of her expensive jacket. "Okay. Like you say, you're good at taking care of yourself. Better than I ever was. There is half your father in you—" Her voice suspended again. We didn't have to say it. We were both thinking, *But he disappeared.*

I pointed at her, thumb up and finger out—the Mick Jagger point-and-shoot she'd used ever since I was little. "Time to go back and pack. I hated that apartment anyway."

Chapter Two

Two weeks later, there I was asleep again, after another night shift. Same time, same weather, same bed—but this time I did not live alone, I had roommates. The apartment was located in Venice instead of West L.A. Fewer palm trees, more sea breeze, otherwise the same close-packed strings of cars out front, same rows of buildings with the ever-present TVs flickering in windows.

The rap at the front door made me bury my head into my pillow. I was sliding back into my dream involving guns, squealing tires and tomato sauce with oregano, when a knock at my bedroom door startled me.

I jerked upright. "What?"

Leslie, my coworker and new roommate, opened the door and popped her head in. "Sorry, Sasha. Some suit asking for you."

"Suit?"

She shrugged, her beaded dreads swinging and clicking as she glanced over her shoulder, and back at me. "Suit. Tie. Briefcase. Something about legal papers."

A lawyer? Asking for me? This did not sound good. *Take-out delivery lawyer service has to cost a C-note a minute*, I thought. But out loud I thanked her for the heads-up.

Once again I surged up from the water bed and yanked my summer duvet around me. Not the beautiful one. That was now packed at the bottom of my closet in my old karate-gear carryall. This duvet was a gen-yoo-wine cheapo in five garish colors, one hundred percent synthetic Earthwear.

I hadn't unbraided my hair from my work shift, so my braids fell around my shoulders, all six of them, with curly wisps trying to escape; the effect, to my eyes, looked like I'd stuck my fingers in a light socket. Oh well. This was not any visit I'd asked for.

When I entered the living room, the mixed smell of simmering spaghetti sauce and stale marijuana toxins slugged me in my empty middle. The pounding I'd thought was in my head resolved into the boom-crash-screech of an action movie on the TV. So that explained the dream.

The sauce smell drifted in from the kitchen, pungent with fresh oregano. The toxins were from Dougie, a long, lanky guy in a filthy T-shirt and jeans. He lay in the middle of the living room, looking at some book called *How to Make a Million off the Internet* as he smoked his doob. The TV blared unwatched across the room.

Marcie, whose name was on the lease, had to rent out the extra bedrooms in order to scrape together enough cash to support this slob—nobody at the restaurant could figure out why. As they say, love is blind. In this case, blind, deaf and dumb. *Especially* dumb.

Dougie spewed another cloud before greeting me. "Hiya, Sasha." The greeting was accompanied by a leer down my body. I clutched the duvet tighter.

"Dougie." I left off the "hi" or "good morning" or any other word that he could possibly interpret as an invitation to hit on me. Not that that would stop him—as long as Marcie wasn't around.

Leslie jerked her thumb at the visitor and then vanished into the kitchen, firmly shutting the door on Dougie's personal smog bank.

I turned to the front door. There stood a young guy in a suit, carrying a legal briefcase. He looked ordinary enough: pleasant face, wavy brown hair pulled back into a ponytail, dark brown eyes, brown skin. Obviously startled by my height. I don't hold that against anyone—I *am* tall. Not a surprise when you come from two tall parents of spectacular make and model.

"Sasha...Muller?" He looked doubtfully down at his paper and up at me again. We were eye to eye.

His using my Gramma's last name was reassuring. "My mother sent you?"

An explosion whacked our ears as Dougie decided it was time to play some trash metal for the entire West Coast of North America.

"Just to sign some papers," the guy said—or I thought he said, not being very practiced at lipreading.

"Why didn't Mom call me?"

He looked puzzled, cupping his hand to his ear.

Now what to do? Take him somewhere else, obviously, but not while I was practically naked. I couldn't just leave him. Dougie was quite capable of grilling him with nosy questions, and I didn't want this suit thinking Dougie had any right to the answers.

So I jerked my thumb toward the inside door and led the way over Dougie's legs back down the hall to Leslie's room. I hoped she wouldn't mind for five minutes.

I stayed long enough to see him perch carefully on the single chair, and dashed to my own room. I picked up my cell, speed-dialed Mom—to get her answering machine. So I thrashed into some clothes, choosing my most comfortable jeans and my *Got Books?* T-shirt. I braided my six braids into one big one, shoved my feet into my sandals, tried Mom again and got the machine. I waited for the beep. "Mom, call me? You sent some lawyer, or was that Roger?"

There. That took care of it. Right? I frowned at the doorknob as if it had become the Great Doorknob of Power, but two hours of sleep prevented me from getting any vibes about what I'd forgotten.

So I turned around, surveying my room. About the only furniture I owned was my water bed, my one indulgence, because it reminded me of my hammock when I was a kid on board a ship with Dad and Mom. But in Los Angeles, hammocks caused too many questions, and I had learned to compromise with things that raised no questions. Water beds raised no questions.

Everything else was garage-sale rejects, or survival stuff like clothing. I had gotten into the habit of always choosing things for practicality and invisibility.

There was another equally strong habit, being ready to jettison everything and run. I set my cell on my bed and reached into my closet for the gear bag I'd mentioned before, which contained my few important items. It went with me to work every day. Figuring a lawyer might need to look at my legal stuff, I hitched the bag over my shoulder, then eased the door open.

The walls reverberated with Dougie's thrash noise, jarring my teeth and bones. I whizzed across to Leslie's room and threw open the door, braced for action...to find the lawyer guy sitting where I'd left him, his briefcase on his knees, his brown eyes tilted up toward me in question.

"Okay." I shut the door. "What've ya got?" The screeching noise diminished to the mindless thud, thud, thud of elementary percussives.

The young man opened the briefcase and sorted through his papers.

"Several items of import," he murmured, the thump of the distant synthesizer drums and the hiss and rattle of his papers muffling his voice.

Import. Did he have an accent? Hispanic, maybe?

"Here."

He held out a sheaf in one hand and a pen in his other, his manner earnest—maybe nervous. Like he wanted to get this done and get out. Who could blame him, with that noise pounding our brains?

"Can you give me a quick overview on what this stuff is?" I was thirsty, hungry and functioning on under two hours of sleep.

"Yes." He stood and obligingly turned so that the papers were not upside down. "Here." He held them under my nose.

I bent to peer at the print. Just as I registered what appeared to be an old rental agreement, five fingers closed hard on my arm. My muscles tightened to whip off a forearm block, light flashed—

—and my body turned inside out, my bones snapped like rubber bands, my head exploded—

Then it all reversed.

Though it had been many years since I'd been wrenched between worlds, I knew instantly what had happened: I'd been thrust through a World Gate.

I dropped with a splat on a tiled floor, gasping for breath. The lawyer plopped next to me, the briefcase spilling the papers out. He groaned as he struggled to sit up. As I tried to recover my wind-scattered wits, I stared at the papers. They were flyers for local sales, a couple of rental signs and—

"You're a fake." I glared at the guy, who ran a shaky hand through his hair, which had jarred loose from the ponytail. Then, as a few more wits moseyed back, "Of course you're a fake. What could be more unmagical than a lawyer?" Hadn't Mom said a young man had come to her? *About your age.* "Well, this is *totally* craptastic. I can't believe I fell for that."

The guy grimaced, rubbing his temples. He looked confused and upset, and a lot younger than I'd first thought. He probably wasn't much more than twenty. "I feel sick."

"Good," I snarled. "I'm so glad your rotten spell gave you the world's worst smackdown."

"Gate...very edge of its reach."

I sighed, disgusted with myself. I'd been braced for the old guys, or if not them, some sinister geezer like Saruman—one glance and I would have slammed the door in his face. But a young, cute guy with puppy-dog brown eyes wearing a tie and a L.A. liberal ponytail, toting a briefcase and talking about legal papers had completely suckered me.

Stupid! I wanted to stomp and yell, but I didn't have enough energy for that, so I settled for a snarky question. "I take it you're one of Canary Merindar's goons?"

We were still speaking English, though his translation spell would probably wear off soon. He winced again, frowned, mouthed the word *goon*, and flushed. "I am not!"

"Only Merindar," I said with false cordiality, "would be slimy and disgusting enough to force me against my will, without my permission, without warning, through that blasted World Gate."

He gulped in air and scrambled to his feet, leaving the

briefcase lying on the magic-transfer Destination tiles. "Emergency. They were right behind us." He pointed at the tiles. "Come on, we've got to go."

"Home." I sat where I was. "Now."

The ex-lawyer tugged impatiently at the tie. "How can men wear these things in your world? I feel like I am strangling. No, you are not understanding. If I take you back, Canardan Merindar's mages will get you. They had a tracer out, and after we performed the ten-year spell your father asked us—"

"So why are you any better? Anyway, I don't believe that about my father. Those two old guys mentioned him too. Going for the ol' sentimentality, pretend you're from my dad? No chance, Lance."

"Lance?" He looked around, as if weapons had sprouted somewhere in the little chamber. The English spell seemed to be fading.

"The point is, I don't recall anyone asking my permission to bring me here." I hugged my bag to me.

By now my other senses were waking up, and the smell of the air coming in the high windows, the sight of stone walls, even the rich colors—so much more vivid than those in L.A.—all made my throat hurt and my eyes sting.

I don't do sorrow well. It makes me surly.

"I—" He flapped a hand, shook his head and opened the single door. "I believe I had better let you talk to Elva." He was now speaking in Khani, the old language, which I had not used for years.

And, like I said before, I had not forgotten a word.

He lurched dizzily through the door, throwing the tie in one direction and the suit jacket in another, leaving me staring through the doorway at a young woman about my age who was pacing impatiently. As the guy launched clothes right and left, the female stopped, gaping from him to me.

"You *found* her?" she asked in Khani. "Oh, well done, Devli." Another fast, puzzled glance. "Ah, which one is she?"

"The daughter. Grown up." The kid—Devli—vanished behind a folding screen painted with a highly stylized series of raptors in flight against a starry sky. Grunts and rips from behind the screen indicated he was getting rid of the last of his Earth clothes as fast as he could.

I shifted my attention back to the female, who had to be Elva. She was dressed in a homemade shirt and trousers, her brown hair wrapped up on her head. Her dark eyes, so much like the guy's, were quirked in puzzlement as she studied me.

"Send. Me. Back." I tried hard to sound polite. "Please."

"Why?" Devli shouted from behind the screen. "When we tracked you down, it was to discover you were not living as a queen and princess should—"

Anger burned through me. "And when I was last here," I interrupted, "the would-be queen and princess were running for their lives, grateful for stale bread and eating it with one eye to the door that might come crashing in. My waitress life might not be prestigious, but it didn't include any weapons or death threats."

Elva flexed her hands. "But—"

"And I am not a princess," I added, more quietly. "Sounds to me like Canary is still king. My father is dead, near as I can tell."

Elva said on a hopeful note, "But we have not determined that your father is dead."

"Either a person is dead or is not dead," I retorted. All these years of wondering, and there still was no answer.

25

"Or is missing—"

Voices shouted from somewhere outside. Elva whirled around.

I scrambled up, still woozy from the world transfer, and staggered out of the Destination chamber into a bigger room. The walls were stone, the floor as well. I was obviously in a castle. Moss-splotched stone walls, arrow-slit windows down one side with age-darkened, rotting tapestries between them, and two huge, very dusty, spider-webbed tables testified to a place abandoned for an appreciable length of time.

"Devli." Elva dashed across the room toward the farther table. "I hear trouble."

"Coming!" Devli squawked, amid increased sounds of frenzied dressing.

She turned back to me. "You need more seemly clothing."

"These are seemly where I come from. And if you send me back, they'll continue to be seemly."

She frowned. "Did I misspeak? You attract attention dressed thus, and it were better if—"

She halted at the ring of iron-shod boot heels outside the main door.

Devli hopped out a second later, trying to fix the ties of a greenweave shoe. Elva reached the table. She picked up a rapier and a saber, tossed the latter to Devli, who let go of his shoe just in time to catch the weapon with both hands.

"Hey," he protested. "That almost knocked me in the head."

"No loss," Elva cracked, and I knew then they were brother and sister. "Now pick up those outlandish other-world clothes, lest you want to signal to every villain within a day's ride where you were."

As she nagged, she picked up the tie and the coat and

tossed them to him. He bundled them with the other things into a kind of knapsack, which he slung round behind him. "Table," he said to her.

Together they sprang to the closer table and shoved it against the wooden door about two seconds before the latch rattled. A muffled curse prefaced thumping and kicking.

My two hours of sleep left me struggling to catch up. "Wait—"

"This way." Elva used her sword to flick up the single tapestry on the inner wall.

Her gesture sent up billows of dust. She sneezed.

"Why should I follow you?" I demanded.

Devli said, "It's either us or King Canardan. I am afraid there is no choice left."

Canary? I'd already made one big mistake. I did not want to risk another. I crowded behind Elva and Devli into the narrow passageway previously hidden behind the tapestry.

An ancient magical glowglobe, dim enough to shed faint light, revealed a narrow, mossy corridor.

Elva had pressed against the wall, and when I passed, she closed in behind me. Except for our breathing and footsteps we were silent as we dashed down the passage, which abruptly jolted right. Another ancient glowglobe revealed a steep, cramped spiral stairway.

We shuffled down into darkness. All three of us trailed fingers against the mossy wall to guide us as there was no handrail. Ech. I was glad of my sandals. The stair moss was even worse than the walls.

Devli thumped into a solid door just before we heard a distant *wham!* from the upstairs room we'd left a minute ago. Devli yanked the iron-reinforced door open. Sudden light blinded us when we galumphed through a stone archway into a courtyard.

Elva pushed past me and led the way, sword up, looking around quickly. "Come on—" she began, motioning toward what seemed to be a stable from the smell emanating from the open door.

A stream of guys in brown battle tunics blasted through another stone archway in the wall adjacent to ours. A few waved rapier-sabers, and several wielded heavy straight swords. These had to be Canary's henchminions.

Devli scrambled in front of me, taking up position beside his sister. The men fanned out, moving in slowly. Some gave me puzzled looks.

Someone barked out a short command. The henchminions raised their swords, some upright, others holding the points outward. A couple waved their swords vaguely. Both those swords looked awfully tarnished.

Devli and Elva valiantly tried to drive the warriors back, but they were outnumbered and not well trained. Neither were the henchminions. From the caution with which they circled in, trying to get past Elva's and Devli's frantic sword swinging, it was clear the orders were to "take" and not "kill" or we'd have been sliced and diced.

Still, the siblings retreated. I also retreated, my bag clutched tightly to me. I was trying to think past my headache—and coming up with nothing because I had no idea where we were, who anyone was. I had no weapons, no sleep, and worst of all, no caffeine to boot the brain.

Just then a cry from across the courtyard caused the leader of the patrol to yell, "Out here!"

Great. Reinforcements.

The henchminions grinned, some relaxing, others

brandishing weapons expectantly. Their leader said to Devli and Elva, "Put your weapons down."

"Not likely," drawled a voice from the archway behind us.

I whirled around. A tall guy sauntered into the courtyard, sword in one hand, long knife in the other. Neither weapon looked tarnished.

Devli sighed, shutting his eyes briefly. "The pirate."

"Pirate? *Pirate?*" I repeated, trying not to twitter. "Pirates I *read* about. I never wanted to *meet* any—"

No one was paying me the least heed. Elva and Devli gripped their weapons with renewed determination, though they didn't seem to know where to attack first.

"Come along," the pirate invited the henchminions, waving his knife to and fro as he passed me by with no more than a glance. "Come on, men! Here's your chance for glory!"

Canary's goons sprang to the attack.

The pirate wore a fringed black bandana, a gold hoop in one ear, a crimson woolen vest over a billowy shirt like those worn by the siblings, only the pirate's shirt had been dyed robin's-egg blue. The vest was both sashed (lime green) and belted. Full black trousers, high blackweave riding boots. I wondered, despite the danger and my headache and everything else, is there, like, a pirate code, where they have to dress like that? I kinda thought pirates, you know, didn't do rules.

Despite his severe lack of fashion sense, the pirate's fighting style left the siblings in the dust. He broke the front patrol line, leaving Elva and Devli to deal with the outer two warriors. Then, as the newcomers spread slowly out, stepping warily, he glanced back once.

"That her?" A brief head-to-toe from light-colored eyes, set well apart.

"Yes," Elva gasped, wiping her brow on her sleeve.

"Useless, eh?" the pirate commented, not missing a beat as he disarmed two of the brown guys.

"We only had weapons for us—" Devli began. A knife, hitherto hidden in the boot top of the patrol leader, thunked into his arm. "Oooh," Devli finished, staggering back.

Elva sprang to her brother's aid.

I hadn't meant to help anyone. I mean, nobody was on my side as far as I could see. But that "useless" comment stung.

"The invitation didn't include swords." Anger smacked away the last of the headache.

I slung my bag behind my shoulder and picked up a rapier dropped by one of the guys the pirate had wounded. I hopped over the guy, who lay groaning, rocking back and forth with a hand at his bleeding shoulder. These rapier-sabers were heavier than the fencing saber back on Earth, but far lighter than the clumsy straight swords.

Straight swords can break a rapier—if they connect. Rapiers are fast. Especially if one knows how to use them.

Ah, there was another. I picked it up as well, and as three men charged at me, whirled both blades around experimentally. Yep, heavier, but good reach and a nice snap to the steel.

Fencing for sport has strict rules. My father had explained to me when I was a child that dueling was also hemmed by rules, but warfare wasn't, a piece of advice that my mother and I had minded when seeking extra training in martial arts. Which also has rules. Different ones, though.

So I used the two blades, the dust on the old flagstones, roundhouse kicks and a fallen cloak all to advantage, pinking all three in under a minute. It was apparent their training was at best rudimentary—counting on numbers—whereas I was hungry, angry, unpadded, and oh yeah, had been competing on fencing teams for the past ten years. Fencing—and winning trophies. Only my fear of publicity had kept me from doing anything professional with it.

And so I ended up fighting next to the pirate as the rest of the attackers came at us, this time with no hesitation. The pirate flicked a smile in my direction and whacked an attacker over to me.

I returned the compliment a moment or two later by tripping one, who lunged at Captain Color-Challenged, took a slice across one arm and a pink in the other arm, and retired from the lists. I didn't kill anyone—I was far too squeamish for that—but noticed that the pirate only wounded as well, taking them with practiced precision out of the fight, but not out of life.

I was breathing hard and sweat ran down into my eyes when the news clue-sticked me that there were no more attackers. They sat or lay, most groaning, some bemused. There were fewer than I'd first seen. A bunch of 'em had prudently found business elsewhere.

The pirate put his point down and leaned on it. "Sasharia Zhavalieshin?"

"No, Snilch Gritchpea," I said crossly, trying unsuccessfully to wipe the sweat from my eyes, but my arm was as sweaty as my face. "I'd like to go home now."

Devli claimed our attention by swaying, then falling face down. Elva knelt and sniffed. "Pepper-poison!" she cried.

And, despite the many years since I had breathed this world's air, there in my mind was the spell my father had taught me. Before I could think I'd muttered it. On Earth, for a time, I'd practiced my father's spells, but they'd never worked, or barely gathered magic. Here, a sudden surge of power ran through me and zapped over Devli in a faint, coruscating light. He sat up, gasping.

Devli and Elva stared at me.

The pirate gave me a pensive smile. "And you want to remain on a world where there's no magic?"

"Well, at least they have aspirin," I muttered. The backlash of powerful magic hit me. I sank to the ground and put my head on my knees.

Chapter Three

"We have listerblossom steep." Elva sounded subdued.

Steep was tea, that I remembered from childhood. Listerblossom, my mother had once told me, was probably related to willow. It was remarkably effective as a fever-reducing analgesic.

"May I suggest a strategic retreat?" The pirate saluted us with his sword. "Half those boys are hiding inside, but they might combine and rush out for some more sport."

"Here." Devli drew in a cautious breath, touched his arm, smiled. Then straightened up. "Hands together. I left a transfer token in a...a place of safety. Brace yourselves."

"Are you well enough to do a multiple transfer?" his sister asked, concerned.

Devli's eyes widened. "Oh yes. Better! Because that wasn't an antidote. There is no antidote to pepper-poison. If you survive it, you sweat it out. *That* magic I don't even know, but I recognize the effect. It's old morvende magic, taught to Prince Mathias Zhavalieshin."

They all stared at me, evidence of the previous generation's problems.

I pressed my hands to my eyes, someone touched my shoulder—

—and we transferred. But this time it was quick, causing no more than an inward jolt and a twinge of queasiness. A short distance, then.

Dim lighting—smell of damp stone—I knew I was underground before I even saw the cave around me. The room was small and round, with several dark archways leading off who knows where. In the center sat a low circular table, on it a neat stack of pressed paper, an inkwell and a quill pen that Devli had obviously set up in case of need. The light came from a glowglobe set in a wooden holder. Next to the paper lay Devli's transfer token, which had given him something to focus on in absence of a regular Destination chamber.

Destination chamber. Glowglobe. More blasts from the past.

"We are safe." Devli bowed to me. "Devlaen Eban, journeymage, sworn to your father's service."

"Elva Eban, navigator aboard the *Flipping Squid.* I—" Elva stopped, and shrugged. "I'm not a mage, but I joined Devli to help." She scowled at the pirate, who leaned in an archway. "Devli's group has been working to find your father, free him and restore him to the throne."

Devlaen whisked himself away somewhere behind me, but I was too tired to look.

Father. Throne. Plots.

Not again.

"Sit down." Elva peered worriedly into my face. "Cushions over in this alcove."

She carried the glowglobe through one of the archways, which opened into a smaller chamber. On the rock floor someone had spread an old carpet, worked in green-dyed wool, and on the carpet had scattered cushions. I dropped gratefully onto the nearest one, next to a short-legged table with ink, quills and more paper waiting, this time little message squares of various sizes. Elva set the glowglobe next to the inkstand.

"*Flipping Squid?*" I looked up at her, trying not to laugh.

Elva gave me a twisted grin. "Well, I didn't pick that name."

The pirate lounged down onto the pillows with an easy swing that suggested courtyard fights were nothing new. "Ships tend to change hands rather often, off our shores. It's traditional."

Elva muttered, not quite under her breath, "So says a pirate."

"Privateer," he corrected.

"But you have no letter of marque," Elva retorted.

"Of course not," he answered, amicably enough. "How can I get one from the real king when he's missing? And I don't think I'd like to apply to the current king since it's his ships, along with various other enemies, who are my prey."

Elva sniffed. "Talk about stupid names." She turned to me, with a dismissive back-of-hand toward the privateer. "Ask his name."

"*Zathdar* is the name of my flagship." He smiled. "It works well enough for us both."

Elva glared. "So why don't you tell us your real name?"

"Zathdar," I repeated, wanting out of that argument before it started. My head hurt too much. I gave him a mock frown. "There wouldn't be any apostrophes in it, would there?"

"Apostrophes?" He pronounced the word in English. It hadn't translated out in Khani.

Seeing that Elva had stopped glaring and was curious, I reached for the smallest square of paper, dipped a quill into the ink and wrote *Z'ath'd'ar* in English.

"Flyspecks." The pirate turned the paper this way and that.

35

"The letters seem clear, but the purpose of the flyspecks?"

"Well, in magic stories at home, heroes or villains have names that begin with Z," I said. "And a lot of apostrophes. Just checking. You know, if you're a hero—or a villain."

Zathdar compressed his lips into a firm line, as if he was trying hard not to laugh. "Perhaps the absence of flyspecks will serve as my proof that I am neither. Just an ordinary fellow—"

"—wearing a red vest with a lime green sash—" I interjected, and he laughed.

"—going about my ordinary business."

Elva snorted so loudly her sinuses probably buzzed.

Before she could shoot an insult pirate-ward, I gabbled on, "'Dar' I recall means 'spring' in Sartoran, at least as a suffix." I paused, remembering my father's patient voice as he tutored me in tents while rain poured down, on the deck of a smuggling ship, in an old castle tower. His graceful hands, as he sketched out the Sartoran letters, which Khani had adopted. "Zath is storm—"

Elva crossed her arms, sitting bolt upright on her cushion. "It means hurricane. Who but a villain calls himself Hurricane?"

"The spring storms that come down on the other side of the continent are the fall storms up north," the privateer Zathdar said. "They come fast and are hard to fight out at sea. It's a great name for a pirate ship. Privateer. So it works for me too."

I turned to him. "Do you have another name?"

Blue eyes gazed back at me, their expression friendly but observant. "Jervaes is my family name." His features were even. I couldn't see his hair, or even if he had any, because of the bandana.

"Jervaes. Sounds familiar. I think." I turned to Elva. "Anything wrong with it?"

She shrugged. "A common enough Sartoran name."

Devli reappeared, smiling with triumph as he held out a heavy ceramic mug to me. He dropped down next to his sister.

The smell was so refreshing it alone almost banished my headache. It also awoke emotions from my childhood, making my eyes sting. I slurped tea to hide my reaction, breathing in the aroma of a field of rain-washed and sun-drenched herbs waving in a gentle wind. The taste was fresh and herbal. I drank the tea down and immediately felt better.

Zathdar the hurricane privateer said, "Why don't you tell us your end of things, so we can put it together with what we know?"

"Sounds reasonable—" I began, but Elva cut in.

"No," she stated, chin up. "At least, not until *you* find your way back to *your ship*."

Zathdar gave her a quick, challenging grin. "Why don't you find your way back to yours?"

Elva flushed. "Because I know my brother's friends. They are all trustworthy. I know they mean to restore Prince Math to the throne, if Queen Ananda doesn't want to rule on her own. If we can find out where he's hidden. You showed up knowing our plans, followed us to the World Gate castle without any invitation—"

"Saved our butts," I put in, trying to keep things fair.

"Oh, I think the three of us could have gotten out without his sword waving around," Elva retorted with commendable bravado, but even she didn't seem convinced.

Especially when Devli shook his head slowly but emphatically. "Bad as those fellows were, we were no help, and Sasharia couldn't have fought them alone. Without him, we'd be in Prince Jehan's grip right now. Or far worse, War Commander

Randart's."

Elva shuddered, then squared her shoulders. "I don't trust this fellow. Too many unexplained coincidences."

"There aren't any coincidences from my end." Zathdar sat back on his cushion and clasped his hands around one knee. "One of my crew heard one of your friends asking questions all around Land's End Harbor, hinting at plots that include mages, World Gates, and the name Zhavalieshin. They reported it to me. Some investigation led me to the mage students. They were quite easy to follow." He nodded at Devli, who blushed.

"It was our fault we kept our headquarters at Cousin Nad's house," Devli admitted.

Zathdar continued. "King Canardan was not too stupid to investigate the houses of the former stewards belonging to the old king, he was probably too arrogant. But obviously that changed. I believe the attack on the old castle—which everyone who knows anything about magic knows holds a Destination accessible to the World Gate—is proof enough that the king's men were right on your heels."

Elva sighed. "All right, so we made some mistakes. But I still have questions."

"Well, why not discuss them on the ride down to the river where I've hidden my flagship? Prince Jehan's men will be busy searching all over, and we cannot hole up in this cave forever."

Elva looked at her brother, who spread his hands, then at me.

I copied Devli's gesture.

"Let's go," she muttered.

Chapter Four

She said those words at the very same moment that, away in time and space through the World Gate, sunshine dancingstar Zhavalieshin (known since her thirty-fifth birthday as Sun, which was the best damage control she could do with that stupid name she'd made legal back when she was twenty-two, complete with lowercase initial letters) picked up her cell phone.

At the hotel-room door, Roger stood patiently. "Coming? We might not get a cab in time to make the curtain."

Sun said, "Sasha has never ignored my calls before. One more try."

Roger murmured, "Maybe she didn't pay her bill?"

Sun gave him an ironic look. "I may be an old hippie. And my daughter is a child of a hippie. But Sasha's too practical to skip paying bills. You ought to know that by now."

"I know you two are half-crazy, with all your talk of World Gates and what all." He grinned, adding under his breath, "But that's part of the fun of being around you."

"Hello?" Sun stood straight, her brows arching in surprise. "I take it this is not my daughter Sasha."

At the other end of the phone, Dougie quickly recovered his surprise at hearing a female voice. "Nah. I was hoping you'd know where she was." How was he to know his dope connection wasn't calling back? Stupid old bag—having a blocked number. Everyone knows only drug dealers have blocked numbers.

"I am Moira Muller," Sun snapped. "Who *is* this! And why are you using my daughter's phone?"

At first Dougie had thought asking where Sasha had been a pretty cool answer—like, lob the ball back at whoever was calling. He wouldn't have to explain why he had Sasha's phone. But.

Dougie said, fast, "I'm tryin' to find Sasha. She, like, took off earlier. With some suit. I thought they were in here all afternoon." He snickered at the idea of lawyers doing the horizontal Olympics—and charging people for their time. "But when I tapped at the door, like, it, you know, opened. She ain't here. Or the suit," he added.

The lawyer again, Sun thought. *Stick to the point.* "What I am to understand is that my daughter was visited by, or is visiting, a lawyer, but that does not explain who you are, and why you are using her phone."

"Well it was just layin' around—"

"Lying."

"I am not!"

Sun said with the quick, sharp consonants that made it clear to Roger, at least, she was very angry. "The phone was *lying* there. Unless it was *laying* baby phones? Use the language properly, and tell me why you have my daughter's phone, and *who you are*."

Dougie cursed the old bag, Sasha, the phone, but only inside his head. He was about to sling her some bull but he remembered a show on which the cops traced cell phones. Crap! Maybe it hadn't been such a hot idea to make his connection with someone else's phone, like he'd first thought.

"I'm Doug. Roommate," he muttered. And, in a whine, "Like I told ya, she like took off with the bozo in the suit, and hasn't come back. Her car's out front and everything. I was hopin' the phone would find her—"

"What is the address?"

Dougie stared at the phone, appalled. What if this old broad really was a cop? He closed the phone and tossed it into Sasha's closet. "Hell." He slammed the door behind him.

On the other side of the continent, Sun looked across the hotel room at Roger. "I have to go back," she said.

"Back to what?" Though he knew the answer.

"To L.A., right now." Sun's eyes were tense with worry. "Sasha would never—" She shook her head. "I have to find her. That strange message she left, and she won't take my calls? Some idiot using her phone, obviously without her permission? I'm afraid I know where she's gone."

Roger flung the hotel keycard on the nightstand. "You're not going to say something easy to hear or to believe, are you."

Sun spread her hands. "If she went out of the world, it means she was taken against her will." And when Roger shook his head, she studied him, saying slowly, "You don't believe me, do you? In fact, you never did."

Roger approached, stopping halfway across the room. "What was I supposed to think? Oh, I never thought you outright lied. And I do know the difference between lie and lay."

The feeble attempt at a joke did not bring an answering smile, only a troubled stare. He half held out a hand, but Sun stood there by the window of their suite in the Omni Hotel, below which the traffic of 52nd Street hissed and honked, voices in at least three languages echoing up the buildings.

He said, "I always thought your story was one of your

41

hippie metaphors. Like your names—the fact that the name you gave me is not the same one as on your passport, which isn't the one you pay your taxes under. All your identities seemed your way of keeping your friends at a distance."

Her brows snapped together. "I was always upfront with *you.*"

"I know. I expressed it badly. I've the time, the money, and I've always enjoyed being your *cavalier servente.* No one else likes the same music, the same art, the same kinds of conversations. And it was those things that convinced me, well, you might change your mind one day. You might want more than a *cavalier servente* with time and money. And the same taste in opera."

"You've been a good friend," she said gently.

"So what's the bottom line here?" Roger asked. "What happens if you go to L.A. and get swept off to some mystery place? Though I can't really believe it. Even the king is easier to swallow."

Sun rubbed her hands up her arms, which she'd kept in fighting shape, though she'd ceased to let herself believe she'd see Math again. Nor had she—quite—believed he was dead. Her one steady conviction over all these years was that she couldn't bear to go back, to search, to discover there was no hope. She'd hoped he would find them. Like he'd sworn, on his honor, on his heart, before he pushed them through the Gate back to Earth.

And left them there.

She wiped her eyes. "I can't answer that. Maybe I've been weak. Chickenhearted. Trying to outrun the past." She drew in a long, steadying breath. "But one thing I can promise you. I'm going to find whoever it was who grabbed Sasha, and I'm going to kick them from here to Pluto. Because even if I don't rack many points as an ex-princess, nobody, *nobody* messes with Mom."

Chapter Five

"Tell me more about these flyspecks?" Zathdar asked presently. "In your world, the flyspecks on a written record signify someone chosen for a great quest? Or signify someone who chooses to thwart a seeker?"

"'Chosen' by the writer." I laughed.

He just looked puzzled.

The two of us were alone. The siblings had dashed off, Devli pausing only to grab the mug from my fingers. Until he asked his question, we'd just sat quietly, me with my eyes shut as I did my yoga breathing in an effort to get rid of the last of the headache.

I sighed, not wanting to explain that I had actually missed Sartorias-deles terribly, so much that I had read every fantasy I could get from the library, and later, the bookstore. Most of those books were delightful, making me wonder if the writers secretly saw another world and just hid it behind the guise of fiction, for whatever reason. I'd read for escape, and also for answers, hoping someone would have a story set here, though I had never encountered one.

To tell the truth, I badly wanted to come back, all my life. But I wanted to come back to Dad, and a happy existence, like my early childhood. I did not want to be taken back without my consent, especially to be thrown into what was beginning to sound like the same mess we'd escaped—only worse. Because Dad was still missing.

Zathdar regarded me with that puzzled look. I did not want to talk about my dad to a pirate. So what was the previous subject? Oh yeah, apostrophes. "Even when you love the stories, when you read a lot, sometimes certain, oh, what we call in English 'tropes' tend to show up over and over. I guess some writers read them when young, and think they have to use the same ones. Like the flyspecks in names."

Zathdar nodded, to my surprise. "The same can be said for ballads, and certain types of music. Yet we listen even so, past the familiar, for whatever it is that draws us." He tilted his head. "Sounds like Devli and Elva are almost ready." He got to his feet, and as I followed him into the bigger chamber, he smiled back at me. "The search perimeter won't have reached this far yet but that assurance will become less trustworthy as time passes."

"Ready." Devlaen pounded in, lugging a knapsack full of jutting corners. Magic books, obviously.

"Ready." Elva appeared from the other direction, a bag over her shoulder. She held an armload of clothing, which she thrust at me.

Since they were all standing there, I slipped the voluminous shirt over my T-shirt, and pulled on a wide-waisted coarse-woven riding skirt, hiding my jeans. The skirt promptly tried to fall off.

Zathdar's mouth quirked as he undid the Day-Glo green sash and handed it to me. The silk was warm from his touch. "And *this* makes me less noticeable?"

All three nodded, Zathdar's smile broadening.

I sighed, then tied the skirt up as best I could. "Ready."

Devlaen led the way down a short tunnel to what smelled

like a stable annex—the clean smell of fresh hay mixed with horse. Again, childhood memories hit me right in the heart.

Elva glanced at my head, then shrugged. I didn't have to look down to see that my braids were fuzzier than ever. Apparently many braids were exotic but acceptable here too, even scruffy braids, for she did not speak, only beckoned for me to follow.

The sun was just about to set when we rode out, Devlaen trying to arrange his bulky pack of books on the back of a skittish young mare, Elva watching in all directions. Zathdar seemed content to glance around once, but I remembered that comment about search perimeters. It surprised me that pirates, or rather privateers, talked about search perimeters. I thought their action was confined to water, which you didn't have to search, since there were no convenient mountains, trees or castles to hide behind.

No, I thought, watching the fringes on his bandana swing gently with the even pace of his horse. *Don't get paranoid because the guy is competent. Competent is good when it saves your sorry tuckus.* Besides, privateers had to train somewhere, and maybe it was as easy on land as at sea. One thing for sure, he was ready for action. He carried a cavalry sword across his back and the rapier in a saddle sheath.

Elva wore her weapon, which whapped against her leg at every step of her mount. Devlaen seemed to be entirely occupied with his bag of books, and while I had my gear bag clutched to me, it didn't contain any weaponry.

We emerged from the hillside opening into light green leafing trees, similar to beech, and I was stunned by the purity of the color. In L.A. you did not breathe such champagne air, or see such color, unless it has rained for a couple of days— something that happens rarely enough in Southern California that it's always a headline news item.

In the distance, on the opposite side of the river valley, a hamlet was built in steps up the sides of the rocky canyon. Some of the single-story houses were whitewashed, some colored a warm shade, like honey-butter. No people in sight. Bad sign? Good sign?

"Where to?" Zathdar asked Devlaen and Elva.

Devli opened his mouth, then looked confused. "I guess Cousin Nad's is out."

"Away," Elva said shortly, and pushed her mount ahead of us all, so that she was in the lead.

"My flagship is anchored right here at the mouth of the river." Zathdar pointed downward in one direction. We were as yet too high to see the river.

"We need to get away." Elva sounded a little desperate. It was clear she had no ideas, either, except that she didn't like his.

We went single file, as the path was narrow, bendy, and the shrubs and trees grew close. I grimaced down at my mount's bony neck, and busied my fingers with untangling the coarse mane hair. Smells, sights, even sounds bombarded me, bringing up memories I thought I'd forgotten. I didn't know which hurt worse, the happy ones or the bad ones.

Zathdar had fallen behind me, going last. When I turned in my saddle, I found him studying me. "So what can you tell us from your own perspective?" he asked, voice lifted so the others could hear. "A summary will do. We know you were small when you left this world."

His slightly tilted head, the faint sympathetic smile, made me aware that I'd tightened up from neck to knees. "Right." I tried for an easy tone. It was a perfectly legit question. "What I remember is King Canary. Uh, that's a joke we came up with,

47

my mother and I, though he hardly looks like any small yellow bird. Do any of you know him by sight?"

"No," Elva said from the front. She frowned back at us frequently.

Devlaen grimaced. "From a distance. In parades."

Zathdar just gestured, his palm turned up, which I interpreted as an invitation to go on.

"Well, he's tall, with reddish hair. Eyes a real bright blue. I remember his smile. My mother says he's handsome, but all I remember is that big smile, and how tall he was. Things at the castle were fun. Then the old king—my grandfather, that is. He finally died. I don't remember him much at all—" I was descending into the personal memories I'd wanted to avoid, and so I shook my head. "He died, as I said. Next thing I knew we were traveling. Then we were on the run. The grownups didn't tell me much, just that we had to be very quiet, and careful. We hid in a forest, we hid on a smuggling ship. My father got us to that old castle. I remembered some of it, though it was at night, during a heavy storm. He sent us through the Gate. Said he'd come for us. Never did."

I paused when we reached a forked path. Elva scowled, running her fingers along her scabbard. She was clearly tense with indecision.

Zathdar said, "Keep to the right, is my suggestion."

"I agree. Left looks like it goes back toward the old castle." Devlaen turned around in his saddle. "That all?" he asked me.

"That's what I remember. Here's the basics of what I know. My mother said Canary began flirting with her as soon as my father brought her over from Earth. Dad was sent to Earth to see other worlds and gain perspective, since he was a second child. Canary had urged him to do that. Mom and I think now that he, Canary I mean, thought Dad would never come back."

"Magister Glathan thought so too." Devli nodded slowly.

We'd reached another branch of the trail. Elva cast a quick look back. Devli shrugged in non-answer.

Zathdar said pleasantly, "Left-hand trail goes down to the river. I feel obliged to remind you that if War Commander Randart is anywhere behind us, his searchers will find that cave retreat by morning. If not sooner."

Elva sent a darkling look at her brother, who said defensively, "How was I to know our rescue party would turn into a war party?"

Elva muttered, "Hold my spot on ship defense, that I can do. Not against the king's entire army."

"Let's go left, sis." Devli gave an anxious look at the mountaintops.

I could have pointed out that Randart's searchers wouldn't be stupid enough to make silhouettes if they were really up there, but kept quiet, and Elva reluctantly headed to the left.

"Would you continue?" Zathdar asked me. "You had gotten to King Canardan and your mother and father."

I shrugged. My story wasn't all that exciting. Maybe he thought my natter was better than sullen silence from up front. "Dad didn't die on Earth. Nor did he carve out a new kingdom, or whatever it was Canary thought he'd do. Along the way on his journey through California, he met my mom, at a Renaissance Faire. Um, never mind what a Renaissance is. Just think of it as people dressed up in costumes. Mom didn't know he was a prince. She was a hippie activist in 1968, because it was romantic and exciting and seemed destined to make the world better. Anyway, they became friends. Same sense of humor. Then they fell in love, and he wanted to marry her. So he sprang the prince business on her and said that getting married over here in this world would make her being a princess more official in the eyes of the people of Khanerenth than a marriage back on Earth."

A distant shout rang through the woods. Zathdar's hand smacked to his blade. He twisted in his saddle, alert as a greyhound, while Elva was still looking around saying, "What was that? Where?"

A voice answered from much closer—a little kid. "We're still berrying, Papa!" and another even younger voice added, "Our baskets are almost full!"

I stayed quiet until we'd rounded the bluff away from the unseen berry pickers, then looked back uncertainly. Zathdar made a polite gesture to continue. "Mom didn't know anything about being a princess except what we get in stories, but she loved him, and the idea of adventure. So they came here. She loved it here, and people seemed to like her. Canary made a big fuss over her, like I said. She thought it was harmless flirtation. Cracked jokes, hand kissing, never carried it beyond public gatherings. And my Aunt Ananda, my father's sister, didn't seem to mind even though she'd very recently married Canary. Though Mom said she was a couple tacos short on her combination plate—"

"What?" three voices asked, right in a row. At least they were listening, I thought, laughing to myself.

"Oops. Uh, Aunt Ananda wasn't very worldly, which didn't seem to bode well for a future queen. And Dad and Mom were really popular, even though Dad wasn't all that much more worldly, for he'd been studying magic for years. To support his older sister when she ruled."

Elva hesitated again.

Devli slewed around to give me an inquiring look as his sister scowled down into the river valley.

Zathdar's expression was impossible to interpret as he

checked the horizon constantly. I don't want to say he was inscrutable—he didn't do Sinister and Mysterious—but his smile was just a pleasant smile, with no clue to his thoughts.

Elva clucked to her horse, and we moved.

"I'm almost done," I said into the heavy silence. "Everything seemed fine to Mom. But she says, what does an L.A. hippie chick know about royal politics? Anyway. When the old king died, Canary stepped forward to rule in my aunt's name because she'd gone crazy from grief over her father. Canary sicced the army onto us, claiming my dad had somehow managed to commit high treason. Isn't that the usual charge usurper kings throw at the good guys?"

Devli spread his hands. "I don't know. I'd just been born."

"My ma says it's traditional," Elva called from the front.

"Don't ask me," Zathdar said when I glanced his way. "The charge I worry about is piracy, even though I am actually a privateer."

"Okay. So War Commander Randart was apparently Canary's old friend from his youth." Three nods confirmed that. "He'd suddenly been promoted to commander in chief of the military." More nods. "He sent what seemed like a zillion soldiers to chase us."

Elva made a spitting motion over her shoulder. I remembered that pretending to spit was a lot like cussing. Actual spitting was worse than any of the sexual cusswords you hear all around you on Earth.

"Oh yeah. At some point someone told Dad that Canary claimed my father had ruined my aunt's wits with his magery, so he could get the throne to himself. I do remember that, because it was right before he took us to the castle and put us through the World Gate. I guess that was the high treason. Until recently there was no further contact. Nada."

Devli's mount stumbled on a rock half-buried in the dusty path, causing Elva's to whicker and sidle. She bent to soothe the animal, and Zathdar said, "What about the magic your father taught you?"

"What about it?" I asked.

The privateer lifted a hand. "Anything of use? By which I mean, to find your father?"

"No."

"I don't know much about magic, but it does seem that spell you used in the castle courtyard was not parlor illusion."

"It is a strong spell, that much I know. Papa wanted to teach me more, but we were always on the run. Maybe he thought I could use that one." I waited for someone to call me a liar. Because I *was* lying, at least partly.

It was true I was not even remotely properly trained. It was not true that I knew only that spell. I knew another powerful spell, one a beginner ought not to have been taught, but Papa had been desperate. And so, though I had yet to discover if he even lived, I kept the promise I'd made to him before Mom and I fell through the Gate away from him. I would keep that secret.

Devlaen sighed. Zathdar returned his attention to the path, which switchbacked down the side of a grassy slope into a forest-covered little vale. Elva, who seemed the least interested in questions of magic, was digging through her pack, and emerged triumphantly, holding a roundish shape wrapped in a length of clean linen.

"Bread. Anyone hungry?"

"Yes," I exclaimed as my guts growled a hallelujah chorus.

Elva split the bread into four equal portions, passed it down the row, and we ate as we rode.

Chapter Six

Sun Zhavalieshin crossed the continent of North America, landing with the rest of the red-eye passengers in LAX on a hazy morning.

She'd had plenty of time to plan out her strategy, since she couldn't sleep. First, a cab. Second, the small mailbox place she and Sasha had agreed on years before, a couple miles from the airport. Nothing much changed in Westchester, along Sepulveda. The constant roar of planes overhead kept the area from becoming too hip and thus redesigned every couple of years, unlike some of the other communities so close to the beaches.

The mailbox place was still there. Sun asked the cabbie to wait, got out in her rumpled suit and ran inside. Her fingers shook as she rattled the lock. She wrenched it open and sorted through the accumulation of trash mail and ads. There, behind her own postcard with the Omni Hotel info, was a postcard with Sasha's latest work and apartment addresses, dated two weeks before. They had faithfully mailed their changes each time they moved, just as promised, in case their cell phones broke, in case email didn't work... They knew it really meant that in case one of them vanished without a trace, there'd always be a starting place for a search.

She gave the cabbie Sasha's apartment address and sat

back, eyes closed. The meter was ticking up ridiculously, but she didn't care. Either she would soon go out of the country or out of the world. Whichever it turned out to be, she had to use up these dollars.

The new apartment was in Venice. With the meter still ticking, she climbed out, immediately spotting Sasha's old rattletrap of a car. Sun paused on the doorstep long enough to straighten her linen suit and touch a hand to her hair, upswept as always. She knocked.

No answer, but she could hear the thump-thump-thump of a stereo inside. So she rapped with the metal clasp of her purse, and this time the door was opened by a tall, pretty-faced young man with a carefully tended three-day stubble. His leer turned to confusion when he looked up from Sun's bosom to her raised eyebrows. "Yah?"

"I am Sasha's mother. Is she here?"

Dougie wavered. His first instinct was to slam the door, but then he thought the woman might call the cops, and the place reeked of weed.

The woman cleared her throat. Dougie's single remaining brain cell fumbled its way back to the present. "Naw. But you can look around if you want." He opened the door, pointed toward Sasha's bedroom and cranked up his death metal so she wouldn't grill him with stupid questions.

She marched inside the room and Dougie forgot her as he lit up another joint.

Sun shut the door against the noise and marijuana smoke, and looked around. Absolutely nothing recognizable except that silly water bed. Sun opened the closet, where a few clothes hung.

Below the clothes, two pairs of shoes sat side by side. Otherwise the closet was empty—no gear bag.

No gear bag.

Sasha never went anywhere without that bag.

Sun spotted Sasha's car keys lying on the bare desktop. She grabbed them up, drew in a deep breath and opened the door. The noise almost blasted her back inside, but she hustled to the front door, glad the lout seemed as determined to ignore her as she wanted to ignore him. There was no use in asking him anything, she wouldn't trust whatever he said.

She stepped out, closed the door and breathed again.

After she paid off the waiting cabbie, she got into Sasha's car. First, a search. No gear bag. The car smelled of Sasha's favorite herbal shampoo, a scent that made Sun's eyes tear, but she had to keep moving.

All right. Wherever Sasha was, she'd managed to take her gear bag with her.

So it was time to follow.

Sun drove the car to the long-term storage facility in West L.A. that she hadn't opened in years. She'd driven by once or twice, always meaning to get rid of the past and start over. But she'd never made it inside.

Now was different. Math was no longer the issue. Sasha was. Sun parked Sasha's car in the last slot and walked inside, her heart thumping an anxious drum roll.

From the thin chain she wore around her neck, she took the key she'd carried all these years and found the storage locker. It wasn't very big.

Nobody else was in the place, not in the middle of a working day. She crouched down, glad of the years of stretches, and opened the lock. There lay the outfit she was wearing the day they blasted through the Gate back to Los Angeles.

She took it out and buried her face in it. The material was

soft, hand-woven cotton-linen from another world. It smelled a little musty, but faint, oh-so faint, remained a trace of the queensblossom rinse she'd always loved to use on her hair, and even fainter, a trace of Math's musky, male sweat, left from that last desperate clinging hug and kiss.

A zap of pain tightened her jaw, but two deep breaths and she had control again. Sasha had vanished, maybe against her will. The longer Sun messed around, the longer her search might be, for who knew what time was doing between here and there?

She looked in either direction. No one. So she stripped out of her middle-aged lady suit and pulled on the old clothes. Their softness and scent were nearly as powerful as magic in sending her emotionally back to her confused younger self, who stumbled through the World Gate into Los Angeles with a grieving child at her side, no money, nowhere to go except home—a quarter century in Earth time after she'd left.

"Mom," Sun whispered, leaning her forehead against the cold metal of a locker.

Her mother had taken them in, though she was old. And trenchantly conservative. You don't change women of eighty, you upset them. Sun thought of her mother's wrenching hands, her angry tears, during their last fight—over her giving Sasha fencing and martial arts lessons. *She needs to be a lady, not a boy-girl, or she'll turn out like you!* At least Sasha had known her grandmother for a year, long enough for Sun to get on her feet and find work, before Gramma slipped away after a massive stroke, leaving them on their own yet again.

Time to go.

So. A quick look down. The shirt was roomy and long, the riding trousers voluminous. An old, faded sash, belonging to Math, was next. After tying it around her middle, she sat on the dusty floor and pulled off her sensible pumps. There was no leather where she was going. And no one had ever seen nylon stockings.

Her old cotton-wool socks fit over her feet, and then the soft greenweave mocs, cotton-lined inside, nubbly outside where the waxy leddas strips were woven. She stood and bounced lightly on her toes, loving the feel. The shoes were flexible, yet gripped the ground. A person could fight in those shoes. Or run. Or sit comfortably through a rainy night listening to ancient ballads—

She shook away the memory, bent down, her first instinct to bundle all her American clothes into the locker. That would not do. Who knew when she'd be back, under what circumstances? Maybe tomorrow. Maybe never. If so, in twenty-five years (for she was paid up that long) whoever emptied it out would find things tidy.

She pulled out the last item, a short knife her husband had given her. She hadn't brought her sword. It would have gotten her arrested in seconds. But the knife she could tie on under her trouser leg.

When she was done she straightened up and opened her purse. Nothing in there was needed except one item, which she slid out and held tightly as she put the purse, with all her money and papers, into the locker. Shut it. Locked it.

And without allowing herself time to worry, she spoke the words she'd never thought to speak, stared down at the gleaming gold transfer talisman in her hand—

Magic ripped her apart and reassembled her on the other side of the World Gate, with all the sensitivity of a giant swatting a gnat.

She landed painfully on her knees and bowed her swimming head. Yoga breathing, in, hold, out, hold. In, hold, out, hold... When her stomach settled, she performed some cautious yoga stretches. Very slow stretches, for fifty-year-old hips and ankles aren't as forgiving about sudden jars as twenty-year-old ones.

Gradually sound and sense returned. She picked up the transfer talisman that had fallen from her fingers and tucked it into the deep pocket in her trousers, then looked around the tower Destination chamber, apparently unchanged all these years, except by wind and weather blowing through the narrow arrow slits.

She stepped cautiously out into the ancient dining room, and there were all those age-darkened tapestries hanging on the walls, as she remembered. Let's see, the old shortcut—hardly a secret passage, as everyone had used it—lay behind the middle tapestry. On the opposite side of the room, the big carved doors led to the grand stairway, and the great hall below.

Where there were voices.

She paused. The voices were male, and at first echoed exasperatingly. The corners of the room were full of dust and spider webs, indicating no one had been around for years. Yet here and there the dust had been disturbed. One of the old tables lay on its side, and the other had been shoved into a corner, its top mostly dust free.

So who was here? Sasha? No female voices—

As the speakers became more distinct, she realized two things. One, they were coming up the grand stairway, and two, Canary was speaking.

Was it really Canardan Merindar? She shook her head. No, she would not mistake that charming baritone voice, the musical laughter. And they were coming *straight here.*

She tiptoed to the middle tapestry and slipped behind it, poised to run.

Moments later the voices abruptly resolved into audible

clarity, meaning the speakers had entered the room through the main door.

"...they had that door locked. Signs they'd been in here. But by the time my men got the door opened, they were gone."

"There's supposed to be another entrance," Canary said. "Probably behind one of these rotting rugs. Leave it for now. Where is the Destination chamber? Ah."

The voices diminished slightly as the two passed into the tower, but Sun heard Canary say, "There's still a strong sense of magic in here. I don't know enough about transfer magic to gauge how long it would linger. Nothing else. All right."

The voices got louder. "Tell me again about the fight in the court. Samdan said it was two men who'd joined those Eban brats."

Eban brats! So Steward Eban, or at least her children, are involved, Sun thought. *She was Math's most loyal—*

Listen!

"...the pirate or the other?"

"The other, fool. Why do you hesitate?"

The second voice lowered into embarrassed formality. "Pardon me, sire. But the reports did conflict. I report only what I heard. I did not witness the fight myself. Samdan maintains he was at the front, but he was first down, a cut over his eye, then another in his knee. So his glimpse was merely that. But he insisted that, beside the Ebans and the pirate Zathdar, there was a young man in strange garb, a white shirt with odd letters. Tall, with a hawk nose, like the old king. Hair worn back in many braids."

They had stopped. Sun turned her head, pinpointed them by sound: standing by the old refectory table that had been shoved into the far corner.

59

"Well?"

"It was Lankinar who insisted this person was actually a female. He said that the clothes were quite strange. Trousers much like deck trousers on ships, yet different, the shirt made like body singlets, but worn with nothing over it. So it was revealing, ah..."

Amused despite herself, Sun wondered how Mr. Official Voice was going to get around the sorts of personal details that no one ever seems to like discussing in official reports to your superior, whatever world you are on. Especially when the personal bits belonged to the likes of kings, queens and so forth.

The man cleared his throat and tried again in a tone utterly devoid of human emotion. "What Lankinar insists is that there was no male body in those clothes, and most of the others now agree. They saw a man possibly because they expected to see a man, possibly because she was tall, possibly because she fought as well as the pirate."

"Hawk nose, you say?" Canary let out a long breath. "Damnation. They're back. Or at least one of them."

"Who, sire?"

"Never mind. Now, my last question. Where is my son? All of you have been avoiding that question," he added grimly, with a hint of the old laughter Sun remembered. "Which is why I had to drop my own work to oversee his. Is Jehan drunk in a tavern somewhere? Or holed up with some pretty minstrel girl who caught his eye?"

"Uh, no, sire. Prince Jehan did detail the extra ridings to us, you'll remember."

"Don't excuse him. Tell me where he is."

"He rode down to Sarendan. A sculptor. Famed, he said. Wanted to pose for him. Present you with a marble bust as a surprise."

Canary gave a bitter laugh, and Sun remembered him long ago saying, *My boy is too much like his mother.* His heels rang on the floor as he moved through the door. "Finish the search, and send someone to remind Jehan that art, though no doubt admirable, must wait on events..." Their voices faded.

Sun leaned against the mossy wall. *Tall, many braids. Hawk nose.* Sasha was here. She was alive. She was also free, and had escaped Canary's clutches, despite a fight.

All right, then. Food first. Sleep. Where to begin the search? The brief reference to a pirate made no sense, but "the Eban brats" did. Obviously Sasha was on her way to Steward Eban. *And so thither go I.*

Chapter Seven

One of the many euphemisms for chamber pot is "necessary". I can introduce the necessary topic once and then never again. It was a relief, oh, what a relief, to be able to use the Waste Spell.

When I was ten and new to Earth, I had to learn about toilets. Let me sum it all up in one word: yuk. The Waste Spell did work—sometimes—as magical influence ebbed and flowed through the Gate. But since using the spell involves saying the word at the same time you let go, well, you can imagine how trustworthy that spell turned out to be on Earth.

We paused and drank from a stream, after which I used the spell, celebrating inwardly at the notion of no more restroom hunts.

We rode on.

Conversation was tense and desultory, mostly between Elva and her brother as they brangled about where to go. I was so tired I only wanted to sleep, so I was content to follow, listen and breathe in the fresh air. Zathdar seemed busy keeping watch.

When it was too dark to travel, we camped in a small clearing under a clump of low-hanging willow. When Elva and Devli began yet another argument about whether or not they could risk a fire, Zathdar said, "You have a Fire Stick, right?"

And on their twin nods, "No one will search for the same reason we're camping. They can't see to travel at night any better than we can. As soon as we get these animals rubbed down, I'll pace the perimeter, make sure the fire isn't visible."

Elva pulled the packs off the horses before Devli and Zathdar led the animals a few yards away to where a stream trickled. Elva took a Fire Stick from her pack. She snapped it into flame and made a gesture that would keep the flame low.

Presently Devli returned and sank down with a sigh. "Horses are fine."

Zathdar returned shortly after. "As I thought, these woods are dense. Fire's invisible on all sides but from up-trail. Whichever of us is on guard could probably hear any pursuit before they could see the glow."

Devli mouthed the word "Guard?" and Elva scowled again.

Zathdar hitched the rapier over his shoulder on a baldric, checked the other blade, then chose a grassy spot from which he could see the trail and us. While the siblings exchanged low-voiced talk about bedrolls, feedbags and stored food, I took out my splendid embroidered blanket to spread on the soft green grass.

In the sudden silence, foliage rustling in the summer breeze and the snap of the low fire were distinct. The ruddy glow revealed three faces staring at the glinting firebirds embroidered in gold thread on the scarlet background, surrounded by silver-edged white blossoms.

"If anyone wants proof of who you are," Zathdar commented, "that banner is it."

"Right now," I said, fighting a yawn, "it's a bedroll. In the morning it goes back into my bag. And no, I won't ditch it. My father gave it to me."

Devlaen stared at me, Elva stared at the firebird blanket

63

and Zathdar glanced in the direction of my bag, then away into the darkness.

Nobody spoke.

I fell asleep so fast I don't even remember stretching out.

Crackling twigs woke me, and the smell of fresh tea. The sky through the trees was low and gray, the air cool and misty. I sat up, shivering, and accepted gladly a somewhat-battered travel cup from Devli, whose face looked as grimy as mine felt. The tea tasted like a fine Gyokoro green tea at home, refreshing and above all, warm. I'd forgotten that summers on this world were usually cooler than Earth's. Khanerenth lay at the eastern end of the enormous continent that stretched a good way around the southern hemisphere. Most people lived on this continent, I'd learned, in part because there was more sun, but in part because some of the northern lands were weird and wild, not conducive to humans building cities.

Elva snapped the fire out, and picked up the Fire Stick to stow away in her pack.

"Where is Zathdar?" I asked.

"He was gone before we woke." Elva grinned. "Hope that means he's gone for good."

"No." Devli cocked his head.

We all heard the thud and crunch of horse hooves on the trail.

Elva flushed, though we could all see that he was as yet too far away to have heard.

Zathdar appeared, leading his horse by the reins. "Time to move briskly. The king investigated the tower himself last night. And he knows you are here." A glance my way.

Elva put her hands on her hips. "You found this out how?"

"I dispatched watchers before I met up with you. I also set

up a possible rendezvous, which I kept while you were all asleep."

"Watchers." Devli said only the one word, but the look he gave his sister made it clear that once again they'd forgotten an important detail in their own plans.

Elva scowled as we mounted up. The horses, refreshed after a night of rest, trotted with head-rocking enthusiasm down the narrow trail.

We were low enough now to see the broad stream that all the mountain trickles were feeding into. The constant rush of white water paralleled us as the trail twisted between steep slopes, green with tough grass, gnarly pine and moss-covered rocks. The mist increased to drifting streamers of fog; the forest canopy was so thick we heard the constant splat, splat, splat of water on leaves.

I stayed out of their sporadic talk, which was mostly about the trail and where the searchers might be.

I was awake and alert enough to consider my options. The day before all I could do was follow along and try to keep my eyes open. Now, though I was hungry, thirsty, still tired, at least I could think.

So...what should I do? No use in going back to the castle. Even if I knew any World Gate transfer magic, which I didn't, if the king's men were there, I'd walk straight into their clutches without them having to break a sweat. And while we'd managed to fight our way free of yesterday's guys, I wasn't going to count on that twice. Especially alone.

That left me with my companions. Should I ditch them? Good thing: they had rescued me from capture in the courtyard. Bad thing: at least two of them had been part of forcing me through the World Gate in the first place. Therefore I did not owe them anything.

We paused once on a cliff, and I drew up beside Zathdar. He slanted a questioning look at me. I said, "I assume the World Gate tower is guarded."

"You can't go back. They're watching for you to do that."

I laid the reins along my horse's neck. The animal obligingly swung round and stopped, blocking the trail so the brother and sister drew to a halt. "Before we go on, I wish you would tell me why you forced me through that Gate."

Devlaen sent a pleading look at his sister, but she studied her saddlebag as though it held the One Ring.

"I told you." Devlaen fiercely rubbed grit from his eyes. "It was a promise made to your father. If he vanished we were to wait ten years, then perform a specific spell. It brought us a letter he'd written, telling us where you and your mother were. But the letter disappeared, and we were afraid the king also got that information. We thought it best to get you two safely back here, where we could guard you." His face reddened. "I know what that sounds like. But we were going to bring you only for your own good!"

I decided against a pithy opinion about what they could do with their notions of "my own good". "Go on."

"My mage tutor was certain they were ordered to offer you anything you wanted if you would go back with them. They were not well prepared. I don't think anyone was surprised when they came back empty handed, but rumor has it the king demanded that they cross over to that world before we could. So when they returned without you or your mother, they had the World Gate transfer magic to build all over again."

My father had told me that transfer magic took weeks and weeks to make. It was actually a complicated layer of spells put on those transfer tokens. "The king's mages being two older guys? One gray haired?" I asked.

Devli grimaced. "Magisters Perran and Zhavic."

"My mother mentioned them once or twice. It seems weird that they knew my mother, yet came after me first. And tried to trick me! Truth, honor, sinister castles, secrets—"

Devli shrugged. "All that is in the records. When your mother first came, she said she liked such things. So the mages tried to lure you with them, the fools."

"Yes, but at least they tried truth and justice. They didn't pretend to be a lawyer!"

"Heh." Devli's shoulders now shrugged up around his ears, which were as red as his face. He said with the air of a guy picking his way over a minefield, "When your mother wouldn't come with me, I had to find you. It took some time, because you'd just moved. And, see, we've notes from your father. About what he really saw on that world. So I had to find you, lay a false trail for Perran and Zhavic, and put together a plan. And. Um."

"Lied and tricked me. Yes. As I just said. What I'm trying to get at is why."

"I told you, they're *after* you—"

Zathdar had been watching the sky, the fog-blurred treetops and the shadowy trail that vanished under the forest canopy. I couldn't see or hear anything amiss, but apparently he heard enough to cut in, "I think the rest of the explanation should wait on more trustworthy surroundings."

Without waiting for an answer, he urged his horse down the trail, and we followed, Elva with many backward glances. Beyond the next bend we found the white water of the river where our mountain stream poured in. The bend after that revealed that the river had smoothed and widened. We rode along its bank. I clutched my gear bag to my side, wishing I had more answers. One thing seemed certain, on land I had more freedom of movement. On a ship, I'd be stuck.

We rounded the last hill and there, anchored fore and aft in the middle of the river, was a pirate ship.

I had the haziest memory of ships from childhood, due to nighttime smugglings on and off, and being hidden in holds. Since then, I hadn't learned much more beyond what I'd read in the novels of Patrick O'Brian, but when I saw that graceful, wickedly lean schooner with its tall, raked-back masts, the long gaff mainsails and the reefed topsail, the narrow hull with the half-deck forecastle and aftcastle, I knew instantly it could be nothing but a pirate ship.

And I longed to be on it.

"Like my *Hurricane*?"

Reluctantly I shifted my gaze, to find Zathdar riding beside me, smiling. I asked, "What chance would you give for me sneaking back into the tower?"

"Why?" he countered, his smile fading, his eyes watchful.

"Because at the very least I need to send a message to warn my mother. I vanished without leaving any word. I know she'll be after me, soon's she figures it out."

He stared down at his ship, brow furrowed. "If you go back to that tower and transfer between worlds, I'd say your chances of leading the king's mages straight to her would be high."

"Oh." I didn't bother telling him I couldn't even do a transfer.

He moved forward again, a kind of nonverbal coercion, and to test it I said, "Aren't you in a bit of a hurry to get us aboard that ship? I mean, I don't see any danger on the road back up on the hill."

Elva's head turned sharply, her mist-washed face wary.

"Just because you don't see it doesn't mean it isn't there."

Zathdar lifted a hand, indicating the forest-covered mountain we'd just ridden out of. "The search will be going out in rings. With the king there himself, instead of War Commander Randart, they will be even more determined to be the ones to nail you down. Then there's the fact that they will have heard from the defeated warriors that I was there."

"And?" I winced, realizing the implications at last. "Oh, I didn't think of that. What, a blockade?"

"I expect the king's messengers are riding belly flat to the ground to all the signal points right this moment, yes. And while I don't mind running a blockade, I prefer to choose the time, and the place, if I can."

"So what you are proposing," I said, "is that we all take ship, and you'll let us off somewhere out of the range of the search?"

"Yes."

"Sounds fair to me." I was relieved at having made a decision. "Lead on."

Elva sighed in disgust. Devlaen did not hide his relief.

We soon reached the pirate ship, which the crew had edged downstream while we were closing the distance. The lee rail had been anchored fairly close to an outcropping. A gangplank had been extended to a broad, mostly flat granite rock. A young boy ran over experimentally as Zathdar rode ahead of us.

Zathdar dismounted and handed his reins to the boy. He hefted his travel pack from the horse and slung it over the opposite shoulder from his blades as he waited for us to dismount.

The boy, maybe twelve, grinned as he collected my reins. The other two left their horses with him and retrieved their packs. I tucked my gear bag tightly under my armpit.

Devli led the way over the gangway. One by one we jumped onto the deck, Zathdar last. Behind us, the boy mounted a horse and led the other animals back up the trail, where they were soon swallowed by the woods.

"That kid going to be okay?" I asked.

"Okay?" Zathdar repeated the English word.

"Safe. Fine. Good."

"Ah. Yes. He's my local eyes. His uncle runs an inn, so the horses will be part of his lending stock before we clear the estuary."

As he spoke the sailors divided into work parties, some pulling in the gangplank, others going to the sail ropes. Zathdar indicated we should go aft, down a few steps with a carved handrail, and into a cabin that spread across the back of the vessel, the walls and stern windows slanting in at a graceful angle. This had to be the captain's cabin.

Elva looked around with the air of an experienced sailor. Devlaen seemed more anxious to keep his balance as he clasped his bulky pack to himself. The siblings halted just inside the door of the captain's cabin, blocking the way.

So I turned my attention back to the smooth, slightly sloping deck. The crew seemed to be mostly made up of young people, females as well as males. Here and there a gray head was visible among the varying shades of brown, black, red and blond. Some dressed gaudily like their captain, others wore plain homespun shirts and brown-dyed deck trousers. These were like hip-hugger bell-bottoms in L.A. Almost all of the crew were barefoot.

On a signal the sails loosed, placketing loudly until the wind caught and filled them so they belled in the slow-moving breeze. The ship surged on the river, water chuckling down the sides.

"Go inside." Zathdar's open-handed gesture was just a tad ironic. "I assure you, there are no trapdoors."

Devli and Elva shuffled farther inside the cabin, gazes flicking warily this way and that. Zathdar's head barely cleared the bulkheads, as did mine. A circular table had been built into the center of the cabin, around which were set cushioned low chairs. I chose the empty one between the siblings. Zathdar left the only vacant chair and moved to the stern windows, through which he peered out at the trail we'd descended.

No pursuit appeared before we rounded a bend and a hill hid the trail from view.

Zathdar faced us. "The short version of what I discovered at my rendezvous is that the king sent his son with a sizable force to take anyone found in the tower. Apparently the prince changed his mind when they arrived just ahead of you and found the place empty. He left the two ridings we met—all inexperienced men—and took the better ones as an honor guard on an art quest southward. He seems to have heard about some famous sculptor—"

Devli snickered in a familiar teenage-boy way.

"—or we'd all be guests of the king right now." Zathdar made an ironic gesture, putting his wrists together as if shackled.

"Art quest," Elva repeated, laughing with her brother. "I've heard all about those art quests of his. What d'you want to wager that sculptor is pretty?"

Zathdar spread his hands, obviously uninterested in sculptors, pretty or not.

"What now?" Devlaen asked.

I said, "Canary has a son? Why would he put a boy in charge of warriors?"

Elva waved a hand. "He's older than all of us. Didn't you know? Canardan Merindar was married to someone else before he married the queen. A morvende. They had a son before the marriage ended. The gossip is, he ended the marriage so he could marry Queen Ananda, and the prince's mother went back to the morvende."

"Well that would explain the prince's interest in art. I mean, what I remember is that the morvende are the deep-cave dwellers who don't have governments, but do lots of singing and painting and archive keeping. And magic."

Devlaen's wistful expression made it clear where his own interests lay.

"I never met any son, though." I shook my head. "I wouldn't have forgotten that."

"But he wasn't in the country for a long time." Elva jerked her thumb toward the west. "He got sent off to those barbarians at the other end of the continent to some military school. When he was done with their lessons in marching, he got sent off somewhere else, I don't know where, but that's not important. The important thing is that he's about as sky-eyed as the queen. Won't set foot on ships. Gets sick. Hates getting dirty, so he won't drill with the castle guard, though he supposedly commands them. The king tries to get him to take charge of guard business, but if he passes by some house with a good mural, or some fine weaving, or hears a new melody, he's as likely to leave the army sitting there in the sun while he chats with some old bard or sculptor or weaver. Especially if the artist is female."

"I'm surprised Canary hasn't killed him," I exclaimed. "Unless he's mellowed since the days he wanted my parents dead. Probably me too," I added.

"Oh no." Elva waved her hands. "He wanted you alive. To

bring up and then marry off to the idiot prince, according to the gossip my mother was hearing from castle people, before she was turned off. Then nobody could complain about your father being ousted."

"What?" I jerked upright. "I never knew that!"

Zathdar said, "It's true. That's why your father had to hide you before he could act."

Devlaen smacked the table. "My mage tutor says the king probably would have killed off Prince Jehan a long time ago if there wasn't a severe shortage of heirs."

"There's also the fact that though he's an idiot, the prince managed somehow to make himself popular." Elva made a disgusted face. "Even though he never gets anything done."

"Maybe because he never gets anything done. Our mother says that the government is a mess," Devlaen put in. "Ma told us the king is now trying to arrange a marriage to any suitable princess who will accept a bumbling fool so he can get grandchildren and train *them* in his wonderful ways."

"Ah, speaking of wonderful." Zathdar indicated the cabin door. Three sailors entered, each carrying a tray. Good smells filled the cabin as they set the trays on the table.

Zathdar slapped together a sizable sandwich between slices of very fresh bread and ducked out. A few moments later his voice drifted back from the deck as he issued rapid orders. The thundering sails and the groan of wood smothered most of his words. I caught a few: lookouts, signals, line of sight. I suspected that the rest of Zathdar's fleet was guarding the river mouth from the sea. As soon as we joined them, they'd be running for open water, spread as far as possible so as to spot any fleets on the horizon.

"So what do you want to do?" Elva asked, recalling my attention. "I mean, after he puts us ashore again."

I needed time to consider my words. I took a bite of a rice-and-cheese stuffed cabbage roll. It tasted like a pot sticker or spring roll.

When my father taught me that last bit of magic, he'd told me there were two plans. The best one was that he'd come himself to get us. The second best would be his old teacher, Magister Glathan, coming for us. That would mean Dad had had to hide in a certain place, but I had memorized the release spell. The magister wouldn't know it in case they caught him and tried to get it out of him.

The worst would be that no one came.

And the worst had happened.

Nobody had said if Dad or Magister Glathan was alive, but I knew where to go to find out about my father. I also knew what to do. What I did not know was whether or not I could trust these people. If Dad was alive but under protective enchantment, what good would it do to perform the spell, just to bring him back straight into danger? "I wish I could contact my mother. She is going to be so worried."

"If they find her, she'll be a prisoner," Devlaen said soberly.

I sighed.

Zathdar reappeared, the fringes on his bandana dancing in the freshening wind. "Soon's you're done I'll show you your cabin." He turned from me to Elva. "If you don't want to bunk in the crew quarters, you can share with her. There are two bunks in the forward cabin."

Elva looked mutinous, but Devlaen half raised a hand as if in supplication. Elva scowled at Zathdar. "I'll stay with the princess. Since you already have a navigator."

Princess. I laughed.

Everyone turned my way.

I waved a hand. "Never mind. It's the princess thing, took me by surprise. Not that I actually am one."

"But people remember. Your father was very popular. That's why we've found so many people to help us." Devlaen pointed to his sister and himself.

Elva grinned. "And so was Princess Atanial."

"Atanial." Sartoran for "shining sun". I'd forgotten that. My throat tightened, causing me to breathe deeply the way Mom had taught me. I didn't know if I wanted her to find out I was here or not, and have to deal with all the memories and the pain of the questions we could not answer.

So I rose and Zathdar led us forward along the gangway. We dodged around busy crew members. I noticed that nobody stopped or saluted or any of that. Some of the sailors (and they looked to me more like sailors than like my idea of pirates) sang as they hauled on halyards, others high on the masts talked cheerily.

The forecastle cabin was narrow but pleasant, with two bunks built into the sharply curving bow. There was storage built below each bunk, scuttles for air and two little fold down tables on either side of the door. Someone had set neatly piled clothing on one of the bunks, both of which had soft cotton-wool blankets on them.

Zathdar stood on the deck immediately outside the door, for there wasn't much space inside. He ducked his head under the low, carved lintel and indicated the pile of clothing with an open hand. "Donations. Hope something fits."

Elva threw her knapsack onto the other bunk.

"There's a cleaning frame down in the crew's quarters. We all share it." Zathdar nodded at my bag. "If you want that stowed below, I can take it."

"No thank you." I kept the bag gripped in my arms.

They looked at me, and Elva said diffidently, "What do you have in that thing, anyway?"

"Just a lot of boring paperwork of the sort you need on Earth. And a few childhood keepsakes."

"Oh." Elva turned away and busied herself with unpacking her knapsack—all three things.

Zathdar leaned there still, arms over his head and braced against the lintel, one hand dangling beside his fringed bandana. He didn't look the least bit threatening, but Elva set aside the knapsack and scowled at him, her shoulders tight, arms crossed and held close.

"I'll send over the remains of the meal in case you get hungry." He turned away, letting sunlight stream into the cabin, and ran up onto the deck to oversee our emergence from the river into the sea.

Chapter Eight

Sun remembered the ancient castle. It had belonged to the crown (whatever family was currently wearing it) for centuries, with occasional zigzags into the hands of rebellious dukes and princes, and once it was a mage school, established by a princess whose older sister was the heir.

On their very first arrival through the World Gate, Math had conducted her all over the castle, relating its colorful history and pointing out with boyish delight various sites of magical traps and illusions. *Ever since the old mage school was closed, the mages keep insisting they got them all, but then people discover new ones. In fact, Magister Glathan—he's my tutor, I hope you will come to love him as I do—made me go through until I discovered one, as my own master's test.*

The one Prince Mathias had discovered was a false section of wall. The false wall was located in the corridor behind the tapestry. That entire wall was dark, mossy stone, looking as unpleasant as it felt. But close to the corner where it adjoined the outside wall, just a few steps from the stairs, there was a narrow rectangle of illusion: it looked like wall, but was actually a doorway.

Beyond that illusory section of wall someone had built a cozy little room.

They spent their first night there, and their last night. The first in a fire of young and ardent love, the last in close-hugging sorrow at the imminence of parting, their tired, bewildered ten-year-old daughter pressed between them for comfort. That they gave. They also kept her between them for safety, which they could only try to give.

Sun turned away from the dining hall, and lifted the tapestry. The passage beyond was moldy, the glowglobe weak, but nothing had been disturbed. She trod to the end, but instead of passing down the narrow circular stairs, she turned to the left and cautiously put out her hand.

Cold, damp air chilled her fingers. Yes, the illusion was intact. She held her breath and plunged through. Safely inside, she clapped once. The glowglobe lit, though it, too, was very dim.

Thick, rotting cloth hung on an old rod over the invisible door. She pushed the curtain along the rod, which would block light breaking the illusion, and turned around.

The windowless little room appeared to be untouched. There was the narrow cot on which Sasha had lain her last night here, after Math had taught her some spells. Difficult spells—far too complicated, one would think, for a child. But Math and Glathan had been desperate, and Sasha brave and determined. Finally she could stay awake no longer and so she fell asleep on the bed, and the mage left to give them privacy.

Math and Sun had sat shoulder to shoulder, guarding their daughter's slumber while they talked and talked, making promises and contingency plans. All in vain.

Sun turned in a slow circle. There was the old carved chest, its pattern of running horses so heartbreakingly familiar. She lifted the lid, sniffing in the scent of cedarwood, and pulled out one of the soft yeath blankets, and a sturdy tunic of Math's that she herself had packed away. It was brown livery, the silver-

and-crimson firebird of the Zhavalieshins stitched on the front.

No more sorrow. You've wept enough. So you are back at last. Find Sasha. And then find out what happened to Math instead of wasting the rest of your life wondering.

She lay on the cot under the blanket, clapped the globe out and fell asleep, waking suddenly when men's voices brought her sitting up. She pressed her hands over her mouth, then remembered the illusory wall. She could hear anyone in the passage outside, but if she made noise, they'd hear her.

"...not much of a secret, if you ask me," came an unfamiliar tenor voice.

"More of a shortcut." That deep, slightly husky voice was familiar, a voice from nightmares. It belonged to Dannath Randart, Canary's right-hand slimebag. "But the king said, add it to the patrol. It and the main stairway through that old refectory are the only way to the Destination chamber, and he seems to think someone is using magic to come or go."

"All right. But what are we watching for?"

Two sets of footsteps started down the narrow tower stairs, and Sun knew the voices would soon fade. She hesitated only a moment, then eased the curtain back and plunged through the icy illusory wall. She tiptoed barefoot to the stairs, grimacing at the feel of cold slimy moss.

"Anyone. Anyone at all. But the king mentioned females."

"Commander? We were all shifted from badly needed coastal patrol to watch a castle for...women?"

Sun followed down two, three more steps. *Come on, Randart, you know you want to tell him,* she urged mentally.

"Yes," War Commander Randart said shortly as he reached the arched tower door. "And if any appear, bring them straight to the king. To no one else. No matter who they are. No matter what they say."

The creak of the heavy door caused Sun to crouch on her step and peer around the angled stairs. A shaft of early morning sunlight outlined Randart's tall, broad-shouldered form. Except for looking older and even tougher, he hadn't changed much. His shaggy dark hair was graying, his hard face lined. The other man was also tall and broad, as you'd expect from the king's own men-at-arms. Younger, though.

He thrust the door open and morning light lanced halfway up the stairs, just stopping short of her toes. They thumped the door shut behind them and the poised bar *thocked* into place.

Sun slipped back upstairs to the secret room. She ripped the tarnished silver stitching from the brown tunic, and the bits of rotted red silk. Mentally she heard Math's laughing voice. *Livery was supposed to be gold. Silver and gold. But for a long time they couldn't get the dyes to match, and so the runners and warriors were galloping around in pumpkin orange, rust, even pink and yellow, if the sun changed the dye. Not exactly impressive! Finally they settled on brown.*

They were still wearing brown, she'd seen. But with the Merindar cup over the heart, and not the firebird of the Zhavalieshins.

She packed her things together, dug underneath the folded clothes and brought up the rapier she'd laid in the chest that last night.

Her hands were calm as she pulled the baldric over her shoulder and shifted the sword to her hip. She undid the knife from under her trousers and strapped it on outside. The little knife came next, tucked sideways into her sash the way Math had taught her so long ago.

She knew who the enemy was now, and where to go. But first she had to get out of the castle without being seen.

After a quick listen at the false door, back she trod down to the tower door that led to the courtyard adjacent to the stable. From the courtyard outside came the muted clatter of horsehooves. Ah, that would be Randart's departure. The watch had changed, and the patrols were just beginning. Now was the time to slip out, before the newcomers were really familiar with the castle and had covered all their blind spots.

And hopefully before they'd had their morning coffee and were awake.

As she eased the door open, she smiled, remembering her discovery so long ago that this world had coffee. Proof that the humans here were indeed from Earth—coffee and chocolate. Her smile was a little sad. She could remember thinking what can go wrong, if a world is beautiful and has magic, coffee and chocolate?

Answer: it also has humans, with all the familiar greed, ambition and intent. Ah well.

Courtyard. Open. There was no better route out of the castle, so she eased along the inner wall, watching the sentry walk opposite. So far, no one was in view along those crenellations. They were probably concentrating the guards around the Destination tower on the other side of the courtyard, inside as well as out.

She slunk farther along the wall, one hand on her sword to keep it from scraping the stone. A flicker in her peripheral vision made her duck behind a hay cart tucked in the corner next to the stable door.

She crouched down and peered between the hay mound and the cart's seat up at the opposite wall, along which walked two guards carrying spears, one of the men wolfing down a bread-and-cheese sandwich, his spear tucked in the crook of his arm. From their shuffling gait and their desultory conversation, she figured they'd just been woken up. The real go-getters were probably searching more methodically inside.

Good. Her job now was to keep it that way.

As soon as they passed beyond the lower tower, she slipped around the cart and into the stable. The animals paid little attention. Stablehands were busy in the loose boxes rubbing down the mounts that had galloped in that morning. She ghost-footed past. Some of the horses twitched ears at her, and one snorted, but the stablehands were too occupied to pay attention.

She found another door adjacent to a tack room, and sneaked out. The long early morning shadows stretched westward, with two silhouetted guards standing at either end of the wall. The road leading up to the stable entrance was a broad grassy expanse, no cover whatsoever.

So she hugged the wall until she reached the north side. The terrain there was rough, overgrown with weeds and brush. None of it had been cleared away for decades.

Picking her way with care—the ground was rocky and rough, and she did not want to rustle the shrubs—she moled away from the castle until she reached the shelter of a stand of young maples on a ridge. Now hidden from the castle's walls by their thick canopy, she slipped onto a narrow animal path and hurried downhill to the stream that fed the castle's water supply, and thence along the stream until the castle was out of sight.

The stream zigzagged steadily downhill. She paused to drink from the cold, clear water from time to time. She clambered along parallel to the stream, toiling uphill when the ground rose.

Her stomach was roiling with hunger by the time she reached flat ground. But no convenient fruit trees grew in the middle of that young forest, which was mostly cedar, maple, with chestnut trees here and there, the trees blossoming. The season was summer, from the look of the bright green growth and the heady sweet smell of bloom. Birds twittered, cheeped and warbled everywhere, hidden by the green canopy overhead. No nuts would fall for months.

At least she'd stumbled upon an old road, shaded by massive oak and maples. Here the air was considerably cooler, and she was no longer being scratched by shrubs, all of which seemed to grow prickly leaves. She stretched out her legs, forcing herself up to a rapid march. Now the plain brown tunic would mark her as a runner. If she came upon any of Canary's men, she would lie like a rug about being a messenger, and hope that old names and castles matched up with present owners.

It was about midday when her ears registered a sound that didn't belong in the rustle of a sleepy forest landscape. Math had told her, *Don't try to identify every sound and sight, only those that don't belong.*

Instinct got the message first. When her mind caught up with the Danger Flag, she discovered both sword and knife in hand. She hefted them, regretting the two years since her last fencing lesson, and faced the three scruffy highwaymen.

Two feints from either side and she knew they were used to working together, though they were slow and out of practice. She'd instinctively turned her back to an enormous thornberry tree, so the three could not surround her. They stayed well out of one another's range as they tried to close in from either side.

She used her old backup tricks: kicked dirt up into the face of the first, lunged at the second, and while he was shifting his weight to block and the third side-stepped to back him up, she whirled and cut low. Her point stabbed the knee of the third guy, who'd shifted to back up his pal.

He let out a howl as his partner slashed down at her. She flourished her blade into a downward block, turning the strike toward the ground.

By then Dirtface had recovered, switched his sword from one hand to the other. Something about that movement caught at her. She flicked a look at his face. About her own age, heavy chin, big jug-handle ears—

"I know you," she exclaimed, backing up, her point hovering midway between the two on their feet.

The pair also halted, Dirtface squinting.

"You were one of Math's men." She waved her sword for emphasis. "Robbing people?"

Dirtface gaped. "Your—your highness?" He turned to the others. "That accent. It's her highness. Princess Atanial!"

Atanial, the name Sun hadn't heard for fifteen years. The last one who had spoken it had been Math, just before kissing her goodbye. *Atan—bright sun—my darling.* And he'd pushed her through the World Gate.

"Hoo." The second one looked away guiltily.

"Still in...practice," the third whispered, voice tight with pain. He sat in the dirt, hands pressed to his knee as blood seeped nastily between his fingers.

She flung down her sword, heedless of the others holding their weapons. "Let me look at that knee. It felt like my point went in too far."

"Oh yes. Oh yes," the man muttered, teeth clenched.

"Well what are you idiots doing holding people up? Math must be dead or he'd die of shame."

Three variations of upset and dismay faced her.

Dirtface, he of the ears, said, "We never heard he was dead.

But he isn't here, either."

The second man, the leanest one, with a thin ferret face, had been silent a while. He jerked his thumb at his taller companion. "Ye recognized them ears. Didn't ya?"

Sun laughed. "Yes. I don't suppose you fellows have anything to eat?"

Dirtface had pulled a length of mostly clean cloth from the pouch at his sash, which he handed down to her. She helped the man she'd wounded to shove up his trouser leg, and she bound his knee snugly.

Dirtface nodded approval when she was done. "If we did, we'd be eatin' and not robbin'."

Sun laughed again, winning rueful smiles from the others. "So here we are. Four middle-aged folks starving in the middle of the forest. Three running from the law one way and one running from the law the other, I guess? Come on, let's at least find a stream. I badly need information." She added wryly, "And to rest my bones."

The two helped their companion up, and they made their way off the road to the river, which ran more or less parallel. They washed faces and hands, and the wounded man soaked his leg in the water, then rebound the bandage. They sat on the grass, Sun with shoes and socks off. She hadn't walked so far in ages. Her feet hurt. It felt wonderful to soak them in the cold stream.

She kicked her toes in and out of the sparkling water, sensing that the armsmen—former armsmen—were uneasy. "I arrived in Khanerenth last night. My daughter is here, apparently in the company of some pirate."

Dirtface pursed his lips. "If it's Zathdar, she'll be held for ransom from the king. If someone else, no telling what's going on."

"What can you tell me about this Zathdar?"

Dirtface shrugged. The second man said, "Rumor from the coast has it he attacks the king's fleet. Keeps 'em in a stir. Messin' up trade. Randart has a prince's fortune on his head as bounty. But no one can catch him. They can't find his lair."

"I mean to find my daughter, lair or no lair." Sun smacked her hands on her knees. "First I need to know a few things. Like, what year is it? What is the last you heard about Math? And—forgive me—but why are you robbing people?"

Dirtface looked at the others, who all deferred to him. "The year is '54. No word of the prince for ten years, now. And we took to the road because there is no other way to fill our bellies."

"So I've been gone twenty years, by your time," she murmured. "It's been fifteen for us. But what's this about no way to earn a living?"

"King"—Dirtface made a spitting motion to the side—"threw us out of the castle guard. Said lay down arms and disperse or he'd hang us all, meaning Prince Math's guard, man and woman. Some found work, others found closed doors and threats. *We* got the doors and threats. Not even a stable would take us."

"It's them ears, see," put in the second man, with a thumb toward Dirtface. "Everyone knows the Silvag family. Personal guards to Zhavalieshins for time out of mind. Big ears, every one."

"True." The third man winced. "And we don't know anything but sword and horse."

"What about teaching at that war school?" Sun asked. "Though I remember it was mostly maritime, still—"

"Closed in '34." Silvag lifted a shoulder.

"Opened again after the Siamis War," the second one said. "But Commander Randart made certain none of *us* can poke a nose near the place."

Siamis War? Who or what or where was that? Obviously she had some history to catch up on. But that could come later. "All right, then answer me this. Do you know where Steward Eban lives?"

"Everyone knows that. Everyone from the old days," Silvag scrupulously amended. "But they watch her place day and night. Especially since spring."

"Well, good to know." Sun forced herself to be cheerful. "Then we'll have some time on the walk to figure a way in, won't we?"

"We?" Silvag said, and Sun saw the wary hope in his face, heard it in his gruff voice.

"Unless you'd rather stay around here and rob people. I want to find my daughter, and then find Math. It looks like he's needed."

Chapter Nine

When I saw Zathdar the next morning, I actually stopped right in my tracks. Poor Elva thumped into me from behind.

She peered around my arm, then snorted. "Ugh. Talk about swagger."

Zathdar flicked his crimson silk shirt, turning this way and that. That shirt was so gaudy it was barbaric with its black and gold embroidery in highly stylized patterns of raptors on the wing. "Handsome, isn't it?" He preened, grinning at Elva. "Bought it in an old pirate cove on the other side of the world. Couldn't resist."

"But...couldn't you have found a bandana to match?" I pointed at the glorious green and gold silk tied round his head. This one had even longer fringes than his last. His trousers were sturdy black cotton-wool, but he made up for that lapse into sobriety with a purple sash. "And...purple with crimson? Wait, I'm asking that of a guy who wore orange and green together yesterday, with a crimson vest. Never mind."

He spread his hands. "My captains on the other ships have to be able to see me."

I turned to Elva. "That does kind of make sense."

"Signal flags make more sense." She eyed the grinning privateer.

"Not in the middle of battle when everyone is too busy to hoist flags. Speaking of which, since the winds are contrary, we're about to conduct morning drill. If you'd like to watch, feel free, but I must warn you that the gangways here will be busy." He indicated the deck running along the rail on either side of the masts, curving in toward the bow.

I pointed at an elegant rowboat on two hoists. "Shall we watch from there?"

He extended a hand and we clambered up into it.

Someone rang the ship's bell in a fast pattern—*ting-ting, ting-ting, ting-ting*—and the crew stampeded to battle stations, some with smoking firepots, others carrying arrows dipped in oil, and bows, and the youngsters with buckets of sand, presumably to put out any fires the enemy started.

There were no cannons, of course. I remembered that from childhood. My mother had explained that gunpowder did not work on this world, whether because of the cooler, wetter climate or because of some magical influence, she wasn't clear. But no cannon meant longer, lighter, faster ships than those of the Earth age of sail—and completely different fighting tactics.

The crew hauled expertly on steel-edged booms—like long knives on poles—to be swung out to cut enemy rigging, and sweep along the rail of the enemy to lethal effect. Archery parties in the tops went through the motions of shooting arrows, and the sail crews practiced snapping sails out, up, around as the captain called orders. The people at the helm caused the ship to veer and yaw.

"Not bad," Zathdar called out when at last the ship rocked in the water, sails reefed, crew watching him expectantly.

He flicked up his eyeglass, trained it on the closest of the consorts, the *Jumping Bug*. Their crew was still running about the deck.

"But not good, either. Again."

The first mate drowned mutters and groans with a high, tweeting whistle. Once again they ran to their stations.

Next he had the other two of his ships attack. This time the bow crews shot blunted arrows with what looked like paper twists of jelly or some red, sticky substance at the tips, which scored hits on crew and ship alike. The ships yawed and slanted even faster, each trying to board the others, to be vigorously beaten back with wooden practice weapons. By noon they were all red faced and sweaty, but their motions were tighter and faster. They had shifted from thinking about what to do to automatic reaction. That's the point of drills, I'd learned during my years at the dojo, and on the fencing floor.

The bells rang a slower pattern, and everyone relaxed, talking as they put away their practice weapons and lined up for water. The captains of the two other ships rowed over and climbed up, vanishing into Zathdar's cabin for a conference. Zathdar kept the door shut, and the helmsman made certain no one walked about on the little half-deck where his scuttles opened to the air.

We climbed out of the lifeboat as the crew returned to their regular duties, the night crew going below to their rest.

Elva scowled and prowled the deck. When the sounds from below the open shuttles indicated the crew had all gotten their midday meal, I asked Elva to join me in the cramped wardroom. I was starving.

The cook, a woman my own age, cheerfully provided us with two lipped wooden plates and a helping of what the crew had had. The way Elva dug in, I suspected that these biscuits stuffed with cabbage, savory beans and cheese were common fare on ships, along with the orange wedges. We ate with our fingers.

"We need to get you safely to land," Elva murmured, after the cook vanished back into her galley.

The mates' wardroom was empty. Everyone was either on deck or else in their hammocks. But I was aware of the canvas doors running down the sides, dividing off the mates' cubbies. (The rest of the crew slept forward and some below.)

"You don't think we're safe now?"

"Oh, I am. I think. I hope." She lowered her voice, glancing at those canvas doors. "But what's to stop *him* from ransoming you for a smacking sum from the king? Or for a pardon and other concessions?"

Ransom! I hadn't thought of that. Uneasily I considered it. Then I said low voiced, hoping the slap-thump of water against the hull, the creak of mast and deck would cover our conversation, "He has a price on his head, right?"

"That's true."

"So he risked his life to come inland to help you out, ahead of the king's men, and he's against Canary. Those are two points in his favor."

She knuckled the sides of her forehead. "That's what my brother says too. But I think something's missing. I feel like, oh I don't know, we're on the coast with a strange chart. The big landmarks are all there, but what about the little ones?"

I looked at her puckered brow, her unhappy posture, and wondered if Elva was a math mind. The navigation image sure pointed that way.

"Listen, if you find any reason to distrust Captain Hurricane, I'll listen. But I do feel obliged to tell you that I'm going to make my own plans as soon as we reach land. That doesn't include your brother's mages or magisters, or whoever sent him."

Elva flushed. "That's fair."

We finished our meal and dipped our dishes in the bucket set aside for them. I watched the brief flare of magic cleaning my plate as it hit the water, and I remembered the cleaning buckets from my childhood. It had actually been such homely little magics, and no grand and spectacular spells, that had caused me to ask my father to teach me. On this world no one had to wash and rinse dishes—or clothes, if you had a cleaning bucket or frame. And the cleaning frame not only cleaned your clothes, but your body as well, right to your teeth, when you stepped through. It felt like the snap of electricity all over you, leaving you feeling as if you'd scrubbed with a loofa and rubbed all over with a thick towel.

I stacked my dish on the waiting pile. There was a step behind me, and a young woman as tall as me appeared from one of the little cabins. I realized I blocked the accessway and moved aside, murmuring a word of pardon.

She ducked her head, giving me a quick, almost furtive look without meeting my eyes, and climbed with practiced speed up the ladder to the deck. I followed more slowly, trying to get the feel of climbing a ladder when the ship swings you out, back, and bucks suddenly from side to side. On deck I discovered yet more drills going on among those not on duty. This time it was personal combat.

The weather had changed dramatically while Elva and I were below. A heavy mist grayed the masts and the sails overhead, turning the blue sea to gray-green. It made the deck slippery, but that did not stop the practice on the forecastle, directly outside of our cabin, where most of the crew gathered round a clear space.

Devli sat on the rail along with several other young men. He'd accepted a bunk below in the crew's quarters, and these were his messmates. That is, the fellows he shared a table with. The pirates seemed like sailors to me. Nobody was cursing and spitting, or teaching parrots naughty songs. In fact, I wasn't sure if this world even had parrots, though I knew that many Earth animals, birds and other fauna as well as flora had come, or been brought, through.

Devli beckoned to his sister, who walked to the rail where he sat, her arms crossed. Next to the sailors, her uneasiness made her seem out of place.

A short girl with bright red hair tapped her sword point on Elva's shoulder. "Want to join in?"

Elva jumped, and shook her head warily.

Her attitude seemed to puzzle the redhead, and I wondered if her feelings were hurt by Elva's attitude. But she turned my way and said more tentatively, "Would you like to get in some practice?"

After years of dojos full of strangers, I was used to this situation. Thinking that rest, food and a workout were the three things I needed most, and I'd gotten the first two, I said, "Sure, thanks."

A big grin was my reward. "I'm Robin, second mate. Why don't you grab yourself a weapon. You'll get a turn anon."

She indicated the weapons locker. It was an admirably neat arrangement that rolled back against one side of the half-deck wall and lashed into place. The locker held three rows of neatly stored steel weapons, ranging from light rapiers to very heavy flat swords of the sort infantry carry. There was one curve-tipped cavalry sword marked off with a red tie.

I picked out a dueling saber, buttoned on the end, and began warm-ups as I watched the two in the center.

It was immediately apparent that they were more enthusiastic than trained. The bout only last a few seconds.

One dropped his sword, the watchers crowed and catcalled with good nature, then they recommenced. This bout lasted longer only because they circled two or three times, watching one another—but not well enough to actually spot openings.

The winner of that bout turned around. His eyes briefly met mine, and the fellow flushed. I wondered if I'd managed to come unbuttoned or unzipped anywhere. No, the sturdy shirt I'd borrowed was laced up to my collarbones, sashed with a plain berry-brown-dye sash. The deck trousers were drawstring, securely tied, so I wasn't flashing underwear. My feet were bare, as I'd kicked off my sandals almost first thing on coming aboard.

An older, gray-haired man said, "You keep pickin' the easy ones. Come on, let's see you work up a bit of a sweat." And he stepped up, swinging his sword from hand to hand.

More catcalls, and the gray-haired fellow promptly and gleefully trounced the younger, taller fellow. Then it was his turn to pick a partner, and he pointed straight at me. "Let's see what your father taught you."

"Well, he started teaching me, anyway." I stepped into the ring of watchers. "Most of my training was gotten elsewhere." I felt self-conscious, but no more than one did during a sparring match for a belt test.

What I didn't say, because I thought it would sound arrogant, was that I'd seen his own weaknesses when he fought the tall, young fellow from Devli's mess, and so I knew where to get inside his guard as soon as he lunged at me in a feint.

I tapped the button against his chest, and he looked down, blue eyes wide in surprise. "Well! Try it again?"

I swept my sword up in salute. The second bout was longer. He was stronger than I, but I had the edge on footwork, speed, and far-better training. Once again I tapped him, this time just above the collarbones, and a whoop went up from the watchers.

"Pick me! Pick me!"

"Hoo, how would you like to die?"

Laughter and more catcalls surrounded me as Zathdar and his two captains on the half-deck aft watched. A short, wiry man with waving dark red hair leaped over someone and confronted me, his slanty eyes slitted with laughter and his grin wicked. Like Zathdar, he wore a golden hoop in one ear. "Try me, Prin—ah—"

I'd forgotten the princess business. Was that why some of them stared at me so much? "Sasha will do."

"Owl. First mate." I saw a sort of family resemblance to Robin, and later found out they were cousins, though almost a generation apart in age.

"All right, Owl, bring it on!"

"Bring?" He looked around. "It? On?"

"Slang for have at it!"

As we squared up, whispers of *bring it on* went through the watchers. Owl attacked me and I closed out everything else.

I won that first one, only because I whipped a hook kick up and nailed his wrist after I dodged a lunge. The crew sent up an appreciative cheer, Owl flashed a grin and we were at it again, this time much faster and harder. I was soon drenched with sweat, several times nearly losing, recovering a heartbeat ahead of defeat, and then returning an attack which he parried, sometimes almost too late.

But finally he launched a complicated strike that I couldn't deflect without straining my wrist. I was just enough off-balance to take the brunt of the hit in my hand and arm. I dropped my blade, wringing my stinging fingers. "Yi! Yi! Yi!"

"We'll call that a draw." Owl lowered his point to the deck.

"Do you usually fight with gloves?"

"Yes," I gasped. "And that's something I'll have to see to right away. But that was a win. It was as fair as my hook kick, right? All's fair in war, but not in dueling? Is that true here?"

A silence fell, at first I thought because of my question, but I saw that Zathdar had joined the circle. "More or less. Depends where you are." Zathdar swung his sword experimentally.

Someone returned my blade, others made room for me to sit on the deck in the first row.

Zathdar and Owl squared up, and began a long bout that was sheer pleasure to watch.

As they traded feints, Elva slid up next to me. "I think you should thump him." She jerked her chin toward Zathdar. "Do him some good."

"Nope," I said, after a flurry so fast I nearly couldn't follow it. Zathdar staggered back, Owl's sword flew and he rolled on the deck. The sword was caught in midair by the tall, blond young woman I'd seen below. She had a strong face, with a Kirk Douglas chin. She returned Owl's blade as she said to Zathdar in an oddly shy manner, "That trick. How do you do it?"

"On your feet, Owl. Move through it slowly."

Owl scrambled to his feet and took his sword in hand. "I pressed inside like this." He made a slo-mo lunge.

"And I blocked here, used my shoulder to blind him." Zathdar whipped his sword in a tight circle, shifting his weight as he came out of the turn with his blade low.

"I saw it almost too late, blocked—"

The two reenacted the exchange, their method recalling good bouts from my dojo days. Most of the crew intently watched each pass.

When they were done, there was general movement, and

again Elva said, "Go on."

I shook my head. "He's better."

Elva made a noise of disgust.

Zathdar said in a quiet voice with considerable amusement, "She's right, you know. Not by much, though. It's those upward blocks."

So he'd heard. While I shut out everything when I engage in a bout, he was aware of everything around him. This is the difference between a lifetime of just dojo-floor practice and a lifetime of using what you learned, I thought. But aloud I only said to Elva's flushed face, "We don't hit above the collarbones in competition fencing, which is why I'm unused to blocking upward."

"Nor do you defend against a mounted attacker, is my guess," Zathdar observed.

"True enough. Plus he's a tad taller and bigger through the upper body than I, so he's got a longer reach. That makes a difference even when the training is the same, but his is better, I think."

"Practical experience." He gestured with a mocking air of apology and flashed a grin. "However. As this is supposed to be learning, want to show them some tricks of the trade from the other world?"

"All right." I scrambled to my feet. "But I saw those hits you scored on Owl. Anyone have a pair of gloves I can borrow?"

Several women offered, but their hands were all smaller than mine. Only the blonde did not offer, though she was my size. A gangly fellow passed me his, and they fit perfectly.

So Zathdar and I squared off, and the entire crew fell silent, even those in the tops, who leaned out to watch.

We began by making a few passes to test reflexes and

strength. On the former we were roughly equal, but he had the edge on the latter. Also, his drill hadn't been confined to the rules, and while I'd seen opportunities to use street-fighting techniques with slower fighters, he was too well practiced high, low, back, in all the places sport fencing forbade. He seemed to be holding back—he was demonstrating. Gradually we sped up, until my arm felt like string and my eyes burned with sweat, and then came the inevitable tap of the point lightly in the hollow of my collarbones.

The crew burst into cheers. "That was fantastic," I exclaimed and flourished a salute.

"Want another?" he offered.

"Nope. I can already tell I'm going to be sore and stiff by nightfall. I haven't had a workout that good in much too long."

He turned away to select another volunteer as I returned the gloves to their owner, apologizing for their dampness. At least there was a cleaning frame below, I thought, sitting gratefully.

We observed two more sessions before the watch bell rang. In the general movement Zathdar appeared at my side. "Come to the cabin?"

"All right." I swung to my feet. "I have some questions."

"I thought you might." He gave me an ironic eyebrow lift before leading the way. I followed that silk, no less eye-blinding for being sodden from the increasing mist, as around us the day watches changed, people talking and laughing, the armorer keeping up a running stream of insults if weapons were not wiped down and put back in the racks to his exact specifications.

The other two captains had long since rowed back to their own ships to oversee their own combat sessions. Zathdar waved me into the cabin, and I ducked my head absently as I passed inside. This time I noticed things I hadn't before: the neatly made bunk, the coverlet dyed various shades of green from pale silver to deep forest. Green was green, but somehow the thing radiated masculine vibes.

Above the bunk at the head end, someone had built shelves, which were crammed with handmade books. Next to the shelves, a silverwork crane taking flight rested on its own little shelf, jury rigged between a bulkhead and the hull. Next to that, in eye-pleasing array, were a series of maps—Khanerenth, Sartor, Colend. Chwahirsland. Some of the western lands that I did not recognize.

Above the foot of the bunk, a shelf held a tiny carving of a tree. It was exquisite, the bark indicated by the grain of the wood, each branch curving up into impossibly tiny and intricate twigs, attached to which were tiny five-point leaves made of green silk.

"I didn't steal that," Zathdar said from right behind me.

I jumped and whirled around, feeling unsettled, as if I'd been caught prying through someone's personal things.

Zathdar did not glance my way. He shifted around me, the crimson silk of his shirt shimmering in the diffuse light from the stern windows. The fabric shaped smoothly over the contours of shoulder and arm as he reached up and carefully took the carved tree from its shelf. "There's a spell that goes with it. You say it, and the leaves rustle. You can listen to them. Very pleasant, I assure you, if you happen to be caught windless out in the deeps, the ship wallowing and no breath of air."

He faced me, holding out the tree in both hands. I shook my head. "It's too delicate. I'm afraid I'll break it."

He turned away again and I whooshed out my breath, trying to find the cause of my absurd reaction. This was a captain's cabin, and little as I knew of ship matters, I did know it hardly constituted personal space, not unless the door was shut (it was not) and the scuttles all closed (they weren't).

He leaned a knee on the bunk and settled the tree just right, the fringes of his bandana swinging against his cheekbone. The books, the green coverlet, the precise slant of the handwriting on those maps, the tree and the silver bird. I'd seen all these the day previous, but then they'd been just things, scarcely noticeable. Now they were *personal.*

Rain began hissing on the deck overhead, which somehow made the space feel even more cramped. Though the rain made a steady thrum, I could hear the sound of his breathing. "Did you steal the ship?" I blushed uncomfortably. I hadn't meant to say that at all.

He grinned. "It's tradition, how pirate ships change hands. But pause and think. Where would you go if you wanted to purchase one? To a kingdom shipyard, asking the yardmaster if he happens to have any pirate ships for sale—very fast, preferably with at least one false hold? No, when navies take pirates, they tend to work the ships into their fleet, captains squabbling over who gets command. Then, er, they tend to be spotted and cut out again by people like me."

"You could have one built."

"But it can take years. If one has enough money. Easier to catch 'em, I'm afraid."

"You said pirate ships. But you claim to be a privateer. How do privateers get their ships?" I asked.

"Steal 'em from pirates." He tapped the earring glinting against his jawline. A ruby stone glittered on it. "You wear a hoop after you've survived a battle, and rubies when you've defeated a real pirate. While that won't scare off other pirates— little does—the ruby tends to ward off the would-bes. Saves effort."

He twiddled his fingers, giving me a wry glance. I laughed, as I was meant to. The moment made me feel slightly less unsettled.

"So." He thumped his elbows on the table, hands flicking open. "Before I get to my suggestion, what do you wish to do?"

"I'd like to be set on land as soon as possible, thank you."

"Even though by now there is a price on your head?"

"There is? But I didn't do anything!"

"It's not what you've done, it's who you are." He gave me an apologetic smile. "I guess what follows is what they're afraid you'll do."

Annoyance flushed through me. "Arrested for a crime someone else premeditates on my behalf? That's got to be a new one even for the local Dark Lord."

"Dark Lord? King Canardan is a king, not a lord. He also has red hair. Or would the 'dark' refer to his clothing? Except that he is reputed to dress well, and the mode, everyone tells me, is light colors."

Once again he made me laugh, and my annoyance vanished. Why bother getting mad, ranting about unfairness? Zathdar already knew it was unfair, and of course he had a price on his head too.

So I said, "There's a reward offered for laying me by the heels whether I'm on land or at sea, isn't there?"

He spread his hands.

"Well, on land, I'm my own person, so to speak. I'd rather *call the shots*—" The words came out in English. "I'd rather be on my own."

"To find your father?" he asked gently.

I lifted my gaze—and met his blue eyes straight on.

101

What is it about the mirroring of gazes? Eyes are just eyes, circles within circles. You meet people's gazes all your life. Then, one moment you look across the table out of surprise or question or maybe even a little challenge, and there are *these* eyes. Your nerves zing and prickle, leaving you intensely aware of your heartbeat, your breathing, your toes crunched in your shoes, your damp palms. Distance is so relative. Whether the other person is a foot away or across a crowded room, you have fallen into intimate space.

I flicked my gaze up to the glittering gold embroidery on his headband. No intimate space here, noooooo.

I said to the fringes, "I have no idea if my father's even alive. No one will tell me."

"He vanished. That's all anyone can tell you." Zathdar snapped his fingers. "The Ebans seem to think you know where he is."

"I can't help that." I shrugged and studied the map of Sartor just beyond his shoulder as if a professor was about to slap a final exam before me.

"There's another matter. Something many of my crew are in favor of, by the way, as nearly all of them are exiles for one reason or another. Far too many are new, as the unrest spreads. Sooner or later someone's going to ask your intentions, so it might as well be now, and by me."

"I'm listening." I moved away from the table and confronted the map, poring over it.

"I thank you for that." I could hear his smile in his voice. "But I was hoping you'd take that as an invitation to talk."

Now even his voice sent prickles through me. This was the last thing I needed. Second to the last, I amended, backpedaling mentally. Worst thing? Capture by Canary's goons. But the second-to-the-last thing I needed was any kind of chemistry with a pirate. *Especially* one who had the worst taste in colors I'd ever known, even in the mega-geek world of graduate school. *That's right, Sasha, make yourself laugh. If you laugh, it's just a silly chemical thing, here today, gone tomorrow. Abso-freakin'-lutely.*

"Rumors have to be crossing the country now, however garbled. If you were to raise your family's banner, many people would flock to it."

That surprised me enough to flick a sideways glance, but I stopped at the bandana. "I don't have a banner."

"You do too."

"It's just a *blanket*. And anyway I have no legal standing."

"You have, let us call it, a symbolic standing in the eyes of many people who want the Zhavalieshins back on the throne."

"So in place of my dad I serve as a figurehead for civil war? No, I hate that, I'm sorry. I don't mean to sound like I'm casting any aspersions here—blood and guts after all was your career choice—but if you're hinting you'd like me to join your fleet here under the Zhavalieshin banner, well, in a word, no. I won't stand by and let my family name be an excuse for someone wanting power to draw brothers and sisters and mothers and fathers and kids, even, to go marching to their deaths. Or sailing to their deaths. Because that's what civil war *is*, when you strip out the rhetoric about who's right and who's wrong." I winced, suddenly realizing that I was giving A-double-attitude to a pirate captain on his own ship. One who could toss me in the brig, and who would stop him?

But he did not sound angry. "Fair enough. Then you must be set down on land as soon as we can. First, though, there's a little matter of a blockade to run."

"Oh. Blockade. Right. But…we aren't exactly racing."

"That's because the blockade will be raised guarding the

103

main harbors, on the other side of the kingdom. And if the king issued the order, you can be sure the orders were sent by magic."

I remembered those magical message boxes. Like email, only with real paper. "Right."

"So we'll make speed soon as we get a favorable wind, but we do need to be ready for anything. Though I have an idea."

"I suppose you can't land me on the coast somewhere?"

"Far too dangerous."

I had a vague memory of my father being told the same thing, back in our smuggling-boat days: lee shore winds, rocks, cliffs... Khanerenth's coastline outside of the harbors was terrible on ships.

"Thank you." I turned toward the cabin door. He did not stop me.

Outside, I found that tall young woman with the blond hair.

"I'm Gliss," she said, before I could speak. "Captain of the tops, starboard. The mates invited the sail captains to mess. And you. If you'll come." She sounded gruff, almost as if she didn't want me to, but her eyes were more brooding than angry.

"Thank you," I said. "Lead on."

Chapter Ten

"Crap. Crap. Crap. Crap," Sun muttered with each painful step.

"Shhh." The admonitory hiss blended in with the patter of the rain.

Lightning flared, revealing reproach in Silvag's wet face. Sun realized she'd been speaking instead of thinking. But oh, her feet hurt so much, so very much—

Another flare, farther off; Silvag held a hand flat toward the ground. *Sit.*

She sat right where she was, mud squelching under her butt. She didn't care. It meant her feet could rest.

The next flare brought a long, rumbling judder of thunder across the sky, and the patter became a roaring downpour. Folgothan splashed down next to her, his bad leg held straight out. Leaning close, she muttered, "Sorry."

He shook his head, drops flying off his gray hair. She'd apologized at least fifty times by now, but the sight of his pain filled her with fresh remorse.

Haxin, the ferrety one, had been looking around carefully during the flashes. Now he leaned close. "He's gone ahead. If it's clear, we'll have a cart back."

He didn't mean clear of enemies, though that was implied.

Silvag had already explained that his wife had expected him to come home with some money. She had said she didn't care how. He didn't know how serious she'd been.

Wincing and grimacing, she peeled off her socks and set her feet out in the warm rain. The sting slowly diminished, and she almost nodded off into sleep when she heard Haxin splash upright, hand on his sword.

"It's us," came Silvag's low voice.

Moments later hands helped Sun to rise. She picked up her shoes and socks, walking barefoot through the mud. Little stones jabbed into her feet, internal lightning flares of agony, but she thought of Folgothan and kept silent. Presently they reached an old cart, pulled by a patient horse. She sat on the lowered ramp, her feet hanging over. Folgothan sat next to her, swinging his bad leg up. Haxin clambered up behind them, sitting by Silvag on the buckboard.

Sun leaned her cheek against the rough wood of the cart and this time she did fall into an uneasy slumber, waking stickily when the cart rolled to a stop. The rain had ended.

She hobbled behind Folgothan, whose breathing was a constant, painful hiss in and out. They entered a low cottage built in a jagged sort of rectangle, obviously each room added at different times, sized according to what materials were at hand.

The small rooms were scrupulously tidy. They passed through two or three. At last she was pointed to a rough-and-ready loveseat, cushioned by mismatched, homemade pillows. She sank down gratefully, but stood right up again. "I'm wet," she said in dismay.

A woman her own age came forward. Her face was square, thin from worry and undereating, the bones prominent. Her expression was forbidding, but after Sun's exclamation she said politely enough, "Never mind that. Those pillows dry out nice."

Sun sank down with a sigh. "Here." She twisted off her opal ring and handed it to the woman.

"For?"

"The household, with my gratitude."

Sun watched the woman's brow clear, and relief pooled inside her. She'd remembered right. People in this country had different attitudes toward work, toward charity, toward a lot of things, than Sun had grown up with in L.A. Silvag's wife might have resented it if Sun had expected her to use the ring to barter for princess things, but a donation to the house was acceptable.

"I'm Plir," the woman said with cautious approval.

"Atanial." The old king had declared that "Sun" was not an appropriate name for a princess. At home when she'd changed her name, it meant paperwork, fees, and standing in long lines at City Hall. Here, a king could change names on a whim. He'd decided that she'd be Atanial, a Sartoran name.

"My daughter is fixing you a bath, your highness. We'll have those clothes through the frame while you soak, and then planning. But first here. Lark, bring it in."

A teenage girl stood in the doorway. Lark was short and strongly built like her mother, with her father's jug ears. Sun noticed she wore her braids firmly back behind them, with no attempt to hide the ears. If anything, the braids framed them. That won Sun over at once. Lark had spirit.

She came in, carrying a mug of listerblossom tea, which Sun took with a word of thanks.

Before long she felt human again. She was clean. The ache of her feet receded to twinges whenever she flexed her toes. Her clothes were still wet, but the evening was quite warm.

The men joined Sun and Plir in another room with a big

table. Haxin was busy repairing what looked like a piece of harness gear. Folgothan sat back, eyes closed, hands loosely clasped around a mug of listerblossom tea. This tea was a pain reliever.

As Lark silently set out bowls and spoons, the others all faced Sun. "Your highness," Silvag began, after a look sideways at his silent companions. "What is it you wish to do?"

"Get to Steward Eban."

Silvag and Plir exchanged a glance—each obviously reading the other for cues—then Plir said, "When?"

"Whenever it's safe." Sun hoped tiredly that would be in a week. Except these people would be scrounging extra food for a week.

"They're watched all the time," Silvag muttered.

Lark eyed the grown-ups. "I'm the only one who goes through. No one heeds me."

Sun regarded her, hesitating.

"Question?" Plir prompted. This off-worlder princess might have abandoned them for twenty years, or she might not have been able to get back. She was withholding judgment.

Sun said, "If the king's people don't heed you, it means they see you. Or are you able to get by them unseen?"

Lark grinned. "It was the first, early on. Nobody looked twice at a girl coming round to sell eggs in a basket. Our one thing is our hens, see. They're all good layers. But we can't live on eggs. So I sell 'em. Or trade, more like. Anyways, now I think I know where the spies be."

"When would you suggest we go there?"

"Tonight," Lark said promptly. "It's not far."

Sun winced down at her feet.

"I have some salve, and we could wrap 'em tight," Plir

offered.

Sun heard that as a hint that while visitors were fine for a short time, they would age as fast as old fish. She forced herself to nod, and to rise. "Thanks. Sooner done, sooner no one worries."

Nobody argued with that.

୫)

Afterward, Sun—Atanial—insisted the less said about that trip the better. Yes, her feet were wrapped, and the salve was on her blisters, but the blisters hurt and her bones ached.

But for all that, the walk was indeed not far. She learned that Silvag had settled outside of the city of Vadnais because his duty rotation back in the old days had him spending five days in the guardhouse, with two days off. And after he lost his job, the house was the only thing they had, so the family perforce stayed there. Steward Eban had moved to the outskirts of the city when she was dismissed from the royal palace. She'd expected to live relatively cheaply and in obscurity, and indeed it was that way for a time, but over the past few years she'd become the central repository for messages, reports and complaints about the outrages of Canardan's adherents.

Lark led them by a circuitous route, keeping up a running stream of assurances that this hill was easy, that stream shallow, and it wasn't much farther.

The two middle-aged folks reflected on what a strong, energetic young teen regarded as easy as they shuffled onward, the rain sometimes heavy, sometimes light, but always making a sloggy mess for their feet.

But at last Lark said, "There it is."

Silvag looked around, decided it was safe and vanished into the darkness. Lark led the way over a gentle hill between carefully tended fruit trees and down through fragrant border shrubs to another long, low house built much like Silvag's.

She and Sun crossed the kitchen garden, past the grape vines and stepped onto a porch entrance where the boots and coats were kept during winter.

"Oh, oh, oh! Princess Atanial." A short woman with silver flyaway hair bustled up. "Is it truly you, highness?"

"Kreki." Sun—no, Atanial. She would have to get used to her name as Math's wife again, and all the assumptions (and the responsibility) the name implied. "Oh, it's good to see you."

She threw her arms around the smaller woman and hugged her, then they stepped back and studied one another. Kreki, blushing at being hugged by a princess, turned her head to call, "Dinner! Anything that can be warmed, and some berries and cream?"

"Sounds wonderful," Atanial vowed with passionate sincerity, her stomach growling.

In the background two servants began taking down dishes and wrapped food, the third servant vanishing through the opposite door.

Atanial turned back to Kreki, whose round face had aged. Her dark eyes were wide and alert, her blond hair now silver. She was stouter, but still moved like a guided missile.

Kreki found Atanial as beautiful as ever, her hair the same wheat color, the fine skin of her face softened by time over spectacularly handsome bones. "Twenty years." Her brow puckered.

Atanial spread her hands. "Mathias made me promise to stay. But he never came back for us."

Kreki Eban touched her lips and glanced toward Lark, who stood in the corner, smiling with the peculiar mix of smugness and uncertainty that characterizes teens who *think* they did something clever, something adult—but the adults might still turn on them.

When Kreki nodded slightly, Atanial realized that their coming this night had some special significance.

Kreki said, "Would you honor us by stepping into the pantry? I'm afraid that's where we have our meetings."

She led Atanial through a kitchen with its central stove, fueled by magical Fire Sticks. A door opened into an aromatic pantry. Ceramic pots and jars held dried spices and nuts. Below those a row of barrels contained wheat, cornmeal and other foodstuffs.

They walked single file between the goods to the back wall, which swung silently aside and led steeply down into a cellar lit by a glowglobe. The dirt walls were stacked with barrels of ale and carefully angled rows of square bottles of wine.

In the middle of the cellar, two men and two women sat at a rough table. Only one face was familiar, an older woman with gray hair, round of body, who stared at Atanial with angry eyes.

Atanial's mind caught up. *It's a meeting of the resistance council. And they think I abandoned them.*

"Mathias sent me and my daughter back to my world because we couldn't stay ahead of the pursuit. After several very close escapes, we discovered that Randart had far too good a hold over the army. We tried to escape on a smuggling boat and nearly got caught. It was only Magister Glathan's magery that saved us. And that barely."

The woman, another servant during the blissful palace days, nodded once. She remembered that.

Atanial went on, "And we couldn't go west, for there were

111

mage traps as well as the entire army camped all along the coast, and along the border mountains, ostensibly to train."

Now one of the two men nodded. They seemed to be father and son, for they looked alike: brown hair and skin and eyes, big jaws, eyes with a downward turn at the corners.

"So Math sent us to my world. Promised he'd come for us. He never did. After fifteen years in that world's time, I believe Perran and Canardan's other pet mage, what was his name? Zha-something."

"Zhavic," someone murmured.

"Thank you. They showed up and tried to trap my daughter. She got brought over here by someone. I came after her as soon as I figured it out."

They all made little gestures of acceptance. Five days in another world could have passed in twenty here as easily as five hundred years. Or even "backward" in the sense of someone from farther back in history on the one world being propelled into the future of the other.

"I think it was your son who brought her, Kreki." Atanial turned to Mistress Eban, who looked down at her tightly gripped hands. "Canardan himself was at the castle with the World Gate. I heard him mention your son. I also heard that my daughter was apparently in the hands of some pirate?"

Eyes and mouths rounded in surprise. Atanial remembered her husband saying, all those years ago, *They aren't trained warriors, or spies. They are ordinary people, trying to invent ways to stay safe from an enemy who doesn't look different, talk different, who might even be in the same family.*

For in the early days Canardan had built his alliance one by one, courting at least one person in every influential family.

She said, "Look. You don't want to talk in front of me. Why don't I step outside while you decide what you can tell me? My plan is to find my daughter. After that, I will find out if my husband lives." Her lips trembled. "I have existed fifteen years without knowing. I can wait a bit longer."

Kreki said in a quick, breathless voice, "We do not know anything about Prince Mathias, except that he disappeared ten years ago. But Magister Glathan is dead. Word is, Commander Randart had him shot in the back. Crossbow. After a truce."

Atanial covered her face with her hands for a moment, then heaved a sigh. "All right. I'll wait outside."

She pushed through the back of the pantry. Nobody stopped her. She nearly ran into one of the servants, a pretty young girl with a long red braid who was busy scooping dried peas into a cup. Atanial excused herself, then went through the empty kitchen to the door.

Outside, the rain had stopped. A fresh, cool breeze soughed through the line of pines planted on the ridge at the edge of the property, just beyond the fruit trees.

Atanial stepped out, breathing deeply. Her feet were a constant ache now, but the pain had dulled.

A faint glow worried at the extreme edge of her vision. She looked up. In one of the recessed attic windows flickered the warm, golden flames of two candles. Cozy. She wished she were in the bedroom behind that window, whether guest or servant's room, large or small. All she wanted was a nice, soft bed—

"Your highness," Kreki whispered from the kitchen door. "They want to talk. Our passwords, signals, what we're doing."

Passwords and signals. Why did that seem wrong? Atanial frowned. The vague sense of disquiet was too quick, undefined. Her mind was too tired and scattered. Her aching feet—Math—Magister Glathan's death—and riding over it all, Sasha and this mysterious pirate—

"Here we are." Kreki opened the pantry again. "You might

113

remember Fereli Kinn, the royal wardrobe mistress."

The gray-haired woman rose. "Forgive me, highness," she said gruffly.

"You thought I abandoned you." Atanial summoned a smile. "And in a sense I did. I beg your pardon. I take it the queen couldn't protect you either?"

"The rumor is she's mad." Mistress Kinn flushed, curtseyed, sat. "So the king turned us all off, except for her three personal maids. No one's seen her since, except once a year, standing by the king, on Oath Day."

"I don't think you knew Arlaen Sharveshin." Kreki indicated the older man. "He was a herald-scribe in our day. His son Tam is in the king's guard now, as our ears."

Atanial noted Tam's brown tunic.

"We meet here when we dare," Kreki said. "And exchange news."

"Like? I mean, what is the most important thing facing you now?"

An exchange of looks. Kreki leaned forward. "The mustering of the army. We don't know if the king intends some terrible purge here, or to invade elsewhere."

The man spoke up, a low rumble. "My son hears rumors of a possible invasion of Locan Jora. Take our lands back." The boy inclined his head.

"But we haven't any word for sure. We cannot get close enough to Randart. He keeps only his own picked men around him. The king is guarded by Randart, by the royal mages and finally by the royal valet, Chas."

Atanial breathed out slowly. "I remember Chas. I caught him in our rooms at least a couple of times, going through Math's things. He seemed to have plausible excuses."

"He's a very tricky spy. So anyway, we keep trying to find out the plans. We fear, from the mustering of supplies and the way training has been going, that this is not a vague future plan. It has a date. Probably next spring, judging from the cloth stockpiled in the border castles."

When no one had anything to add, Atanial turned to her own issues. "Tam, you're in the guard. What can you tell me of this pirate holding my daughter?"

"Nothing." Tam spread big, callused hands. "Nobody can figure out where Zathdar came from. He was suddenly there, some years back, attacking the king's fleet. Breaking trade holds."

Kreki said to Atanial, "What I was just reporting to the others is this. I received two notes from my son. One two nights ago. Hastily written and sent by mage-box. It was only two lines, to tell me that their particular group had been discovered long ago by the king, but they had left the tower after a fight. Your daughter and the pirate defeated the guards."

Atanial gripped her fingers together. "That sounds like Sasha."

"I received another note, even shorter, last night. Again just two sentences. The king apparently knows about the resistance group run by my nephew Nadathan, who is also a mage student. The other stated that the pirate—he calls himself a privateer—declares that his family name is Jervaes."

"Common name deriving from Sartoran origin," Arlaen rumbled. "Various versions all over the southern continent here."

"At least that sounds somewhat civilized. I mean, he offered a family name, right? Didn't call himself Slubbertegullion Squid-Guts or Bloody-Skull Liver-Squisher, right?" At the others' puzzled looks, Atanial sighed. "So no one knows his motive, beyond piracy?"

No one spoke.

"Another thing to find out." Atanial's stomach growled. When would that dinner arrive?

"We thought we ought to tell you the passwords and signals," Kreki began.

"Oh! Like the one in the attic window?" Atanial pointed upward. *That* was what had tweaked at her.

The others gazed in dismay.

If only she wasn't so hungry! It was hard to think. "Two candles? Window?"

Arlaen rubbed his jaw. "We did not post any candles."

Tam lunged to his feet, his face blanched. "Not our signal."

Arlaen's eyes widened in horror. "We have a spy here."

Kreki glared at the others. "Who is the traitor?"

They stared back, their faces shocked, angry, puzzled.

Arlaen whispered, "Tam. He has to get out." He gripped hold of his son and muscled him, protesting ("Let me fight! Let me fight!") toward the door. Then he stopped short, Tam stumbling with a subdued, "Ow!"

Arlaen said, "What if the spy is out there? How can I get Tam out?"

"It could be anyone. Even the servants," Atanial added, remembering the young woman just outside the cellar door when she left previously. *But no one pays attention to servants*, Math's voice came, with gentle irony, out of the past, the time they all disguised as cooks when Randart had driven them into a trap... "The girl with the red curls. Servant. Pouring peas. She didn't act surprised when she saw me. Did you tell her anything?"

Kreki breathed out. "No. But Marka has been with us for at least five years."

"So how much does she know? You say your nephew was betrayed. And I overheard that Canardan was hot on your boy's heels when he came to Earth. Well, your son told me so himself. Though I didn't believe him at the time."

Arlaen gazed at his son in dismay. "They'll put Tam here up against the wall." His voice lowered, rough and husky. "They'll have to."

His agony was the agony of any parent. *What happens to your child happens to my child,* Atanial thought, but her mind moved rapidly to memory, and then to action. "Tie up that red-haired girl and take her clothes. Tam, you are about to turn into a girl. *Fast.*" The order was out before she could stop herself.

This time everyone sprang to action, the men vanishing through the doorway.

Kreki thrust a wad of papers into Fereli's hands. "We have to burn these." She scratched a light, dropped the flame onto a ceramic bowl, and they began ripping.

Aching feet forgotten (well, not actually, but ignored) Atanial slammed through into the pantry, then stopped short at the barrels. She'd left her sword in the wagon back at Lark's house, and had forgotten about it. Now she had no weapon but the knife, and that she was reluctant to use unless her life was definitely threatened.

Math had said once, *I'll keep training Sasha, but no steel in her hands until she knows the cost. Flour and pepper, yes. We'll teach her to blind them and run.*

Blind them and run. Atanial was beginning to sort through the bags when Kreki banged out of the pantry, bearing a long, wicked knife, and marched into the kitchen.

Her nerves firing with warning, Atanial followed her through another narrow storage room, this one full of bed and bath linens, and up a creaky old stairway. Kreki's speed increased until she was almost running. When she reached a narrow doorway, she burst into Marka's tiny bedroom, saw the two candles in the window still burning and raised her knife.

The red-haired girl lay on the woven-rag-rug floor with her hands bound and her mouth gagged. Kreki brought the knife down. Atanial froze in the doorway, a squawk of protest forming in her throat. Then Kreki's hand came up, brandishing the red of a long, curling braid.

Atanial leaned against the wall, and even the Sharveshins, in the middle of ransacking the girl's clothes trunk, reacted with relief. Tam sank onto the bed, and Arlaen pressed back against the slanting attic so he would not make a shadow on the window.

Kreki squatted down next to the terrified girl. "Give me one good reason why I shouldn't kill you now, you despicable traitor," she uttered in a trembling voice.

Atanial looked at Tam, who uncertainly clutched a gown. Her mind was moving again, more rapidly than before. Kreki was clearly too angry to think. Tam's gaze averted from the girl on the floor. If she was a spy and he was a spy, had there been some quiet time between two attractive young people, both willing to hear and receive information, perhaps while exchanging kisses?

Atanial watched Marka's tear-filled eyes flicking between Kreki's knife and the boy on the bed, and knew she had it.

She cleared her dry throat, wishing they'd actually gotten to eat that dinner. Or at least sample some ale. "Marka must have had a reason." She smiled ruefully down at the girl. "Of course she had a reason. I'll bet it was a good one, too. She doesn't look like she did it for evil reasons."

Now Atanial had all their attention.

Atanial knelt next to Marka, who studied her with the tense forehead and squinted eyes of pain, anger, fear. Confusion.

"Let's have that gag off," Atanial murmured. "You won't yell, will you? You don't want to die, and no one wants to kill you."

A tiny nod.

Atanial took out her own knife as Kreki gripped hers upraised in silent warning. The girl gasped, working her lips and tongue as Atanial said, "Your reasons might have to wait. But here's the important thing. Do you really want to see Tam dead?"

"N-no." Marka gulped on a sob.

Tam opened his mouth, but his father gripped his shoulder in warning.

Atanial said, "They probably have us surrounded by now, don't they? You comforted yourself with the fact that they have orders to *capture* us. But think about it."

"They wouldn't—they *promised*—"

"My dear, you've been living a lie. Surely you can understand that they might lie to you? Just like they asked you to lie to the Ebans and the others?" Atanial glanced Tam's way.

Marka licked her lips, fresh tears coursing down her cheeks. "You think they have orders to kill me?" Her chest heaved with sobs.

"If the orders came through the War Commander," Kreki said decisively. "Yes. He hates spies, though he uses them."

"The king?" Atanial asked softly, wondering how much Canardan had changed.

Kreki shook her head. "He hates actually doing away with people. Which is the only hope *we* have," she added with irony.

Atanial turned back to Marka. "But Tam they would execute right away, because he's in the guard. Do you want that to happen?"

"No."

"All we need are the passwords to get Tam through the line," Atanial said, and Kreki gasped. She hadn't thought of passwords, but she had not spent as much time around Randart as Atanial had, back in the old days. He'd always used codes and passwords.

Fresh tears welled in Marka's eyes, dripping into her ears.

Atanial brushed the tears away. "We're going to leave you here, but hidden, so they won't find you. After we leave, you can get yourself free, and away. And do whatever you need to do. But at least get Tam through that line, or he will be dead by morning."

"Hackleberry," Marka whispered, her anguished eyes lifting toward Tam. "The password is *hackleberry*."

Atanial looked up at Tam. "Take Lark with you." She nipped the braid from Kreki, shook it so it unraveled, pulled a sash from the half-spilled contents of the trunk. "That around your head tying on the hair, a bonnet over your head. The skirt on your waist. Get through the lines now. With Lark. She's got to get home and warn her family."

Tam and his father fixed on the sash and hair in a matter of heartbeats, and then Tam dashed out, wrestling the skirt into place.

Atanial used another sash to bind Marka's mouth, but far more gently.

"All right, the rest of us have to cause as much confusion as we can so Tam and Lark can get through."

They left Marka on the floor, her candles still burning in

the window. She promptly wriggled under her bed to hide.

Atanial did not see Tam or Lark as she made her way through the house to the front door. The front parlor was dark, which gave her eyes time to adjust. She eased the door open a crack and peered out. At first the night looked peaceful, but as her night vision got better she saw movement among the pines, heard a sudden rustle in the orchard.

The king's men were advancing into position.

She shut the door as Kreki joined her. "What did you see?"

"We're surrounded."

Kreki breathed out a shuddering sigh.

"What are we facing here?" Atanial asked. "This was a meeting in a private home, no weapons present."

"What I fear is that he'll have us handy to blame for all the current problems," Kreki said. "Economy is in ruins, trade by sea impossible."

"Due to this Zathdar, no doubt, who has my daughter. Well, one thing at a time. Here's what I think. You tell me if it makes sense. If Canardan can make me vanish without anyone knowing, whether by death, magic or throwing me into a deep dungeon, his life is much easier."

"Just what I was thinking." Kreki determinedly kept her voice calm.

"So everyone out there needs to know who I am. Warriors gossip same as anyone else. Gossip is on my side. Second thing, we must buy that boy time to get through the line and well away before they discover the ruse. So...why not playact a pair of stupid old women too dumb to see the danger?"

"No playing on my part. I should have been more careful. I should have suspected something like this. It's been too easy." Kreki's fingers trembled as she brushed her hands down her apron. "Let's get busy."

She clapped, and a small glowglobe lit the parlor.

Atanial opened the front door wide, making sure she stood directly in the center, so her entire body was silhouetted. She lifted a hand and made a business of peering outward.

Kreki came up next to her, polishing a candlestick on her apron. "What is it, your highness?" she asked in a carrying voice.

"I thought I saw something. A light."

"Impossible. Everyone is here. Must be a gleam from the stars, reflecting on the leaves of the peach trees. Do you have peaches in *the other world?*"

"Oh yes. But not as good as the ones here! *My husband Mathias* once told me peaches were brought *through the World Gate.*"

"But which way, *your highness?*" Kreki shrilled. "From *your world?*"

"Now, that I do not remember." Atanial laughed as she leaned out, looking around dramatically under her hand, though the light glowing directly above them made it nearly impossible to see anything.

But she heard rustles. One by the barn, another out by the pines. The crack of a twig.

"Rain is gone." Kreki lifted her hand and began peering upward with theatrical earnestness. "Will be a lovely walk if you decide to move on tonight."

"But my feet hurt," Atanial foghorned, lifting her bandaged foot. A flutter behind her ribs had to be squelched, she must not laugh. But this was almost fun.

"Oh, *Princess Atanial,*" Kreki exclaimed, loud enough to be heard from the pine ridge.

"That's what I get for marching for days after years of no walking at all. But I met so *very* many *nice people* on the way, who seemed *glad* I have returned. If only I'd thought of it years ago."

"Oh! How many did you meet? I know all the valley families."

"Too many to count! Oh, but I am so very hungry—"

"Dinner," came a wry voice from out of the darkness, "can be ordered day or night at the royal castle. That's the good thing about royal castles. Welcome back, Sun."

Both women whipped around. Atanial bit her lips against a curse, even a retort. The king himself! She was supposed to be surprised. Were those kids through the lines yet?

"Who is that?" she called uncertainly, doing the peering business again. "*Canardan*? My goodness, is it really *you*?"

"I'm here to personally convey a royal invitation, Sun." Canardan Merindar strolled toward the house, stopping just inside the circle of light.

He was taller than Atanial remembered, his hair a dark auburn, the waves ruddy in the light. He had certainly not gone to fat.

She lifted her voice. "I am here to get my daughter. If you try to stop me, well—" She spread her hands.

"But we can find your daughter together." Canardan lounged a step closer. "Come along, Sun. You really don't want trouble any more than I do."

He used the name "Sun" with a humorous, intimate tone that Atanial disliked just a little more each time she heard it. "No," she responded cordially. "I do not. Therefore, if you let these people go on their merry way, then I won't make any trouble. It's not their fault I seem to have come at the wrong time and headed straight for the wrong place. No one here knew I was coming, I promise you that."

Canardan sighed. "Take 'em." He waved a lazy hand toward the house.

A gaggle of old folks had a snail's chance in the salt mines against a determined band of trained warriors, especially determined as the ironic eye of their king was on them. But at least it was the king, and not War Commander Randart, which meant the oldsters had a better chance of staying alive. And so they gave the escaping young pair their very best effort to prolong things by running around, yelling and ramming into walls, furniture, warriors and each other.

Fereli retreated to the kitchen and threw pots of preserves at the ducking heads of the young fellows trying to corner her. Despite the danger, bubbles of humor fizzed inside her chest when she saw how those big, brawny youngsters hunched and covered their heads each time she took aim.

Arlaen got into the act by groaning and clutching his bad hip as he yanked furniture in the way of the dashing warriors, sometimes tripping them up. He'd apologize, reach to help them, and then knock jugs and plates and baskets onto them. They scrambled about amid showers of crockery, beans, nuts, and once a satisfyingly effective dusting with ground pepper.

Kreki shrieked at the warriors to spare her curtains and rugs, disconcerting them mightily, and Atanial ran around the outside of the house twice, bobbing and weaving, until she stumbled over an unseen cabbage in the garden and measured her length on the carrot tops.

Strong hands picked her up with respectful care. Swords rang, and she smelled healthy young male sweat many times over as she was closely ringed.

Fairly soon the others were brought out.

"This all of 'em?" Canardan asked.

"All we found, sire," responded the captain.

Atanial counted swiftly, then compressed her lips firmly to hide the balloon of relief inside. The prisoners were the old folk and three servants.

No Tam or Lark.

Chapter Eleven

Sore does not begin to describe how I felt the next day.

In the past the only thing to do was work out harder. Over the next couple of weeks—it was easy to lose track of the flow of days on the sea—Owl and I led the personal weapons practices in the mornings, and he conducted drills in the afternoon. Zathdar was there for some of the sessions, and on other days he took his captain's launch away to inspect his fleet, and to scout ahead.

After the first few days, I nerved myself to climb the shrouds—the ropes connecting each mast to the hull on either side—to the platform on which the crew stowed sails for the higher reaches, and crouched with bows during defense practice. This vantage was splendid, the movement of the ship more dynamic, the view farther, the graceful geometry of the sails quite spectacular.

The masts had three levels—mainsails, topsails and topgallants—with a smaller platform at that third section of mast. I climbed up there the morning Zathdar returned from his inspection and scouting foray, clinging to the mast as I accustomed myself to that breathtaking swoop and loop. The wood was rough under my cheek, weather-beaten for countless years, the nails all handmade, each therefore distinctive. On the platform and the side of the mast, unknown hands had carved initials and short words, most of them in unfamiliar alphabets.

Finally I dared to lift my head and look outward. Exhilaration rushed through me at the sight of the vast ocean sparkling in the sun. The deck looked so small below!

"Boat ho," called the lookout on the other mast. "Captain returning."

I shifted. There was the narrow launch, its single sail a long, pure curve as it scudded lightly as a gull, water foaming up in an arch down either side.

Gliss swarmed up with the ease of a flitting bird and scowled at me. "You shouldn't be up here."

"Why not?"

"Because you're a land rat. If you fall, we get the blame."

She turned away before I could speak and slid down a backstay to the deck. That was a trick I was not about to emulate.

My exhilaration was gone, doused by a vague sense of guilt. I climbed laboriously to the deck, clinging with iron desperation as the pitch of the ship swung me out over the water.

When I reached the deck, Zathdar had already closed himself in his cabin with Owl and Robin. The crew in the middle of changing watch nodded and smiled at me, most of them familiar now after days of the practice sessions. They were all fairly friendly. With one exception, Gliss.

Elva was deep in conversation with the navigator at the helm. Having seen almost nothing of Devlaen over the past few days, I explored the lower levels of the ship and discovered him shut into a tiny cubby in the hold, busy with his books under the light of a single swinging lantern. The cabin was hot and stuffy.

"Why are you stuck in this rat hole?" I asked.

He blinked at me. "Studying." He placed his finger on a page covered with tiny handwriting. "Trying to design us some transfer-note boxes. It's more advanced magic than I've learned yet," he admitted.

"For Zathdar?" I asked.

Devli flushed, and I suspected his sister had accused him of throwing in with the...if not the enemy, with the not-quite-allies.

He said defensively, "Well, if he wants to communicate with us, I don't see why he shouldn't. And if I design them, I can make sure there aren't any suspicious wards or tracers on them. So the king cannot intercept our messages."

I shrugged. "Sounds reasonable."

He relaxed a little. "Why do you want to be on land?"

"Find out if anyone knows if my father is alive."

"And then?"

"I don't know. Depends on what I hear."

"So you won't search out your father yourself?" Devlaen asked, his expression intent. The lamplight threw his face into relief, making him look older.

"I was ten years old when we left. That was twenty years ago, your time." And when he started to speak, I deflected: "I would like to sit down somewhere and catch up on history before making any plans."

Devli leaned forward, his expression eager. "But I could tell you that. We study history when we learn magic. I could *show* you just why we need—" He reached a hand toward me.

Maybe he reached just to gesture, but I backpedaled fast. *He's a mage, Clueless! A dedicated one. What's to stop him from grabbing you right now?* "I apologize for interrupting your studies." I backed out to find Gliss coming down the hatch.

"Captain wants you," she said shortly.

When she turned to climb back up, I put an arm across the ladder to prevent her. "Gliss. I am not your enemy."

She looked down, scowling. Her broad cheekbones glowed with dusky color.

"There is something I am missing here." I sighed. "Please tell me."

"You are blind." Her scowl turned into a glare before she dropped her gaze to her hands. "Or you're making game of me."

"No. Think of me as new to this world. I don't remember a whole lot before I left."

She shrugged one shoulder sharply and mumbled something in which the words, *the way he looks at you,* could be made out.

"He?" But I knew whom she meant. I'd sensed that my zings were not just my own attraction. I'd felt those looks from Zathdar. Though he had done absolutely nothing about it, the vibe had been there just the same.

"Zathdar's bright blue eyes." If I expected her to be honest, I had to be honest back. "I can't help his looking. I promise you I didn't try to get him to look. I don't know if that helps." I fingered one of my braids, which were beginning to frazzle in the sea air, despite being rebraided just that morning. "I don't even know how relationships work, on this world. I was ten when I left. And my mother only talked about how rotten Canary—that is, King Canardan—was."

Gliss crossed her arms and leaned against the bulkhead as the ship gave a lurch. "That's pretty much what Zorala says. I was seeing a *princess* coming on board. Showing us all up. Crooking her royal finger at the captain."

Zorala, one of the cooks, was older, weathered, and seemed

to find the crew's interactions as good as theater.

"I'm not a princess." I tried not to sound sharp. "You can blame my parents for my being good at self-defense. My father started that when I was this high." I held my palm down. "And my mother kept it going. As for finger crooking, seems to me that neither royal nor street-sweeper fingers will be any more successful than the other if the captain doesn't want to be crooked."

She hitched her shoulders under her ears, up and down.

"Look, Gliss. Here's how my female code works. I should say that there are many female codes on my sorry planet filled with dysfunction"—the closest word was *distortion in conduct*—"but here's how I see it. If there's a she-and-he twosome, and I find myself attracted to the he, then I wait for her to let me know if there's any hope. Otherwise, hands off. She has to tell me, not him. But if they're not a couple, well, fair's fair. Not that I mean to go after your captain. I'm not sure I like anything but his looks. Definitely not his taste in clothes, and I'm not so sure about this pirate business. But, for my information only, are you two a couple?"

She looked down at the deck. "No." She faced me squarely. "Said on hiring there would be no dalliances with the crew. But sometimes they say that, and later..." She shrugged.

"Yeah. I know that men change their minds. So do women. Look, I want to get off this ship onto land, and live my own life. Whatever that might be. Fair enough?"

She didn't smile, but at least she didn't look as angry. "Fair enough." She climbed up so fast I don't think her feet touched the rungs but twice.

I followed more slowly. Just as well I would soon be gone. Political enemies were bad enough. I didn't want to make a personal one, just because Mr. Pirate might turn out to have a roving eye.

So I did my own arm crossing and cold manner when I entered the captain's cabin. If Captain Hurricane noticed, he gave no sign. He was in the middle of studying a chart, barely glanced up, his manner absent as he said, "My messenger finally caught up with us. The king sent the navy out to blockade the main harbor, as I'd predicted. We're maybe a day from their outer perimeter. Here's the news. He knows you're here on my ship. The navy is ordered to be on the watch for us."

"How are you going to break through the blockade?"

"By joining a big fishing fleet. We've been running parallel to one these past few days. By morning we will be a different ship. I must request you to spend the rest of today and all of tomorrow in your cabin. I cannot risk you being seen on deck. You are too recognizable."

"Who on the fishing boats would know me from anyone else?" I asked, not hiding my skepticism.

"We're going to run a quick errand before we land." He looked out the stern windows, as if something important was happening on the choppy seas.

"All right." I knew he wasn't going to tell me what his "errand" was, not after I'd refused point-blank to become part of his plans. "If you have something to read, I would like to try to reacquaint myself with Sartoran writing. Preferably something that might catch me up on local history."

He frowned at the chart table, fingers toying with a quill pen, then shook his head. "Nothing on board." When my glance strayed to those bound books over his bunk, he said with a quick smile, "Not histories. But if you like, when we land, I could scout you out one."

Thus obliquely asking my plans. Right. As if I'd discuss them! "Well, let's get to safety first. And to land," I said with

131

hearty cheer, my gaze drawn irresistibly... And when his eyes met mine the inward jolt made me shift my own attention to the open scuttle, then to the statue.

Yet the afterimage remained of his open-necked night-sky blue shirt with the gold and crimson embroidery of leaping dolphins round the hem, the green-and-white-striped deck trousers, and a sash riding loose on his narrow hips. The sash at least matched his headband, though both were purple with yellow fringe. More specifically I was more aware of him inside those clothes, the contours of muscle shaping the shirt, the long lines of his legs looking very good in those deck trousers. I wondered if he had buns of steel...

And stalked out, utterly disgusted with myself.

Chapter Twelve

Elva wasn't there when I woke the next morning. I eased one of the vapor-blurred scuttles open a crack, bringing in a strong whiff of fish. I was surprised to discover the surrounding waters full of boats and ships, tall masts surging slowly on the sea, sails belling in the same direction.

When I peered out at the foredeck, fine rain misted my face. Under a low, steel gray sky, the crew labored at dismantling what seemed to be another ship. The *Zathdar* with its clean lines had transformed into a clutter of barrels, nets, old sailcloth, and the topgallant masts laid along a gangway. The masts looked stumpy now, and the rigging had been altered completely to the triangles of fore-and-aft, which made sense for fishing cruising, where you stay closer to shore and want to maneuver better. These sails were old, some of them splotched with mold, patched in other places.

What startled me most, though, was not the crew. They looked pretty much like always, except the piratical splashes of color were gone. The big surprise was the captain. I almost missed him, but the angle of shoulder and neck, the distinctive stance snapped my attention back to the man tending the wheel.

If those buns of steel existed, there was certainly no sign of 'em now. He wore a grubby pair of canvas trousers bunched up round his waist and tied with a rope, some kind of knitted stockings (complete with gaping holes) and aged deck shoes. His shirt was a sun-faded brown, with a long vest over it containing a lot of pockets. As usual he'd tied a bandana around his head, but this was a narrow length of brown cloth, below which at last he'd let his hair hang down. I could see why he bound it up. His hair was an ugly hank of tangled, matted brown, coarse as horsehair, constantly flapping in his face.

My hottie radar still bleeped, even with the nightmare hair.

Elva appeared from belowdecks, brow tense with worry. Behind her, Devli looked excited and happy.

"What is it?" I asked.

"Let's go inside, where we won't get yelled at or knocked out of the way," Elva grumped.

"We were locked below," Devli said to me.

"How should I know he was serious about that? He's never been serious about anything," Elva protested.

"I *love* the idea we might be famous. Like, our faces drawn onto wanted posters and spread round the fleet." Devlaen grinned like a kid.

"What's going on now? I take it we're not staying with this fishing fleet?"

"A raid," they said together, Elva with eyes rolled skyward and Devli bouncing on his toes.

"What?"

"We joined the fishers just long enough to get inside the blockade. Now he's going to run a raid. On a navy ship back out on the perimeter." Devli hopped again. "Hiding behind one of the little islands."

"Zathdar is an idiot," Elva added.

Her disgust was a candle to the sun of my anger.

Despite the captain's request that I stay in my cabin, I marched out into the fine, cool rain, but not before I saw the triumphant look Elva shot at her brother.

It took me a little time to thread my way between the crew members busy dismantling the mess so artistically arranged on deck, and forming long lines of rope haulers along the gangway as the topgallant masts were being raised again.

The seas had gone gray, and the mist was thickening fast, obscuring the other fishing boats. The nearest was a blur maybe two hundred yards away.

By pausing, ducking, swerving, side hopping and squirming, I managed to make it all the way aft, where Zathdar stood at the helm, rain dripping off his matted clumps of hair, his eyes narrowed as he peered into the gray gloom that smeared the line between sky and sea.

I stood for a long moment, struggling to get firm control of my temper. Bitchiness never helped anything, I knew that. So far, being mellow at least got me some answers.

So, when I knew my voice would be neutral, I asked, "How can you see anything?"

"He's out there," Zathdar said.

"Yes, and I was hoping you'd explain about that."

He regarded me with faint surprise. "I told you we had an errand to run. You have an objection to my running a raid on one of War Commander Randart's most poisonous snakes?"

"I thought your errand meant changing the sails or something. Do you"—I tried to maintain a semblance of cordiality—"have an objection to keeping your word? You did say when we broke the blockade we'd land. I see no land, and your errand seems to be taking us farther out to sea."

"We're in the bay." He gestured with one hand, a wide

sweep. "And I saw the perfect opportunity. After my raid, we'll land. I promise that."

If we're successful, I thought, but I knew how that would sound, so I retraced my steps.

Devli and Elva waited inside the cabin, she sitting on her bunk, he at the tiny fold-down table. "Well?" she asked, as I sank onto my bunk.

"We land after this raid." I raised my fingers in air quotes, to which they reacted with mute question. "He says."

Elva scowled. "If we are alive."

"He said I could help." Devli chortled. "So I'm gonna wear a disguise."

Elva turned on him. "What?"

"Perhaps I could cast an illusion or two." Devli rubbed his hands. "Anyway, I'm going. When else will I ever get to be on an actual pirate raid?"

"Wear an eye patch," I suggested, aware of my heartbeat accelerating. My brain was catching up on reality. Me, a waitress, whose most accustomed battles were against L.A. traffic, was on board a *pirate ship*, heading straight for a *raid* on a naval ship.

"Eye patch?" Devli broke into my dark thoughts.

"Pirates have to wear eye patches. And peg legs." I got up, and sat again. "I suspect it has something to do with cannon balls, and no, I'm not explaining that."

The watch bell changed, and Devli vanished on some other errand.

Elva hunched on the other bunk, obviously brooding. We left the door open, watching the swift alteration of the ship back into sleek piracy, as the last of the fishers vanished into the gray haze behind us. The crew got the topgallant masts fidded, the sheets rattled down and the sails set, after which our speed increased with bucking surges, a fine spray arcing on the low, lee side of the ship.

The wind had increased with the rain and we tacked at a dramatic slant. An island emerged out of the gloom, a mere shadow at first, one at which we appeared to be aimed. My nerves twisted slowly into knot-gutted tension as the wind and current brought us closer to it with what was rapid speed for ships.

Chasing another ship is not like a movie car chase. It's a kind of hurry-up-and-wait affair. You run around on deck getting ready, while the ships slowly, inexorably sail toward one another.

The first danger was weathering that island, as we skirted much too close to its rocky cliffs on the in-running tide. I could see the individual twigs making up nests on which birds sat; other birds cawed, dived and flapped about. Zathdar stayed at the wheel, speaking to his crew in short, sharp sentences, while we tacked at that rooftop slant close to the island, and about the same time my tension racked up to high anxiety at the sight of those breakers rolling away toward the rocky shore, the last cliff slid by and we were in open ocean again—revealing our prey. It was a three-masted clipper, easily twice the length of Zathdar's *Hurricane*.

Even I, who knew little about ships, could sense the navy ship's anticipation of an easy kill in the way some sails jerked up and others came down, and the ship hauled its wind in every bit as tight a curve as our own. They were coming on the attack.

So imagine their dismay when, vaguely on the still-gray horizon (it was now late afternoon, not that you could tell where the sun was, but the light was steadily more diffuse) two nicks appeared.

The other two pirate consorts.

Zathdar had sent them the easy way, to form the other half of the pincer. We'd been the bait.

We began to close with the clipper. Devli reappeared, looking ridiculous in a blond wig like an old dust mop and ill-fitting striped trousers (yellow and green) with an outsized shirt of a taxing shade of orange. "He has enough disguises to equip the city theater down there," Devli exclaimed happily.

"You look like an idiot," Elva retorted.

"Sure, but I don't look like me. In case they have wanted posters issued. Oh, *how* I'd love to see one, if it's really true," he added longingly. "And how much of a price on my head."

"Probably two copper tinklets. Three more than you're worth," Elva said with sisterly disrespect.

Devli grinned, flipping his curls at her. "You're sour because you don't get to go. If you acted friendly, I'll wager he'd have you along in a trice."

Elva wavered, which surprised me. Then she shrugged. "And leave Sasharia counting her toes here? Seems fair enough that somebody stays to keep her company."

Devli turned to me. "I wish he'd let you come," he said shyly.

"Thanks. I think." I gripped my hands behind my back. "But no thanks."

Brother and sister widened their eyes in surprise. "But you're good," Devli observed.

"Good at practice. I've spent years and years at it. That does not mean I want to let somebody try to ventilate my chitlins. It only means that maybe I'm ready for it if it happens." I was desperate to keep my voice even. How could I be the only one scared spitless? But from all I could see, I was.

Devli's brow puckered. "You were so *good* in the fight at the transfer tower."

I thought back, remembering only a blur of tiredness that jolted suddenly into a super-powered adrenaline rush...powered not only by inept guards trying to capture us, but by the intense awareness of that derisive pirate whose first word about me had been *useless.*

I wasn't going to say that my main motivation had been to show him how wrong he was. Nope, nope, nope.

"Accident," I stated. "I was half-asleep, running on instinct. I am supposed to stay out of sight. Remember?" And in a thoroughly cowardly, absolutely desperate attempt to change the blasted subject, "Elva would you give me a rundown on what's happened in the past twenty years?"

"If you like." She looked perplexed. "In a general way, at least."

To keep my hands busy so they wouldn't shake, I began to unbraid my hair and comb it out. One braid at a time, wincing and cursing under my breath at the snags. Back in L.A. I'd be doing this job after a good treatment with a whole lot of conditioner, but there wasn't any here.

"How far back shall I go?" Elva asked, and then, her eyes rounding, "If you'll pardon my saying so, you have a *lot* of hair."

"Oh yeah. My dad was a frizz-ball too. Made Einstein look bald—never mind who Einstein was. Let's say that where I come from, big hair is totally *uncool.*" The word came out in English. There wasn't anything close. "I made the mistake of cutting it when I got mad at my mom, not long after we got through the World Gate, and for a couple of years I looked like a walking mushroom. Growing it long at least weighs it down, and I can braid it."

She grinned as I yanked out another braid, which sprang into determined curls adding to the mass hanging down my back to my butt. When I pulled it straight, I could sit on it.

"All right. Well, in '36, two years after you left, there was a strange incident we call the Siamis War, but it wasn't a war, it was more of an enchantment, and extended over the world."

"Oh yes, someone mentioned that. I wondered if 'Siamis' was a place or a person."

"Someone from Norsunder. An original Old Sartoran, I mean from four *thousand* years ago." She hunched her shoulders. "He was young-looking and handsome and charming, and he enchanted people by just thinking at them."

"That sounds nasty." I watched the archery teams climb to the tops.

"It was. Though nobody remembered much afterward. It was like we all lost a year. I was a toddler, so I didn't really notice anything, but the adults still talk about it, and they're worried because Norsunder is on the move, they say."

"That sounds even worse." The clatter of arrows and weapons from outside brought us to the cabin door as the archery teams took their places on the mastheads and readied themselves.

"Yes, Devli says the mages—" Elva stiffened, her face blanching.

I leaped up and joined her, my hair half-combed in a curling mass, the other half in ratty braids, as the deck crew lined up along the rails, weapons at hand.

Things had changed far faster than I'd expected.

Our pirate schooner lurched toward the navy ship, which looked enormous as it loomed steadily closer. The fading light in the west was augmented by lanterns hung high. Zathdar's crew waited, motionless except for nervous hands on weapons, quick head-turnings. Ah. So they were scared too. I could see it in tightened shoulders, in stiff fingers, shufflings, and restless checking and rechecking of weapons.

For some reason the sight of their tension actually eased some of mine. So I was not the only scared person on board. The proximity of violence, deliberately chosen, jetted a mingling of emotions through me, most negative, but somewhere in there was anticipation. Even readiness, I could feel it in the way my muscles tightened along my spine and through my back, a feeling akin to the moments before a match at a big competition, but at a fuel-injected hyper-level.

Zathdar spun the wheel. Sail parties brailed up two sails with lightning speed and the ships thumped together, yards and rigging entangling, masts creaking. We all staggered, then shadowy figures crouched below the rail jumped up and swung over to the navy ship from ropes. More ran across entangled yards to the other ship, roaring and howling.

"Inside! Shut the door!" Owl bawled at me as he ducked under a swinging lantern, sword raised. He and two others took up station in front of Elva's and my cabin, obviously on defense duty. Either that or to keep Elva and me from running to the navy guys.

The mass of surging figures shouted, fought, leaped to and fro. Annoyed as I was with Zathdar, the name Randart had scared me. I had no intention whatsoever of leaping from Hurricane's frying pan into the fire of Canardan's sinister war commander.

But Zathdar didn't know that. Where was he, anyway?

The lanterns shone through the ropes in wild spider-web patterns, creating intersecting geometric light patches and shadows, making it impossible to tell the surging figures apart.

At least the darkness has to be hiding blood and guts...sure don't see any, don't want to see any—

I peered around the cabin door.

The tweet of a whistle—a roar of triumph—and twenty or thirty armed silhouettes jumped down from the navy ship's higher deck. A surprise squad of marines held back as reinforcements leaped over the rail onto our ship and fought their way down the deck, outnumbering the defending pirates.

"They know you're here," Elva said flatly, and I threw open the door.

Owl twisted round. "You know Randart does not mean safety for you."

My jaw was locked, teeth gritted. "I'm out here so I have room to defend myself. I. Do not. Want. To be. *Anyone's.* Prisoner."

From overhead a colorful figure swung, and Zathdar landed on the yard directly above us.

A quick exchange of glances between him and Owl, then: "Here!"

Zathdar flung a cavalry sword through the air toward me.

One sharp thud of heart against ribs and years of kata training took over. I knew sword forms. I knew how to throw and catch a spinning sword. You don't take it standing still, but match movement, and so I flowed into kata mode and clipped the sword out of the air, bringing it down with a swoosh before the first naval warrior reached us.

He leaped back, joining his companions, who were all in brown uniforms. For a moment they all stared at me, eyes so wide twin lantern flames reflected in them, their heads turning slightly as I swung the saber back and forth, back and forth, trying to get the feel for its unfamiliar weight and shape.

"That's the one," the lead man said. "Take her."

My heartbeat shifted into overdrive, drumming in my ears.

Owl, two of his sailors, and Elva (who'd ducked into the cabin and returned with a knife) formed a line in front of me, all of us keeping clear of the others' reach.

"No kill," Owl ordered hoarsely.

Elva sent him a distracted glance. "I thought that was all hot air."

"No. True," he snapped. "Why do you think the bow teams are waiting?"

I remembered them, crouched there overhead. I realized no arrows had been loosed.

Yet.

I swung my cavalry saber, which was much heavier than I was used to. I noted the red tassel on it. This was the one from the weapons locker that no one had touched. Zathdar's fighting blade! But he was nowhere in sight.

A short, barked word and the navy guys rushed us. Then time stopped. The universe narrowed to my trembling fingers, my chi breathing, and the cut and thrust of swinging steel.

No kill? No chance to ask. It made me faster, surer, because I fought as I always had in practice, only one step harder. I did not care if I hurt anyone, I didn't want to kill anyone—

—and they were not trying to kill me. Disarm, yes. Wound, even. But not to kill.

And so I parried, blocked, deflected, kicked, punched, nicked, thumped (and used my knee once to unfair but effective advantage—sorry, guy) but I never stabbed.

The endless moment stretched into a roaring blur as sweat stung my eyes and my throat rasped raw. Abruptly I swayed there on the deck, whooping for breath, peering this way and that for the next target, but there were no more targets. There were only four people lying on the deck, either unconscious or wounded. The rest retreated fast, vanishing over the rail as a mass of gathered pirates, fresh from the supporting ships, chased them aft.

As the navy guys swarmed back to their own ship, the battle shifted to the other deck. I rushed to the side, Owl next to me, in time to witness the end of a saber duel between Zathdar and their captain. The latter's sword clanged to the deck, Zathdar held his point at the man's throat and shouted something that was echoed by a woman at the other end of the navy ship. She was one of Zathdar's other captains.

The result was weapons clanking and whanging to the deck, hands rising in the universal "I surrender. Don't hit me!" The king's sailors were obviously not going to test the pirates' willingness to stick to the rules at the price of their captain's life, and I wondered if that was out of loyalty or fear.

Zathdar flicked a look our way.

Owl moved with the speed of someone who had received orders. As I leaned on the rail, still breathless, the pirates dragged the unconscious navy guys to the rail and attached them to ropes to be boomed over to their own deck. Meanwhile Zathdar prodded the captain and they vanished into the clipper's broad cabin.

The pirates herded the navy below the clipper's decks, then closed and barred the hatches. After that they moved about, some purposeful, most just talking, pointing, demonstrating with their weapons, the restless rattling about of people shedding adrenaline.

Devli emerged from the hatch, papers clutched to his orange shirt, his unlikely blond mop bouncing as he bounded toward the place where the two rails ground together on the pitching waves.

On a sharp whistle, pirates swarmed aloft to free rigging and spars; others got busy hacking, chopping, tearing, cutting ropes. They were doing enough sabotage to ensure no chase would be made without a lot of repairs first. Some returned to the *Hurricane*, carrying pretty much anything the navy guys hadn't nailed down. There wasn't much to loot on a navy scout, but they'd done their best.

Elva joined me. "Ow," she said reflectively, binding a length of cloth round one forearm. "I hope that's the last pirate battle we're in. No matter what my brother says."

"Tell me about this no-kill order." My brain had gone oddly numb, and my hoarse voice sounded far away, like someone else.

"Oh. That. It's just, the Fool, that is, Prince Jehan, who is supposedly in charge of the guard, the navy and I forget what else his father wants to duck the blame for, *supposedly* issued this command to their forces that in any skirmish they can't kill anyone until our side, that is, the resistance, does. He *supposedly* doesn't want our countrymen killing one another if it can be avoided. It seems to be the same for the pirates too. Anyway, I always thought it lies. Canardan's people trying to whitewash their rotten reputation. But I guess it's true. For the navy and army, I emphasize," she added, her brow furrowed. "Not for War Commander Randart's private guard."

The two ships jolted, staggering everyone on both decks, then parted with a groan of timbers. I wondered if Zathdar had made it back just as a colorful figure emerge from the navy captain's cabin. He climbed up the shrouds, caught a rope I hadn't seen in the wavering light from the lanterns (it was quite dark by now) and swung over lightly, landing on the topsail yard just as two arrows hissed through the air from the other ship.

He caught one of the backstays, slid to the deck near us. A last arrow thunked into the coaming round the fore hatch directly behind him, then someone on the other ship shouted an order, and there were no more arrows.

Zathdar gave us all one comprehensive glance. "All right?" He addressed everyone, but his glance rested last on me.

"Alive," I said, and Elva echoed me. Then I drew in a deep breath. *Keep it neutral. You still have to land.*

But I had to ask. "Was it really necessary, this raid? Or just, you know, your typical pirate idea of fun?"

"Oh, let's say that this fellow has been doing a bit of piracy on his own." Zathdar tipped his head toward the ship. "Under orders from the war commander."

His manner was too airy, a contrast with that tight gesture. Plainly I was not the only one keeping crucial info behind buttoned lip.

He grinned at me. "And you think I look strange." He took the cavalry sword from my unresisting fingers, stepped back and flicked the point through the air a yard from my head—an ironic salute.

I clutched at my hair, felt the one side with ratty braids dangling down, the other a tangled mass of frizzy curls, emphasis on the tangled. Total big-hair crisis! I had to laugh, the sheer, squeaky laugh of a sudden rush of knee-whacking relief. It was really over. My muscles turned to Smuckers' finest.

"Well done." He flourished the sword as he smiled at us all. But again I had the distinct sense he was talking to me.

Then he turned away, lifting his voice. "Captain's punch for every hand!"

The sailors responded with a loud, hearty cheer as Zathdar bent to yank that last arrow out of the coaming. He straightened up, flushed with triumph. "Come down in the wardroom to celebrate?"

Again, he did not quite address me, but the air in my general direction. Owl, overseeing the last sweep of the deck, raised a hand in agreement. This was a general invitation, not a private one. He'd said it would take place in the wardroom. No harm in that.

Then Zathdar turned my way. "Join us, Sasharia?"

"Sure." And to Owl, who was rubbing his hands and laughing under his breath, "Captain's punch?"

"Oh, it's good." Owl chuckled. "But it'll knock you back if you're not careful."

The crew divided up into two parties, with off-duty crew members carrying food up to those on duty. The watch captains crowded around with us at the battered table in the wardroom, roaring again as the grinning cook muscled in a huge tureen of something that smelled like citrus, with hard liquor undertones.

A variety of cups, mugs and glasses passed from hand to hand, everyone dipping into the tureen. Next came the sounds of slurping and sighing. The punch was a blend of berry, citrus, wine and a raisiny liquor that was very smooth going down, with a delicious bite. Warmth rushed through me, smoothing away the aches.

"Good, eh?" Owl dug his elbow in my side.

"Mighty good." I sipped again, then realized they were all more or less watching me. So I lifted my glass to the table. "Great job, peeps!"

The *peeps* came out in English, but no one seemed to care. They gave another cheer. In such a small space, their enthusiasm hurt the ears. I gulped down more punch, feeling

147

hot and a little dizzy as everyone started talking, the adrenaline-comedown sort of chatter I remembered from my competition days. "Didya see...?" "...and then I took my sword and..." "He was goin' for Sage, so I grabbed up a stool and..." Everyone wanted to air their own bit, to praise the others and be praised, and—as the punch loosened tongues—more of the compliments came my way.

I smiled and saluted and returned compliments about skirmishes I couldn't possibly have seen, because the flushed, smiling faces and bright eyes surrounding me so plainly expected it. And deserved it too. They'd won, we were safe.

But as the talk got wilder, the compliments sent my way took on a certain familiarity of expression. "Thought you'd finally take action," the cook said, giving me a friendly nudge with a powerful arm. I nearly fell face-first into the tureen.

"Knew you'd come out fer yer Dad," the forecastle captain boomed from the other side of the table. "He never forgot us that haven't any titles, no he did not."

And after a general (though less energetic) "Hear him, hear him!" one of the top hands thumped her mug onto the table.

Then red-haired Robin declared, "When you raise your banner, Princess, we'll be right behind you."

I tried to force a smile, and shot a suspicious look at Zathdar. He had been watching me. He gave his head the smallest shake, turning his thumbs outward, and I knew he hadn't said anything to the crew.

They didn't act like people ordered to drop hints about my princessly obligations, and anyway, it was all coming back to me, how people thought here. When you were born to a title, you had a responsibility along with the title. Your job was politics.

I left as soon as I could, aware of Elva's unhappy face over at a side table, where she sat with Zathdar's navigator and bosun. She followed me in silence.

I tramped wearily to my cabin, Elva behind me, wincing as she flexed her fingers. Titles—expectations—obligations—politics chased round in my head like dizzy mice.

A long drink of water, then I lay down, shut my eyes and firmly told myself that answers were my dad's job. I just had to find him.

Chapter Thirteen

While Atanial was on her way with her royal escort to the royal castle at Vadnais, back at the Ebans' home Marka, at last free of her bonds, crept downstairs. She'd gotten safely under her bed by the time she heard the smashings and bangings of searchers in the lower rooms. She hadn't known who was searching the house, but those words the tall, beautiful woman with the accent had said echoed over and over in her mind, *Living a lie.*

Then the tromping feet came upstairs. Two pairs appeared in her doorway, and one pair kicked roughly at her trunk. A young man said in a bored voice, "Here's the room with the signal. But the girl is gone."

"As well," someone else said.

As well. She knew what that meant. They'd had orders to kill her.

Tromp, tromp, tromp. The heavy boots clattered down the stairs. The crashes and bangs below ended. The door slammed, and the house was silent.

Marka was alone. Wondering if she would ever stop crying, she went back to working steadily at the knots.

Dawn painted the world in dreary blue streaks as she passed through the ruined rooms. She paused in the kitchen to grab some of the spilled food, drink from the water barrel, then eased out into the vegetable garden, where cold air promised rain. Her newly bare neck was chilled, and fresh tears rolled down her cheeks at the thought of her shorn hair—and Tam bearing it away. Maybe flinging it with disgust into a fire. *Stop it. Get home, warn Mama and the others.*

She thought of Mistress Eban's absent kindness. She thought of Tam, his grin, his hands. His kisses. Her beautiful hair that he used to run his fingers through, calling it ribbon-silk...

Her chest ached with the sobs that boiled up, but she couldn't let them escape. At least she had never told the king's man Tam's name, or anything about him. She could be glad of that. She would have to be glad of that.

She crossed the boot-trampled vegetable garden and scurried up the trail through the orchard, leaving barely a rustle.

Atanial slept through the next few days, only rising to drink some healer's tea she found waiting (the smell had woken her up), eat the meals she found on a tray and go right back to sleep. She was in a room, not a cell. The bed was clean and comfortable. Everything else could wait.

She let another week go by while she avoided the king's messengers, either pretending to be asleep, or claiming she still was unwell, as she recovered her strength and wondered what to do.

Then came the morning that Commander Randart entered the king's outer chamber, pushed past the scribes and runners, and scowled at the crowd around the king.

Canardan bustled his bureaucrats through the immediate business, and dismissed the rest with a laugh and a joke.

When the last had departed, the king motioned for Randart to shut the door. He sighed inwardly at his old friend's scowl. "What now?"

"Courier from Ellir." Randart sank into one of the cushioned interview chairs. "Zathdar seems to have slipped inside the blockade."

Canardan slammed a hand down on his desk. "Damn! How does a *pirate ship* 'slip' inside a blockade?"

"My scouts think he might have mingled in with the fishing fleet coming back from northern waters. Though no one reported any vessels standing out or otherwise drawing attention."

Canardan sat back, his breath hissing. "What else?"

"Zathdar reappeared on the other side of Mais Island."

Canardan pressed his hands to his eyes. "No. Don't tell me."

Randart waited, smiling grimly while the silence lengthened.

"All right," Canardan sighed, flinging his hands outward. "Tell me."

"The report is sketchy. Just arrived by transfer note." Only small pieces of paper fit into the magical notecases, which made for very short reports. "But he seems to have cut out the *Skate*. Took it just long enough for his rabble to strip it of supplies while he tried to pry details of the mission from Bragail."

Canardan laughed somewhat bitterly. "I wish him joy for his efforts. Bragail has too many secrets buried to hand any pirate a shovel."

"Except, if I read this aright"—Randart held up a folded bit of paper—"Zathdar began by flinging at least a couple of those secrets in his teeth."

Canardan leaned forward, hand out. "Let me see that." He frowned down at the paper... *The pirate said 2 words, "Chwahir" & "Glathan", so the cptn. endorsed Z's order to leave them alone in t/cabin. We went below, under swords of pirates.* "Glathan. I suspect we will never cease to regret that."

Randart shrugged. "Only way to deal with mages."

Canardan rubbed his eyes, trying to press back the pangs of a burgeoning headache. The kingdom was unraveling under his fingers. It would take a grand gesture of kingly proportion to wrest triumph out of disaster. One possible gesture was upstairs, having been left until her blistered feet had healed enough for her to walk.

Giving Canardan time to consider what to say when they did meet again. He'd been reflecting on those blistered feet from a cross-country run that everyone in the castle—the kingdom— apparently knew about before he did. He had begun to suspect she was avoiding him, but that was all right. He was still considering what to be done.

Bringing him to the present. "What about my son? No message from him?" Canardan flicked his solid-gold notecase.

"Yes, the courier had word about him as well. He sent one of his runners straight to Ellir, promising that the prince would be back by the beginning of the midsummer games." Randart added wryly, "You haven't heard from him directly because he seems to have been caught napping by some highway robbers along his path in the south, and he was robbed of everything, including his notecase."

Canardan groaned. The headache was worsening with every word he heard.

"Well, he did send his guard to the World Gate tower, so he cannot be blamed for a shortage of personal protection," Randart offered, inwardly despising that absurd order about not killing the enemy until they killed first. For Randart, there was no consideration for fellow countrymen, much less pirates or brigands. If you stood against him, you were an enemy. Enemies deserve death. Clear and simple.

Canardan snorted. "No, he can be blamed for being an idiot who cannot defend himself against a couple of bush skulkers. But he will be a married idiot as soon as we lay hands on that girl. We'll make it a grand festival, with public pardons handed out like roses."

Randart did not hide his surprise, or his displeasure.

"Carefully chosen ones," Canardan said swiftly, mistaking the direction of Randart's ire. "Anyway, as soon as Jehan shows up in Ellir, we'll know where he is. Send a message to him to stay put for the midsummer games. He can wine and dine the winning cadets, he can hold musical parties, he can visit every poet and painter in the city, but he is to *stay put.*"

"I'll send a dispatch as soon as we're done."

"We're done. Go yourself. Hunt down that pirate. I don't care if you use the entire fleet. The Chwahir plan is a disaster, blockading doesn't work, and we can't even get our trade protected, so you, my friend, are going pirate hunting, and when you do find them, kill them all. Make certain not one is left alive to come back here and blab all over about our villainy. Against *pirates.*"

Each considered how unfair that was.

"The only one I want left alive is the girl, and you bring her directly to me," the king ordered.

"Consider it done." Randart got up and left.

That night, Atanial awoke abruptly, aware someone was in her room.

If that's Canary, I will scream so loud they'll hear me in Sartor. She sat bolt upright in bed and yanked the covers to her neck.

A shape passed before the faint starlight glowing in her window, a female shape. Stout, with an ill-confined cloud of frizzy hair.

"Ananda?" she whispered, astonished.

"Yes," came the queen's soft voice. "No, do not light a candle. I am believed to be sleepwalking. It's part of my madness."

Atanial gave her eyes a vigorous rub, then she patted the bed, which was large enough to sleep a family comfortably. "Come. Talk to me. I'm glad you're still alive."

"Oh, he would never dare touch me," Queen Ananda said dryly. "After all, it's my name that brought him the crown, even if he put his Merindar chalice on all the shields and carriages. He's no Zhavalieshin. Neither is his boy. Though I wouldn't mind if Jehan were," she added in a reflective voice.

"Jehan?" Atanial prompted as the bed shifted and the queen settled, hands clasped around her knees. "Tell me about him."

The two women regarded one another in the pale starlight. The queen knew she was unprepossessing, but then she'd always been unprepossessing: short, plump, her hands broad, her nose a hawk beak, her hair an uncontrollable frizzy mat of yellow. Her brother Mathias was the tall, well-made version of frizz and nose who'd gone away and come back with this stunning beauty from another world.

"I know him little. What I do know, I shall tell you anon."

Atanial heard the hesitation in her voice and misconstrued the reason. She exclaimed impulsively, "First I want to say this. I never saw you after your father's memorial. This is twenty years of your time too late, but I apologize if I ever made you suffer."

"No," the queen murmured. "You didn't. I knew what Canardan was after when he flirted with you. I only fooled myself once, when I believed his blandishments during our courtship. But I didn't know what real love was until I saw you with Math."

Atanial bowed her head until her brow rested on her knees, which she'd brought up under the covers. Her voice was muffled. "Then my flirtation with Canary must have looked doubly bad to you."

"I could see you keeping it light and merry."

"Yes. And no. He is amazingly attractive, or at least was." Atanial sighed. "So flirting with him was fun. Dancing close to the fire. I thought you didn't care, I thought you didn't notice, I thought I could in some way help Math. And oh, I have to admit I liked the danger. But he burned me good, right along with Math."

The queen nodded. "I know that, and I have my own confession to make. I believe it is my fault that you and Math had to run. You see, I told Canardan the night my father died that I was going to renounce the crown in favor of Math."

"You did? We never heard that!"

"Of course not. You only suffered the results. I thought I could deflect Canardan from taking power, but I had misjudged everything. Including his reasons for marrying me."

"Oh, Ananda. I'm so sorry. So that's behind the mad-queen story?"

"When he said I went mad with grief over my father's death and my brother's treachery, for five years he made sure I saw no one in order to deny it. I did not have the wit or ability to resist. So life went on, passing me by. I became a nonentity."

The queen shrugged, her voice briefly ironic, reminding Atanial momentarily of Math. "Maybe I deserved it a little, though I never asked to be born to a title. But I finally realized that the guise of madness was a convenience for us both. He gets the power he wanted, and I have my freedom within these walls. However, taking power has not proved easy for Canardan. Things have gone wrong for him, especially in the past few years. Ever since Jehan came back. Canardan's become very determined as a result."

Atanial said abruptly, "Bringing us back to Canardan's boy. Is he good to you, at least?"

"Jehan's not really a boy. Though everyone thinks of him as one. It's that white morvende hair, the dreamy manner. He does have a tendency to veer off and follow bards if they sing well enough, I hear, or artists if they're pretty and paint well, but yes, he's always been kind to me."

"Then I won't hate him. But if I can find a way to defeat Canary, I will."

The queen paused, staring ahead for a long moment. "Canardan's got the castle on double watches. Everyone, *everyone*, knows you are back. And that you are here. So you have become a royal guest. Which is why you are in the royal-guest wing here, though no one at all sleeps in any of the rooms either side of you, and the tower is guarded at all the stairways. It's also warded, I believe."

"Thank you for the warning."

The queen rose. Her voice was soft and dreamy. "He's going to offer you everything. Including my life. He would keep that promise."

She drifted to the door.

"Ananda, wait," Atanial whispered, not daring to raise her voice.

But the queen had had her say. She vanished, and by the time Atanial had wrestled out of the covers, run to the door and cautiously eased it open, no one was in sight.

Atanial wandered back to the bed. That was weird, that was definitely weird. She sensed the woman had more to say, but if so, why not say it?

Because she thinks I might buy Canary's line. Even at the price of her life.

It was jolting, uncomfortable, and if looked at a certain way, kind of insulting, but Atanial would not let herself go there. She herself had misjudged the queen in the past, so she had to accept without rancor that that was a two-way street.

Atanial threw herself on the bed, knowing she should arm herself with sleep, but that seemed impossible. She wiggled her toes. Her feet did feel a lot better, thanks to the salve they'd given her after that first marvelous bath.

She could get up and look now, except if she lit a lamp in order to check Queen Ananda's words, who might be watching?

Remember, you are a prisoner.

She dozed eventually, but that thought was still with her when she woke. Pearly blue early morning light pooled on the spectacular rug in several shades of green and gold with highly stylized flowers interwoven.

Atanial threw back the coverlet and padded to the wardrobe. Her feet no longer hurt. The wardrobe was almost as large as the bedroom, into which someone had brought quite a number of trunks.

Canary had had an entire day to set up this pretty prison before he'd closed his trap on the Ebans. She needed to remember that too.

But, she thought happily when she threw back the first

trunk and saw the gorgeous silk inside, there was no reason she needn't take any armaments offered her.

It was a stylishly gowned Atanial, her hair pinned up with pearls, who received the runner come to invite her to breakfast with the king, as he had every day.

It was time to face the enemy guns.

"Please, tell him I'd be delighted. Or better, why don't you escort me? Though I remember the castle fairly well, I don't know which rooms he uses."

The young man blushed as he bowed.

Atanial placed her hand confidingly on his arm and tripped along the hall. She mentally counted up all the armsmen she saw, sure there were some out of sight.

Prisoner, she thought, at the same moment Canary glimpsed her floating down the big marble stairway to the terrace where he had the servants set up a breakfast. Nothing private. Not that there was any privacy when every single pair of ears was cocked in this direction, and every pair of eyes jostling to catch a glimpse of the famed princess. Let them see a kingly welcome.

With covert appreciation he noted that only her face had aged, but its lines were those of intelligence, of laughter, of hard-won experience. Her hair was the same sun-lit yellow as the old days, and her body under that blue silken stuff formed the same strong, enticing curves that had caught his eye two decades ago.

He forced his gaze away and smiled, and she smiled, and he indicated the table, beautifully laid out with the best gold-edged porcelain, the best golden utensils, a crystal vase with fresh-picked rose buds.

She sat, arranging her skirts.

He waited for the silent servitors to set out the platters of hot food. Then he waved them away.

"Feeling better?" he asked.

"Lovely! So catch me up on the news." She tipped her head and charmed him by plopping her elbows on the table.

"Local news?" he asked, with some irony.

"Oh, no. World news. What have I missed?"

"You missed a couple of brushes with Norsunder." He poured out perfectly steeped Sartoran tea for her, himself. "All the mages are yammering about a real strike one of these days. But they've been yammering for the past decade, and nothing has happened yet."

"That sounds nasty." She cradled the fine porcelain cup in her fingers, sipped, smiled over the gold rim of the cup. "Tell me something nice. What is the news in Sartor?"

"From what I've heard, Shontande Lirendi is busy courting Yustnesveas Landis."

"If I knew that Carlael of Colend had a son, I had forgotten. I hope he is not as mad as his father," Atanial said.

"No. Not in the least. He is also a throwback to Matthias the Magnificent." Canardan added sardonically, "Even my cloud-brained son noticed, when I sent him west to Alsais to get some diplomatic experience. Said every female within riding range is in love with him, and half the men as well. Certainly every princess of eligible age seems to be waiting for him to throw the rose, which leaves the rest, like my boy, out in the cold."

"If he's that beautiful, what are his chances with Yustnesveas of Sartor?"

"Well, no one knows. But there's been some diplomatic fluttering about the fact that she'd never leave Sartor, and he'd never leave Colend, so the only solution is those two combining kingdoms into one of the biggest empires this world has ever known, even in the old empire days."

Atanial whistled as she set down the cup and lavishly piled crispy-edged oatcakes onto her plate.

"But there are those who don't think anything will come of it." He helped himself, and for a short time there was no sound but the distant chatter of birds as they ate. Then he lifted his fork, watching appreciatively as she got a second helping. "You still have a splendid appetite, I see."

"Of course," she said equably. "When the food is as good as this. And when I've gone without as many meals as I have." She gave him a mocking salute with her teacup.

He grinned. "Tell me about your girl. She a good eater as well?"

"Yes." Atanial added honey-butter to her oatcakes.

"That's not exactly informative."

"No." She helped herself to some sliced peaches.

"Will you at least listen to my suggestion?"

"Talk away. It's your palace, and your invitation." She made a wry gesture indicating herself there on the chair in her splendid gown, and gave him a lovely smile. "We'll call it an invitation, since you've been nice enough to include a scented walk-in bath and trunks of clothes and a fine room in your durance vile."

"Now, Atanial," he chided. "I'd rather have you as an ally. Much rather."

"In what plans?"

"Recover Khanerenth's past glories." He lifted his hand, taking in the palace. "That's it without embroidery. We're a sinking ship. Trade disrupted, neighboring kingdoms call the prices, and they don't cut us any deals. Threat of war with Norsunder. Chwahirsland has Shnit Sonscarna back on the throne, which has been no good news to anyone."

"I hadn't known he was gone."

"Oh, for a while. But he came back."

She remembered the horrible reports of Shnit of the Chwahir. Now *that* was a truly evil king, no ifs, ands or buts.

But he wasn't the issue. Khanerenth was. "Recovering lost glories sounds nice, but what does that mean? Past artistic achievements? Past trade agreements? Surely not lands that have been settled by treaty."

"Negotiating with bad governments, trouble—" He held up a hand. "I know you're about to come at me with some remark about my governing, but you don't actually know anything except gossip from the Ebans. You can sit in on my interviews, talk to my treasury steward, make up your own mind. At least I've held on. Locan Jora, the others northwards, they keep changing kings like foot warriors change their socks."

"That can't be good." She ran her fingertip round the gold edging on her cup. "So what do you want from me?"

"An introduction to your daughter. Just an introduction. Let her meet my boy. See if they suit. Good diplomacy, join the families, promote peace. Heal the problems here."

Atanial laughed. "How can I arrange that when I am in your castle, surrounded by half a wing of good-looking young men and women brandishing spears?"

"But you are free to go any time." He opened his hands. "Go and find her, with my good will."

Chapter Fourteen

I woke up feeling sticky and hot. The ship wallowed like an old tub. There was no wind. Yet I heard a curious scraping sound, too rhythmic to be weather.

I got up, grumpily wishing that they hadn't seen fit to give me this fancy cabin with a (sweltering) bunk, when a hammock would have been so much airier. Second, I wished I'd warmed up before the swashbuckling of the day before. And how did I get *that* many bruises? I didn't remember taking any of those hits, but they sure ached now.

I peered out of the scuttle. Sun dazzle splashed off the water with eye-watering brightness. There was no hint of a breeze.

A party of tired-looking sailors sat on the deck under the shade of a slack sail, honing the weapons. There were two or three kids about twelve or thirteen aboard. They had been hidden below during the fighting, on Zathdar's orders, so they too seemed grumpy as they carried polished, sharpened weapons to the weapons locker and then brought another to each crew member holding a whetting stone. When I remembered how much drinking had gone on the night before, I suspected headaches were also part of the general malaise.

With a total lack of energy I straightened the bunk. I couldn't complain about a generous gesture—

My thoughts fled like frightened birds when I opened the cupboard below my bunk to get out a change of clothes and saw my gear bag had been moved.

Could that have been the ship? No, it couldn't. I'd tucked it just so. And it hadn't moved during that storm early in our journey.

While I was down in the wardroom, someone had come in and searched my stuff.

Elva was already gone from the cabin. I was alone. I yanked out the bag, ripped it open and unfolded the exquisite embroidered coverlet. There were my things: my Earth clothes and sandals; a carved wooden box containing the jewels Mother and I had carried through the Gate; a child's simple flute (called a *recorder* on Earth) that my father had given me, but hadn't had time to teach me to play; and plainest, but by far the most important, a seashell wrapped in homespun cloth. Just the sort of memento a child would carry, Magister Glathan and my father had decided when they prepared this magical token, and taught me the spells...

It was there. It was safe. I wrapped it back up and replaced the things, then replaced the bag.

Nothing was gone, but there remained the fact that someone on board this ship had nosed through my stuff.

I left the cabin, grimacing as the glare and heat hit me. The heavy summer air was thick with the scents of brine and wet wood, half-dried canvas, and sweaty people. I dodged around the work party and wandered to the shrouds, the heavy ropes attaching the foremast to the hull. These thick ropes smelled of sea and hemp and oils. The round wooden deadeyes showed the effect of wind and weather, but beneath, the stroke of adze remained.

I held onto two of the shrouds, staring down at the water

plashing gently against the side of the hull as I mentally reviewed the night before. Who had been at the wardroom table with me? I could pretty much remember them all, mostly by images of flushed faces as they deprogrammed, like after any kind of sudden big event, whether an earthquake or a big competition. Zathdar had been in the wardroom all the time I was there. Same with Owl and Robin. Okay. So...now what I had to consider was why I suspected Zathdar first.

Movement at my side broke my concentration. Elva held out some toasted bread with melted cheese. "Hungry?" she asked.

I took it with a word of thanks, and she put her hands through the squares made by the shrouds and the horizontal ratlines, leaning her forehead against the twisted ropes. "I know better than to down that punch. I should have drunk the crew's ale," she said sourly. "He gave them the best. Ellir Gold."

"Well, if they're going to raid, why not the best? I take it then you didn't notice who came and went during the party?"

She gave me a glance of quick concern. "What's wrong?"

"Someone went through my belongings last night."

She didn't ask how I knew. She looked away, her shoulders tight, and I said, in blank surprise, "Devlaen?"

She shrugged, her face pink with embarrassment and guilt. "He was gone for a while, and he seemed, oh, like a scolded pup, when he came back."

I let my breath out. So that's why Elva had looked so miserable last night. "I didn't think it of him."

"I suspect his magisters ordered him to. He says they think you have some kind of magical knowledge that you aren't telling anyone." Her tone expressed disbelief and disinterest. She was a navigator, knew nothing of magic and cared less. "You suspected Zathdar," she added with faint triumph.

165

"Not because he's done anything I consider particularly untrustworthy. Opposite."

She fingered the taut shroud. "I don't understand."

"Because my distrust makes no sense. I don't trust him because I like him more than not. I, um, grew up, let us say, hearing about handsome and untrustworthy men."

"You think him handsome? I don't. Anyway, you mean kings." She made a thumbs-down gesture.

"Well, yes. Not only Canary, either. For a time when I was about thirteen my mother was angry with my father for not returning. She got past that, but I guess it had its effect." I whooshed out my breath. "I really have to get over it as well. I mean, Zathdar was there all night. I saw him."

"He could have had someone search your things," she said.

"Yes, but is that really characteristic? From what little we've seen, if he wanted to, he would have searched it himself. Right in front of me."

"Yes, that's more his style." Her tone made it clear she did not think the better of him for it.

I wiped my sweaty forehead against my sleeve. At home I would have jumped in the shower. Now I turned away, my braids swinging against my back, and finished the bread and cheese as I made my way below to the cleaning frame shared by the entire crew. It was made of wood, fitted into the door to the crew quarters, but laden with magic spells. I stepped through, enjoying the snap and tingle of magic whisking away dirt and grime and I guess bacteria.

The air was hot and stuffy down there, the night crew swinging in their hammocks, their deep breathing audible. I paused in the companionway, listening to the thump of feet overhead, as I considered Elva's words. I'd completely forgotten those two older men who'd first knocked on my door at my previous apartment, before Devli appeared at the new one and tricked me.

Except those couldn't be his tutors. They had to be Canardan's mages.

Again I'd overlooked the magical side of this struggle. I had to consider it now.

Devli had magical communication, and he'd been sitting in that hold doing magical stuff. He might not have been making a communications device for Zathdar at all, whatever he'd told the privateer. What if he'd been secretly making a transfer token, like to get two of us off the ship and to his magisters?

Also, I'd been seen by the navy guys. Did *they* have magical communications? What I had to consider now was the fact that not only did Canardan know about my presence, but these magicians did as well. Magicians for and against Canardan, busy with their own purposes. And I did not really know what their goal was, once they'd brought me to this world.

"Problem?"

I lifted my head. Zathdar lounged on the ladder above, one arm lazily blocking the hatch so that no one else could come down. He was back to his scarlet shirt. A shaft of sunlight shimmered with a ruby glow down that extended arm, highlighting its latent strength.

I said, "Devli seems to have received orders to search my stuff."

Zathdar made a slight grimace. "I didn't think of that."

"Here's another thing to consider. He could, say, receive a transfer token in a note box. If he cannot perform a double transfer himself. He's a nice kid, but I don't want him anywhere near me any more."

Zathdar looked up at the bright blue sky beyond the

sagging mainsail, the light stippling the dark sweep of his lashes until he blinked. "I can keep him busy down below, if you stay on deck. We only have a few more days of travel as soon as the wind picks up."

"Will the wind pick up?"

"It's already beginning." He tipped his chin behind me. "We'll have to tack and tack eastward, but north should be a swift run."

"East?" I exclaimed. "I thought we were going west. Aloca Bay lies west, I know that much."

"But the king has Aloca guarded by too large a force to slip by."

"So where are we going?"

"Ellir."

"What? Isn't that one of the king's strongholds?"

"Well, it is. In a sense. But have you ever heard the old saying 'hide in plain sight'?"

"I think our version is 'The safest place for the thief is under the sheriff's bed.'"

He grinned. "That's it. I obtained the latest merchant codes from our friends aboard the *Skate* yesterday, and so it will be a sober trading vessel that makes landfall at Ellir, nice and law abiding. The muscle in Aloca will be searching every vessel. We land in Ellir and do nothing to draw attention."

He hoisted himself up, and I followed after. A faint coolness feathered my cheek. A breeze, just as he'd said. The water in the distance ruffled in little wavelets, whitecaps frothing, color more greenish than the deep and placid blue below us.

"What about the blockade?" I watched one of the slack sails stir, then bell slightly.

"Here comes," someone called from above. Owl bawled out

an order, and the sail party scrambled to make the most of the rising breeze.

"The blockade is broken." He gave me a quick grin, a long dimple flashing beside his mouth down to his jaw, and a corresponding flash of warmth kindled my innards. "They're on their way to reinforce Aloca."

I took a deep breath. Pirate or privateer, there was no future here. *Move along,* I told myself, and I climbed past him. He did not try to stop me, but launched in the opposite direction, gazing upward and calling a command to the team shaking out the topsails to catch the rising wind.

Chapter Fifteen

By the watch change, the wind was blowing hard straight along the coast, and so we tacked in a dramatic zigzag back and forth, using the westward bend to propel us gradually northward. The whistle tweeted, feet thumped. Soon came the agreeable roar of voices from below as the day watch ate their meal and the next watch scrambled from the hatches, looking around and sniffing the air.

Devli was nowhere in sight, neither he nor his sister. I stayed at the rail, out of the way, enjoying the wind. When a hand struck my biceps in a friendly thump, I was startled to discover Gliss there, the wind combing through her blond hair.

"Thanks for not blabbing," she said gruffly.

"No one's business."

She brought one shoulder up, her smile surprisingly shy. "You off at Ellir?"

I nodded, expecting her to express relief, even if covertly, but she said, even more gruffly, "If you change your mind. Till you're—well, until. You could join our watch. Women are good in the tops because we're fast."

"Thank you." I was gratified and surprised. Not even the reminder of my assumed princessly duties implied in that "until" could upset me. I was just going to have to accept that everyone else had expectations of me. That didn't mean I had to raise a banner and lead an army.

I shoved that subject to the back of my brain, knowing it would sit there and leer at me. "May I ask you a question?" On her cautious nod of assent, "Did you set out to become a pirate—a privateer—or did it sort of happen?"

"You didn't know?" She looked surprised. "Everyone's heard of Zathdar's fleet. People want to sign on. But it's tough, first to get an interview, then to pass their tests."

"No, I hadn't any idea. Our invitation was the kind that you don't refuse." She gave the weak joke a perfunctory smile. She was a very serious person, I realized. "So why does he have such a small fleet?"

"He trains people and then sends them out. Other ships're glad to take us on. It's the training, see. And he doesn't keep people long. On account of the price on his head. Except for Owl and his captains and watch commanders."

Odd. Why would a privateer train people and send them away? Training costs money, at least on Earth. You don't train people to be as fast and tough as these and then just send them off, unless...

"We've got allies if we need 'em. They know a couple of signals, see. Like when we broke the navy's threatened alliance with the Chwahir last winter. He says three is more maneuverable." She shrugged. "But if he needs a fleet, well, they're out there."

How do you build a fleet when you haven't a king's budget? You train them, send them out with a couple of signals...

I forced my thoughts back to Gliss. "So you started with life on the sea?"

She shook her head once. "Born in the hills between what they call Locan Jora and Khanerenth. Fighting all the time. Too much of it. Got tired of all the family alliances bickering, worse,

171

the landholders versus the plains people who have always ignored borders, ignore them now, and will always ignore them. So. Ran away to sea. Fishing boat, ten years. Then got voted in here, a year ago."

I whistled. "Now that I know what your invitation is worth, I thank you again."

She squinted upward, frowned at something going on with one of the upper sails and pushed away without another word, swarming up the shrouds like she was flying.

By nightfall we were skimming northward at exhilarating speed. The sky was clear, the air balmy. Three of the day crew brought out instruments, sat on the railing of the forecastle half-deck, and began to play. Some of the crew sang songs in round, in which I could hear the difficult but distinctive Sartoran triplicate chord changes and beats. The teenaged crew members started dancing in twos and threes on the forecastle, one boy alone on the capstan, blithely ignoring jeers and even a couple of metal ale cans potted at him, which he dodged without missing a step.

Owl stumped up beside me. "C'mon, Princess, give us a dance."

"Not much of a dancer." I grinned. "I'm afraid if I get up there and swing my hips around like people my age do at home, every single ale pot would be tossed at me."

"You get up there and swing them hips, and they won't be tossing ale pots." He wiggled his slanting brows.

That made me laugh, but I (easily) resisted the temptation to make a fool of myself.

Zathdar appeared at my other side. I was leaning against the rail with my elbows propped behind me. He leaned next to me, his profile etched against the taut foresail as he watched the dancers jig and twirl round and round the capstan. But I could feel his attention on me. He asked in his mild voice, "No dancing?"

"I'm afraid of what it says about my upbringing that I wouldn't know what to do at a grand ball, but put me on a dojo floor and I'm ready to rock and roll."

Dojo and *rock and roll* did not translate, but he didn't question either of them.

I said, "So did you have a pirate mom or dad?"

He looked up in mock exasperation. "How often do I have to remind you that I'm a privateer?"

"Who dresses like a pirate."

He angled that quick grin again, the dimple accentuated by the golden light of the swinging lamps overhead. I was vaguely aware that Owl had gone from my other side.

"A pirate," I added firmly, "who has no sense of color."

He put his hand to his bandana, which was the long green-and-gold one hanging down his back, the fringes blowing around his slim waist. "Who says green and red is not eminently sensible? Why, in the worst rainstorm, in the thickest action, Owl and Robin only have to look round once and find me anywhere."

"Including in nightmares."

There was the dimple again. I looked away, but I was laughing.

I heard his laugh, a soft chuckle, almost under his breath. His elbow companionably bumped against mine as the ship lurched, and again the fire of attraction crackled through me. But he made no moves.

"Here's an added boon. With this crimson shirt, see, if someone nicks me it doesn't show. I can lie and gloat that they missed. Protect my rep that way."

I laughed again. It was an unguarded moment, at the end of which our eyes met, and his smile turned pensive, his gaze held mine—light blue as the water under a guileless sky—and I had to exert all my will to look away, or drown.

Yeah. I know it sounds stupid, but I really did feel like I couldn't breathe. I was hot and cold and tingling with proximity, with possibility. But I looked away, and as the feelings settled down to the glow one gets when the physical self—whose needs are as simple and direct as those of the creatures around us who do not speak—recognizes equal attraction.

Zathdar said, "With this wind, we'll make landfall day after tomorrow before dawn, on the early tide. I suggest you disembark with the cargo and make your way into the town on the other side of the brewery. If you like, I'll meet you at the Gold Inn, which is run by the brewers. I'll give you any news I discover. That should arm you for whatever you decide next."

"Thanks," I said to the planking of the deck.

When I breathed again, he was gone. I lifted my head in time to see him duck under his cabin door, fringes rippling in the wind.

Owl drifted up next to me. "Why don't you go after him?"

He was so direct yet managed to be so unconfrontational I was not tempted to say, *Why don't you mind your own business?* as I might have to anyone who sneered or leered or made some sort of innuendo.

I said, "You have your life here on the sea. Not for me to say if it's right or wrong, but it's not really mine. I have to find out what mine is."

"You don't want to try to find it here?" Owl raised a scarred hand. "Cause is a good one. More than that, or maybe less, I've never seen him tempted to break his own rule before."

I remembered what Gliss had said about his not being involved with crew.

"Maybe that's why I should go away." I tried to summon a smile, but Owl squinted at me, not smiling back.

My mother said when I was about sixteen: *Here's the truth of my experience. Attraction happens, and it's glorious and good when it happens back. For a short time if the body has picked a bore or a brute, long if the mind and the heart can also match. Because attraction, though it might seem to change the world, is not love. Love is the match of all three. Body. Mind. And spirit.*

How could I find a meeting of the minds with a pirate without talking myself into a pirate's life, at least for a time?

I faced Owl. "Whether bad or good I cannot say, but I do know a lawless life on the sea is not my future. And I'm not the kind who can have a fling then leave without a second thought."

He looked up at the sails then back at me, his narrow jaw working. His ruby-set golden earring, won in pirate battle, glinted against his jawline, emphasizing some tension, perhaps some unspoken thought. "Fair enough."

The armorer was singing a bawdy song in a sweet, soulful tenor when I retreated to my cabin. I lay on my bunk, hands crossed behind my head, watching the light-stippled reflections of water on the ceiling of the cabin as bare feet danced on the deck overhead far into the night.

On the day of our landing, I woke to the sound of bawling commands and busy hammers and saws coming through the open scuttle. Not our ship. In the mellow blue-gold light of dawn, a big brigantine slid by, its deck and masts alive with an enormous crew all busy.

I got up. Elva was already gone, her bunk made. I hauled all my bedding down to the cleaning frame, put it through, lugged it up again to make my bunk neat. When I stepped out, once again the ship wore a disguise, this time as a slightly down-at-heels merchant. Our masts were stumpy, a single sail on each. The barrels (most of them empty) neatly lined the rail. The crew all wore dull variations on homespun shirts and brown-dyed deck trousers.

Everyone was quiet, self-absorbed. I found Elva sitting on a barrel and joined her, turning my attention to the busy harbor as we threaded slowly through ships of every size and type, each a little world filled with people busy doing things.

"This is Ellir?" I asked.

She pointed at the martial outline of a fortress topping the ridge of hills behind the port. "That's the garrison and also the academy. Supposedly—"

"I know, belongs to Prince Jehan. Whenever you start with 'supposedly' I know Canary's son is fumbling around somewhere behind."

She grinned. "Well, truth is, he does seem to preside, though I understand it all is really run by Captain Randart, the war commander's brother."

"Yuk. More Randarts? Ugh."

"I didn't even mention War Commander Randart's nephew Damedran, who's supposedly the best of the academy cadets. Devli says the mages all think Randart wants Damedran as heir instead of the Fool. Except that Randart defends the Fool. Which is another thing against him."

"That doesn't make sense. Canardan *is* the king, right?"

Elva said soberly, "Yes, but whatever Randart wants, he gets. There was supposed to be no killing, that was promised. Yet Randart was angry when they didn't catch your father, and so he made sure Magister Glathan died. He broke his word to do it. Had the magister shot in the back. Bolt from a crossbow.

Right after making a truce."

Magister Glathan—dead?

My father had to be either dead or imprisoned by his last-resort spell. A spell he could not free himself from.

Unless things had changed after Mom and I left, that meant I was the only one who could free him.

If he lived.

I grimaced. Magister Glathan was a vague memory, but he'd been kind and patient with me, and I remembered how much my father and he had talked, how much my father had admired the mage. "That's horrible."

"Anyway, no one knows what Randart wants, except Randart. We'll find out when he gets it." Elva rubbed her arms just above the elbows. "I wonder what can be taking Devli? It's like he married those messmates of his. Never was away from them once, yesterday."

"Where is the brewery?"

"See that big stone building up at the very far end of Market Street? Market Street starts at the base of the main pier, which is just past where that yacht is docked."

I peered under my hand, and whistled. "That's gorgeous. I've never seen such a beautiful yacht."

"It belongs to the Fool," Elva admitted.

"I thought someone said he gets seasick."

"The king gave it to him. He's seldom on it, and only long enough to entertain some of his artists." Elva waved a dismissive hand. "But he has a crew complete with a Colendi cook just sitting around waiting all the same. Anyway, you can see how Market Street runs along the foot of the ridge. See the academy on top of the ridge? The brewery is just below the far end of the academy. Sometimes when the wind comes off the land, you can smell the malt being made from the barley."

"Does Prince Supposedly run that brewery too?"

She looked surprised. "You didn't know? It's entirely run by old sailors. If you get wounded young and can't sail, you have a place there if you want it."

"Beer made by drunken sailors?"

"Oh no! No one is more serious about brewing than an old sailor. Drink a drop on duty and you're out. Which is why Gold is the very best. Ships come here from all over the continent for the year-ale, the darkest. Best barley from the hills, best hops, everything the best."

"So the Gold Inn is good?"

"The food is great. You should have their corn muffins, all slathered with honey-butter..." She sighed. "Why, you going there?"

"Zathdar said he'd meet me there, if he hears any news concerning me, and I could go on my way. I thought that pretty nice of him."

She pursed her lips. "I think it pretty crazy. He's probably the most wanted person in the kingdom, and War Commander Randart, they say, would pay almost anything in reward money to lay him by the heels. I thought he'd stay hidden below while we're here."

"Well, the offer is all the more admirable," I said, lightly enough.

She frowned at me. "But you can't be going like *that*."

"Like what?" I fingered my braids. "Oh. Right. I never thought of that."

"I'm sure someone here will at least give you a bandana for the hair." She paused, frowning again, and stared up at the castle all along the ridge, the stone lit with mellow color by the rising sun behind us. "No, I'm sick of everyone yatching at me about my guesses," she muttered. "Never mind, I'll just check on my own. Here's the important thing right now, you do need a disguise."

The bosun tweeted, causing a stampede of running feet. The masts creaked, sails loosened, whacketted and slumped. A crew got the anchor atrip, then on command let it go. Underneath us the chain roared until the ship jerked. The anchor was down. We stopped moving, except on the gentle swell.

While the sails were bunted, the anchor crew began booming the longboat over the side. I went below for the last time. The sail mistress had told me that I could have anything but they usually traded, and so I left my Earth clothes. I didn't want the extra weight, I couldn't wear them, and they didn't mean anything to me. Let some pirate puzzle over a T-shirt with *Got books?* on it.

I picked out a sturdy forest green tunic that came down to my knees, below which I wore the deck trousers I'd been given, and found some castoff mocs that fit. I donated my sandals. Maybe someone would think the Earthwear an exotic fashion touch. I chose an old floppy sailor's hat that someone had abandoned. It not only hid my hair but half of my face.

By then the boat was lowered, and the ship boy on duty came shyly to offer me a ride in the first trip.

I reached the rail and looked back at the deck. Some of the crew waved, and one or two saluted. Zathdar was not in sight.

I waved, tucked my gear back under my arm and clambered down the side to drop into the boat. I thumped clumsily onto the sternsheets and sat with my gear bag in my lap as the crew took up oars and rowed for the passenger dock.

Chapter Sixteen

Go and find her with your good will—and your worst spies.

Atanial did not say that out loud. She was not certain how much real freedom she had or what Canary might do if she broke the appearance of a truce.

She did know that if she left, it would either be under guard, or else he'd have people following her.

So she smiled sweetly at King Canardan. She smiled sweetly at the two big guards who escorted her back to her chambers when Canary regretfully excused himself to his day's work.

Back in her room she flung the brass jewelry holder against the fireplace stone, counting under her breath until a maid came running in, and she smiled sweetly at her.

Five seconds. The listening ears were close.

Atanial knew better than to confront the servants. They were doing what they were told, whether by will or coercion right now did not matter. "Oops." She picked the brass plate up. "I dropped it."

She set it carefully on the carved wooden bureau, next to the pretty ceramic vase that she would have loved to smash. But she couldn't bring herself to indulge her temper that far. At home, where things were manufactured, maybe. Here, human hands had shaped this vase, another pair of hands had painted the intertwined ivy leaves all around it. If she did any dropkicking, it would be the seat of Canary's fine linen trousers. Or better yet—

"Is Commander Randart anywhere about?" she asked.

The maid's eyes widened, and Atanial realized that not only was she being watched, but every question had to be reported.

"I wanted to ask him if I could witness a military review." Once again Atanial summoned up her sweetest smile, though by now her face ached. "I used to adore watching those handsome young things march about."

"I can ask, your highness." The maid curtseyed, her eyes frightened at the mental echo of Randart's name.

And by noon the word came that Canary was going to escort her himself to review the midday change of the palace guard.

So they stood there side by side on the rampart above the great parade court and looked down at all those earnest faced young men and women sweltering in their faultless battle tunics, and Atanial thought, *Yes, I'm getting the message about who holds the reins here.*

But again she smiled sweetly as they marched, did an impressive sword form, and presented their spears. And that sweet smile was ready and at her command when they descended to walk along the row on close inspection, and she forced Canary to stop every so often, while she asked harmless questions: *How long have you been in the guard? Where do you hail from?* She took care to listen to every answer as if her life depended on it, and she looked into every pair of eyes, willing the person behind them to see her. She thanked each speaker as if they'd given her wings.

And maybe they would, despite the fact that she did not see

Tam among them. Someone would have to help her. She needed to figure out who and how, without endangering anyone, because two things were immediately clear: one, she had to get away; and two, she was about ten years past vaulting over ten-meter walls and castle rooftops in order to do it.

So the next best thing was to get to know as many people as possible—and inspect the castle to see what escape hole might exist.

She ate alone. Neither king nor queen came near. Someone had placed some books in her sitting room—every single one at least a century out of date.

But old as they were, those books still reminded her of the third option, the one she tended to forget because she didn't understand it.

Magic.

She read until the midnight bells rang, then withdrew into that splendid marble bath, locked the door and glanced at the scented, slightly steaming water.

First things first. She dug the transfer token out of her bra and examined it closely. There were no more Gate transfers left on it. Whether one person or two came through, the transfer energy was spent. That much she knew, for Math had told her as much before their parting.

The question was, did the transfer use up *all* the magic, or could the thing still sense wards? She'd been told not to risk using the token if it sensed other magical presences around it. She held it up, remembering how Math and (at first reluctantly) Glathan had tried to convince her that magic was not the equivalent of electricity. Magic existed somewhere in the interstices between light and molecular movement, but she thought of it in terms of battery storage and voltage and switches. It was the only way her mind could comprehend what it could do, if not what it was.

She walked around the bath with the token, and noticed a tiny flicker of light around its edges. Ahah. So it did work. And what's more, she had wards around her, of some sort.

More than that she could not tell. It hurt unexpectedly, remembering Math's childlike glee when she showed a modicum of ability with some little magical trick, now forgotten. His Albert Einstein hair seemed to bristle and crackle with his delight. But tempering that had been Glathan's obvious distrust during those early days, when they first came through the Gate. Later that altered to grudging acceptance, and finally to a truce, and even a measure of trust.

And now he was dead.

She set the token carefully down and took a leisurely bath. Dressed in the soft cotton nightgown they'd left for her, she took the candle and the token and walked through the rooms she'd been given, watching how the token flared briefly with green color here, reddish there, and once a sharp blue snap.

A network of protective wards, just as Ananda had told her. Maybe only wards to let someone know when she crossed the threshold, but possibly stronger ones, meant to prevent her from doing magic, or prevent magic from reaching her.

Now she knew where they were, at least. She tucked the token under her pillow and snuffed the candle so she could sleep.

The next morning she toured the kitchens, asked questions about the baking and cooking, tasted and complimented everything. She saw that there was little chance of egress there. The kitchens were directly adjacent to the expanded guard barracks.

At noon she toured the housekeeping area and introduced

herself to Mistress Eban's replacement. The woman was so stiff, so wary, Atanial knew immediately she'd received stringent orders, and kept her questions confined to cloth, weaving, sewing and the current styles in Sartor. By the time Atanial had inspected the lyre-backed chairs with the cushions embroidered with queensblossom, the woman had unbent enough to flick a look her way.

Atanial gave her a smile, but left knowing she'd met defeat there.

Canary invited her to dinner.

Again they were alone.

By then she was ready to begin the first tier of questions.

"Where is Dannath Randart?" she asked.

Canardan grinned. "You want to see him again?"

He looked so ironic she replied tartly, "I was hoping he'd dropped dead. Preferably with a bolt in the back."

"So you heard about that, eh?"

"Who hasn't?" She spread her hands and then grabbed up a fresh corn bun, noting as she did the faint color along Canardan's still-handsome cheekbones. "I find it utterly reprehensible, and frankly hope that he's on the other side of the kingdom."

"He's going out to sea," Canardan said. "Far enough to keep you from one another's sphere."

"My second question is, what have you done with Mistress Eban and the others?"

"Nothing, as yet. That depends on a number of things. Including you."

"If you dare try to hold their lives hostage in order to force me into something, I will shout it from the rooftops." Her fists
184

thumped on either side of her plate.

He patted the air between them. "No, no. I know better than that. I should be more clear. I believe more lives will be saved if I keep all of you safely here until the kingdom settles."

She sighed. "Even if you do find Sasha, and if by some miracle she agreed to your proposal, how could a marriage possibly settle the kingdom?"

"It would go a long way toward reestablishing good will." He saluted her with his wine goblet. "Join the names, all that."

"But if you do get her, and threaten my life—"

He looked skyward. "What did I just tell you? I might add that my wayward son, who seldom notices a wall until he smashes into it, would probably object as loudly as your daughter. He thinks he's quite a catch. When he isn't following bards around, he's off flirting with every pretty face he meets. And apparently they all seem to like him. No princesses, though," Canary added regretfully.

Atanial couldn't help but laugh. "It sounds like he'd much prefer a minstrel."

"If she's pretty and she paints, he would probably marry her out of hand." Canardan gestured with his butter knife.

"When do I get to meet him?" Atanial put her elbows on the table and her chin in her hands. Math's voice came back from all those years ago, *Jehan's a fine boy. And smarter than his father thinks, despite all the daydreaming.*

To which Glathan had said in his gruff growl, *Maybe because of it. He learned early to keep his mouth shut. But we don't know if what he's thinking is to our benefit or not.*

Which is why I'm going to write him, since no one else seems to be doing it, Math had said, and despite Glathan's shake of the head he'd been true to his word.

What Atanial had never found out was whether the boy all the way across the continent had written back. Math had never mentioned him again, and Atanial wondered now if that was because of Glathan's disapproval, or if the correspondence had ended with the one letter.

The pause had grown into a silence, Canardan frowning into the middle distance. But he was watchful for all that. All she did was look up, and the flick of her eyelashes seemed to release him from his reverie.

"I'll see what I can arrange, but right now he has duties at the academy." Canardan drank, then set his goblet down, his thumb aligning it with an absent stroke just beyond the point of his knife. "Do you remember the midsummer games?"

"The cadets and their demonstrations. Relay races through the hills. And the yacht races in the harbor."

"Well, we've had to cancel the yacht races, but the relays and the rest will go on as usual."

"Why no yachting? I thought the academy is where you got your navy captains as well as your guard captains?"

"Yes, and we'll hold 'em anon. But the merchant codes were gotten by a pirate a few days ago, and we have reason to believe he might try to slip into either of the two main harbors. Those same codes are being used by countless legitimate merchants, so we don't know if he's coming or already there in some kind of disguise. We already know he has a way of stealing in, doing untold damage and slipping out unheeded." Atanial saw the telltale signs of anger in the tightened skin at the corners of his eyes.

Her brow furrowed. "Is this the pirate who holds my daughter?"

He spread his hands. "How can we know? He doesn't exactly communicate with us."

"Back to your son." She set her goblet down. "I'd like very much to meet him."

As a distant bell rang, Canardan got to his feet. "Speaking of whom. I thought we might see if one of his charities is worth what I pay out. Are you finished?"

Atanial rose, shook out her skirts and took his offered arm. Canardan led her through the informal dining room, made of pale peach marble, through the formal dining room that she remembered from the old days. Then it was silver marble to match the Zhavalieshin silver-and-crimson firebird. They walked along the balcony above the main entryway to the palace. From there he took her through the private door to the royal box above the private theater, which was tucked behind the palace's enormous ballroom.

Canardan appreciated her surprise and delight when she saw the lit stage, empty and waiting. The rest of the low circular tiers of chairs were empty. Only their box had a single candle. Two liveried servants stood by, one with wine, another with extra cushions, as Canardan guided Atanial to one end of the beautiful rosewood couch with its fine velvet cushions. He sat next to her and nodded at the servants.

They poured honey-colored wine in the goblets on the little tables at either end of the couch, and set out porcelain plates of tiny lemon-and-custard pastries, layered delicately so that one could take a bite without experiencing any gooshes of custard or splatters of crumbs. Next to the plates, crystal vases of just-budding white roses breathed a delicate scent.

All very thoughtfully arranged, she thought. For?

Another campaign.

Down on the stage, a master illusionist stepped out in the black gown of his calling, and sat upon a stool at one side. Prince Jehan's "charity" was a company of first-rate players.

The custom for the master illusionists to come forward onto the stage instead of remaining behind had been introduced twenty years before, so people could watch the magician at work making the scenes. The old days of one or perhaps two rudimentary illusions cast and left up for the duration of the play were gone. The subtle metamorphosis of scene sets behind the players had become art, as it had been centuries before.

In the intervening twenty years, the gestures had taken on stylized grace, reminding Atanial of a person on Earth performing poetry in sign language. Hidden musicians played on flutes and horns, evoking a garden of birds. The stage glittered with a rainbow splash of color as a setting coalesced into being.

The setting was a garden terrace, with tiers of flowers at various levels. Atanial recalled something about Sartoran gardens, how they might take a century or more to properly mature. Colendi gardens could take even longer.

The players strolled out, wearing layers of silk fashioned in complicated folds, the colors subtle gradations of shades from rose to gold. They gathered around a young man in layers of celestial blue.

Atanial tightened all over, bracing for some obvious message aimed at her through the performance, but before very long even she, relatively ignorant of this world's history, recognized the legendary story of the brilliant Prince Tivonais of Sartor. If he lived, it was a couple thousand years ago.

This was a musical comedy, about the one woman who did not surrender to his incredible charms. Any message was about all the varieties of human passion and love. Atanial sat back and relaxed, chuckling at the ancient jokes about human actions and reactions that hadn't changed much in millennia, whichever world you happen to be on. She sipped the wine, which tasted like liquid gold.

Gradually her focus on the stage widened to include Canardan so close beside her. One of his hands tapped out a counter-rhythm to a dance, while players whirled and stepped and leaped on stage. She heard his breathing as he leaned back, eyes shut, during a beautifully sung lament.

As the play drew to its end, Tivonais sang his serio-comic song about loss. The singer revealed just the right touch of mockery in the relative sorrows of a handsome prince who has everything and everyone he wants. He asks for a single gift from his beloved, a white rose.

While Atanial tried to remember if the white-rose custom among new lovers came before the play, or if the play establish the custom, her body was aware of fingers tracing, ever so lightly, along her shoulder. Her *other* shoulder. A well-shaped arm touching her back.

It was pleasant—she had to admit it was pleasant—that despite the years, the dashed hopes and disappointments, the betrayals and chases, he was still attracted to her. Either that, or he was a master tactician.

But recognition of your opponent's skill in battle is not cause for surrender.

For a moment she considered jumping up and screaming, *You're trying to seduce me!* Oh, how fun it would be to see him embarrassed. Except he wouldn't be, he'd laugh. No, the embarrassment would be all those players down there, now taking their bow for their audience of two. They did not deserve to have their beautiful work reduced to a mere hissing of gossip along the corridors.

She stood. The fingers lifted away. She clapped loudly, then scooped up the white roses from the crystal vase and tossed them one by one down onto the stage.

Below, the young man playing Tivonais, perhaps still in character, made a debonair gesture as he bent, swept up a rose, kissed it and saluted her with it.

She kissed her fingertips and flung her hands out wide, and the other players all clapped too.

Tivonais took another bow. Atanial was aware of Canardan standing beside her, clapping as well, his profile sardonic.

The players bowed a last time, then filed off, the exquisite acoustics carrying back the sound of their whispering.

Atanial turned away from the empty stage and walked to the door, perforce Canardan following, his blue eyes narrowed with not-quite humor as he made a gesture dismissing the waiting servants.

She waited until they were gone and said, "Yes, I felt it. No, I won't act on it. Yes, I was a pompous twit when I first came here all those years ago, but I do not have to justify any actions except—" Even here there were pitfalls, for she dared not suggest that Math was alive, that she might know where.

Nothing but landmines around.

The awareness chilled her spirit like nothing had for years. But she was not a girl in her twenties any more, to indulge in screaming stomping fits because she's so very right while everyone around is wrong, wrong, wrong.

She held her hands out to him, palms toward him. "Age builds its own internal cities, you have to admit that. Whatever your castle walls are made of, I don't know. I don't know if I can believe you if you try to tell me, because there lies behind us the matter of the past. Here's what you can believe from me. Between the garden of appreciation of your attractions—and they are there, as they always were—and the road to action is the wall round my own castle, a wall deep and high, called trust."

190

He had the grace to take her hands and the poise to lightly kiss her fingers. And let her go.

Then he walked away, and the silent servants conducted her back to her rooms.

Chapter Seventeen

War Commander Dannath Randart arrived in Ellir not long after midnight. Two days of very hard riding, sleep and meals scanted while the horses were changed at military posts along the way, brought him tired, aching and irritable to the west gate, which is where the guard barracks was located.

Randart's vile temper eased slightly when he saw the walls patrolled by alert guards, the gatekeepers awake and speedy once his trumpeter had blown the king's signal.

He jumped off his sweaty horse and left his troop to rouse the stablehands, striding upstairs to the commander's tower. He arrived at the same time his younger brother Orthan did, Orthan fastening his tunic with one hand and carrying his boots with the other.

"Dannath," Orthan Randart said by way of greeting, blinking himself awake.

"Any word on Prince Jehan?"

"His personal guard arrived at sunset." Orthan fell heavily into his chair behind the desk. The joints in the wood creaked. "But the prince wasn't with 'em. Apparently there's some girl somewhere outside of town he simply had to visit. But he promised to be along by morning."

Randart sighed, and when a hastily dressed cadet runner arrived, he ordered coffee and whatever food could be made hot the fastest.

As soon as the boy was gone, the war commander shut the door and set his back against it. "News?"

"Nothing." Orthan indicated the darkened window, which overlooked the harbor. Tiny lights bobbed slowly on the water, lanterns legally required on bows, sterns and foremasts. "Nothing."

"As expected. Well, continue mustering the fleet, except for those at Aloca. I'm going out in force. What's the status of the games?"

"Officially or confidentially?" And when his brother shrugged, Orthan smiled. "Officially, everything is in order. Ready to begin. If the prince does show up. As for our business, Damedran will take every prize."

Randart thought of his huge, husky nephew, but did not smile. "What about archery? Is he at the top there?" On the war commander's orders, Orthan had been drilling his son with extra lessons, but though Damedran was a brute with sword, stick and grappling, he couldn't seem to get the eye for superlative shooting.

"He'll win," Orthan said.

"He's finally good enough to best the Valleg girl?"

"No. But it seems she suffered a broken arm. Won't be competing in the games."

Randart frowned. "He didn't—"

"No, no, absolutely not. He knows better now, he really does. No, apparently she was was offered a drink or two celebrating someone's Name Day, while she was on stable duty. She tripped over...her own feet. Damedran handsomely offered to cover for her—gave the watch commander an excuse. Officially there's no disgrace, and unofficially she's in his debt."

Randart smiled at last, thinking, *Now that is the thinking of a good future king.*

His brother saw that smile, and knew what it meant, but they did not say the word "king" out loud.

Instead they turned their attention to logistical concerns—guard rotations, patrol of the harbor, searchers covert and overt as ships continued to come in, though they didn't have much hope of nabbing Zathdar in the act.

The last errand runner left the room. When they were safely private, War Commander Randart said to his brother, "Here's the truth. I don't really want to catch the pirate lurking around the harbor. I've been given a free hand to take the entire fleet, and I mean to sweep the whole sea of all suspicious ships. 'Suspicious' defined as those crewed by names well known on resistance rosters. Zathdar has far too many allies out on the waters. Some judicious slaughter might be salutary to the entire maritime world. At the end of that, if I find the pirate, fine. I'll consider it a job well done."

Orthan grimaced at that mention of judicious slaughter, but he had learned never to interfere with his brother, who was, after all, the king's right arm. Orthan himself was only a headmaster and garrison commander, positions he felt far more comfortable filling. Training boys and running a garrison, he could do. Judicious slaughter?

But Dannath Randart did not see his brother's grimace. He was too busy sorting through the reports on Orthan's desk, reading the headings, then re-sorting them in his own priority order.

When he was done, he said, "So patrols as normal, no assiduous searches. I want the best men rested and ready for the launch of the entire fleet. We'll form a pincer between here and Aloca. We'll gather them all together and get rid of them."

His mood had improved by the time he downed the potato pancakes a sleepy cook had put together. He swallowed his coffee and withdrew into the command suite to catch some rest, waking at the dawn bells.

He'd been through the baths and was pulling on a clean uniform when a runner reported, "Prince Jehan has arrived."

In the commander's office the brothers exchanged brief glances, and then War Commander Randart said easily, as befitted the prince's best advocate in the kingdom, "Request his highness to honor us with his presence, if that is his royal desire. Or we could join him wherever he wishes, to go over the king's orders."

The cadet vanished.

A short time later there was the sheep, the nickname ostensibly chosen for his white hair. War Commander Randart knew his brother liked the prince, despite his brown velvet war tunic that had never seen any semblance of war, that long white morvende hair hanging down his back, and a diamond in his ear. Popular Jehan was, but he was also more a fop than a commander. Why couldn't Orthan see that?

Orthan sighed. He wanted his son to be king, but he didn't want anything bad to happen to the prince. Somehow...somehow, he hoped, it would all work out. Until then, no use in worrying. Dannath would have his way no matter what.

"What color would you call that?" Jehan asked, indicating the pale shade of the ocean.

"Blue," Randart said with obvious patience. "Your highness, forgive me but it might be better if you don't...visit civilians...when we're under orders."

"She sings," Jehan explained.

Orthan restacked already neat papers, keeping his face

195

hidden. The runner cadet in the corner watched, his eyes wide.

"Have you ever heard Faleth ballad-style?" Jehan continued, head to one side. "It seems to have its roots in Ancient Sartoran—"

"Very well, very well, perhaps another time, your highness?" Orthan soothed, eying the war commander uneasily.

Orthan completely misunderstood his brother. The king persisted in believing Jehan might one day wake up and exhibit even a faint interest in the requirements of a future king. The king believed it, Orthan hoped for it in a vague way—and Randart watched for it.

If he discovered any hint of competence in Prince Sheep, Dannath Randart would arrange for a fatal accident. He really did not want to have to do that. Not in a kingdom where every single person who wasn't plotting was busy gossiping. Far better the king suffer one more disappointment, and get so angry he took care of the heir problem all by himself. And there would be a trained heir, at the top of the academy, loyal, strong, handsome: Damedran Randart.

"We can talk about ballads later." The war commander pitched his voice to be heard by the cadet runners on duty outside the office. He was very careful to present himself as the devoted friend and supporter to the prince. For the benefit of all those listening ears, he added in a gentle, coaxing voice, "But your highness, the king has requested me to convey his wishes to you. Now, about the games..."

Everything according to plan.

Chapter Eighteen

The ship's boy rowed me to the main pier, which was very long, with small boats coming and going to drop off or pick up people whose ships couldn't afford closer-in anchorage fees. This meant a hefty hike ahead of me.

The two sailors at the bows tied us on, and the ship's boy touched my arm. I stared in surprise at his crimson face as he mutely held out a bag that chinked promisingly.

"Thank you," I said.

"Collection took up by the crew." He blushed even more, if that was humanly possible.

I took pity on him and climbed out, confining myself to a little wave, and I set out to weave my way through all the busy people on the pier.

The long pier led me past the capital ships pulled alongside. One had to be the navy's flagship. I kept my head low, scarcely looking at it, though no one paid me the least heed. But I felt as if eyes crawled over me like bugs as I hustled past its length.

I slowed a little when passing the prince's yacht. In beautiful wood carved with laughing dolphins all round the rail was embodied the power and arrogance of princes. The yacht was a work of art, and it had the best docking spot in the entire harbor. Yet it was obviously empty of any royal butt sitting in its exquisite cabin. Its crew looked bored as they polished the gleaming wood and flemished their ropes.

I forgot about yachts and princes as the crowd thickened. I'd reached the quay at last. I was finally on my own.

Ellir was filled with warriors. This was a dismaying sight, all that brown, as they strolled in the crowd. Their hands were usually filled with pastries or drink, but every one of them carried a full complement of weaponry.

Whether they were on guard, about to embark in the navy ships I could see anchored in neat rows along the inner bay, or on leave for the academy games, I did not know, and I did not want to find out. I gave myself a mental shakedown as I trod down the warped wooden boards of the long pier, trying to get my land balance back. A good look around made it clear that civilian sailors dress in every imaginable style, tending toward the loud when on shore looking for fun. The career doesn't select for the delicate and dainty, so there were plenty of women of my size around.

The one thing that I feared might catch attention was my gear bag. Though I'd rolled it to be as small as possible, the faint sheen of its plastic weave could draw the eye of anyone searching for the unusual, and so I stopped at the very first vendor who was selling baskets and paid what I suspect was a thumpingly dishonest price for a scratchy, loosely woven affair that I soon hated, but it did its job by successfully hiding the gear bag stuffed into its depths.

This purchase also used up most of the coins in the bag. Either the basket maker was an outright thief or I'd been given enough to cover a day or two's meals. But that made sense. Sailors would figure a day or so on land, and then one hires out for one's next voyage.

Or maybe the Purple-and-orange Pirate would give me

some more of his ill-gotten gains when he met me at the Gold to tell me the local news. Did I want handouts? No. I would cash in some of my gems, or work my way along the road. But I was curious about what he might bring.

For now, I'd just enjoy the market street, which wound in a kind of slightly skewed crescent along the foot of the rocky ridge. Ellir Harbor, overlooked by the combination academy and garrison, was a jumble of old stone buildings and jerry-rigged tents and claptrap houses, most of the latter painted with bright colors. The stone buildings housed the long-term businesses, most sea-related. The rest was seasonal trade, set up in colorful stalls and tents between the dilapidated buildings. Half of the market noise was from these people singing, shouting, waving bright colors or sending enticing smells to lure the crowds who made up the other half of the noise as they strolled by, talking, looking, laughing, flirting, eating, drinking and shopping.

Once chasing. "Thief!" someone cried and the shout was taken up around me.

Moments later the hapless pickpocket was brought down by a pair of brown-tunicked warriors, almost at my feet. Who would be that stupid, or that desperate, to try thievery right under the view of that intimidating castle?

I never saw the culprit's face. A crowd of guards immediately surrounded him or her, and muscled the miscreant away presumably to some lockup. It began a train of thought. What kind of courts did they have, and jails, and sentences? I'd asked my mother a few questions over the years, but Canardan's versions of social government might be different from the Zhavalieshins'.

It was my growling stomach that shifted my attention from the general scene to the specific. I found the moneychangers directly below the gates to the castle, which ought to dissuade all but the most foolhardy and reckless of thieves. There were several to choose from. I drifted along until I spotted a moneychanger where not only coinage was being changed, but valuables of various sorts, including gemstones.

For the first time in all those years, I pulled out one of the more modest gems from the box and brought it to the biggest tent, where a short, thin, stylishly dressed young woman about my age seemed to be handling stones of all kinds. I laid it down, my fake story all ready.

She squinted briefly at it. "Colendi cut, what we call the deep-water sapphire." She named a price.

I'd already noticed that though bargaining took place in many of the market stalls, here there was a standard price for pretty much everything. Not wanting to call attention to myself in any way, I agreed. She counted out three twelve-sided gold coins, fashioned after Sartoran coins, and eleven silver six-siders, then a handful of thin hammered coppers.

I stuffed them all into the bag the ship's boy had given me, and returned to my shopping. Now to see what this money was actually worth.

The sun was directly overhead when I finished buying a good pair of shoes, cotton-lined greenweave that the cobbler adjusted to fit my feet exactly. I traded in the worn old mocs, which would be recycled.

Hunger forced me up the street toward the Gold Inn, which was large, loud, and the first smells that reached my nose were baking cornbread and braised onions. My stomach growled as I passed inside. It was decorated by sailors—deck prisms in the walls, the heavy, pointed glass gleaming with refracted colors, which banished indoor gloom. Old helm wheels high on the walls, bulkheads curving between the alcoves, booths divided off by fences made of worn oars. The chairs round the smaller tables were all cut from barrels and cushioned with old sailcloth.

The heavy, heady scent of fresh-brewed beer underlay the scent of brick-oven baked chicken pies, and bread, and some kind of pepper-and-garlic savory fish chowder. I sat at a long plank table on which cadets and sailors had carved initials and witty sayings in at least three alphabets. A party of weavers took up most of the table, well into a celebration for newlyweds, judging from the toasts.

The waiter, a kid of about ten, tapped me on the arm. "What'll I bring you?"

"Cornbread with honey-butter, dark ale and fish chowder," I said.

He dashed away, as one of the weavers made an obscure joke about damask and brocade, and everyone laughed.

Two toasts later the boy returned with a tray on which the cornbread steamed, fresh from the oven. The weavers began singing a plaintive song in Sartoran triplets about a wandering silk-weaver seeking the source of "rainbow colors true".

A sip of a spicy, almost raisin-flavored ale, a bite of sweet cornbread, and I was lifting my spoon to try the chowder when a brief glimpse of a familiar face in the crowd caused me to pause, spoon in the air.

Elva? No, couldn't be—

She vanished behind a crowd of sailors who suddenly decided to dance a heel-toe stomper right there in the middle of the floor. I dropped my spoon when Elva reappeared, braids flying, brown eyes stark in a face so pale I thought she was going to be sick.

"There you are." She clutched my shoulder. "Get out. Get out."

"What?" I looked down at my food. "What's wrong with the—"

She pulled my wrist, sending my spoon flying. "You've got to run. Now."

"Why?" I snapped, getting up to retrieve the spoon.

"Because I followed Owl. I had my suspicions." She made a terrible face. "He met up with *him* at the stable—" She waved a hand toward the far side of the brewery.

"Him? Zathdar?" I stared at the brewery, but just saw barrels of ale.

"Zathdar!" Elva repeated scornfully. "Oh, you're in for a storm, right enough, if you don't move." She dropped onto the bench next to me and muttered into my ear, "It was a stable, at the other end of town. Up behind the old castle and the warehouses. I *saw* him. They didn't see me."

"Saw who? Owl or Zathdar?"

"Both. But he—he—he ditched the bandana. And the horsehair wig. He's got white hair—the brown velvet with the king's cup. Crown over it. Diamond—" She touched her ear where Zathdar had worn his pirate-battle earring.

Heat flooded through me, followed by a sudden and dreadful chill.

"Don't you see?" Elva looked wildly around, and while the unheeding weavers sang of love and loss, she growled, "He's *Prince Jehan Merindar.*"

"But that's impossible."

"I thought so too. But I *saw* him. He went straight to the castle. The guards on the walls gave him the royal salute, clear as anything."

Whoosh! My first reaction was the self-righteous, fire-hot anger of betrayal, followed by the sickening, almost lip-numbing humiliation that comes of realizing one's been taken for a fool.

I grabbed my basket and followed her between the tables, the singing weavers' plaintive melody blending into the heedless roar of voices behind me.

Out in the street, glare and the rising dust of early afternoon nearly blinded us. I blinked, breathing hard as silhouettes resolved into people, horses, carts, dogs, even a family of geese squawking and flapping. Children danced in a ring to the flitting summer melody played upon a pipe. In front of the last booth before the open road, several women teased a handsome fellow in a brown tunic who seemed to be trying to buy an embroidered scarf.

All oblivious, most of them happy, and very much in the way as I scanned and scanned, resisting Elva's tugs. "This way," she urged.

I faced her earnest, anxious brown eyes and knew that Devli waited somewhere, a transfer token in hand. "Thank you for the rescue. But I think I'll take off on my own."

Her face reddened. "It's Devli. Isn't it? You don't trust him."

"I'm sorry, Elva, but I just don't trust those giving him orders," I murmured as a cart full of melons rolled toward us, shoved by a brawny fellow not watching where he was going.

She moved to one side. I ducked to the other side of it so I wouldn't have to see her reaction, and dove into a pack of sailors, several of them wearing battered floppy hats much like mine. I still felt outlined in neon, though so far the few guys in brown tunics around were not searching, merely sauntering.

All right, Sasha, you got what you wanted. You're alone. Pick a direction.

My pack of sailors headed toward the brewery. I stayed with them as far as the door. That sense of being watched intensified, so I slunk round the back of the Gold's stables and peered out, scanning with care.

The marketplace lay to my left, a long street of tent booths below the high palisade of sheer rock on which the garrison and academy bulked. The market street crested to the right, below the bluffs on which the academy barracks ended in the furthermost tower.

The road on the other side of the crest stretched in a lazy arc, paralleling the rocky shore against which long breakers creamed and crashed. Lines of wagons inched their way in a string that curved through mellow grassy fields to the horizon, the only tree in sight a single clump of willow growing beside a stream winding toward the shore.

No cover whatsoever, but at least that road lay outside of Ellir and its bazillion warriors.

I slipped away from my crummy hiding place and headed straight for that high point, beyond which freedom beckoned.

But right before I reached the top of the market street, not five hundred yards from the low stone wall that marked the boundary of the city, my shoulder blades itched. My danger sense had gone into the red zone, urging me to turn and fight.

I just knew I would hate what I saw. But I had to look.

Past the dancing children. Past the strolling flirts, the bargaining marketers with their baskets, past unheeding cadets and warriors obviously on leave, past the dogs and geese and sailors. I stared straight into a pair of familiar blue eyes, now framed by drifting white hair.

Too late.

Too late, but I turned on my toes and sprinted for freedom, despite the faster footsteps behind me—much faster.

When I reached the top of the road, the footsteps had almost caught up so I plunged into a crowd of prentices in one last attempt to shake my pursuer, and risked a glance back.

The stinker was maybe ten steps away. He hadn't yelled, and though some of the people he pushed past turned to stare, and one or two began to call out in protest, stared, then quickly backed away, no one interfered.

The oblivious prentices didn't part for me. They shoved past and stampeded toward the brewery, leaving me alone to face the enemy.

Prince Jehan caught up in an easy step, and stopped an arm's length from me.

So for a long, measureless moment we stood there facing one another at the top of Market Street, the last of the prentices flowing around us with exasperated looks and a wry comment or two that neither of us paid the least attention to.

All the things I could say chased through my mind. *You liar! Go ahead and strike me down, see if I care!* And perhaps most useless of all, *I hate you!* But I said nothing for a breathless, anguished eternity, as the market crowd walked, strolled, sauntered, pushed, shoved, talked, sang, sighed past us.

Prince Hurricane stood there, waiting for me to speak.

And so I said, "You must really love making everyone look like a fool."

He flushed as if I'd slapped him. But then flicked his head, as if repudiating my words, and retorted, "You have no idea what you're talking about."

"Oh, so you're not a liar and a poser?"

"I never lied—"

"No, *Prince* My-family-name-is-Jervaes?"

"But it is." He spread his hands and flushed again when I took a quick step back. "My mother's name."

"Oh." Well, that was a nasty little oopsie, but I plowed right past. "So you managed to tell one bit of truth. What did it cost you?" Take that!

"Listen. Just listen." He half raised a hand in a gesture of appeal, but when I stepped back, he dropped it to his side. His side, at which he wore a sword. And a knife through his sash. Neither of them touched, much less brandished. Nor had he whistled up his brown-coated minions. There were certainly plenty of them about.

But I couldn't bear another terrible, sickening sense of betrayal, and so, without examining the motivation behind that I said, "No."

His eyelids lifted slightly, giving me half-a-heartbeat's warning. Before I could draw breath to move, or even to yell, a thick winter quilt blotted out the sun and my world was perforce confined to hot, enshrouding darkness that smelled distinctly of mold.

I began to struggle, though it was futile, writhing and kicking until a familiar voice muttered next to my head, "C'mon, Princess. It's your old friend Owl. You can kick me all you like when we get back to the ship. If you can reach me. But you can't be allowed to get us all killed."

Killed? Say what?

I stopped struggling as I considered that, but before I could decide I didn't believe it, something efficiently wrapped me up into a giant cocoon, and *thump!* I fell onto something wooden. Things thudded round me, and a horse clopped. I was in a cart, which jerked and rumbled at a sedate pace back down the street, my face streaming with sweat in that suffocating quilt. I was so tightly wrapped it was useless to yell. No one could hear me anyway.

Chapter Nineteen

Atanial was considerably surprised to receive a visitor.

This time it wasn't night, but morning. She'd done a long session of yoga and had emerged from her bath to discover Ananda entering her room through the servants' door.

"Please pardon the intrusion. But this is the only way to have private converse."

Atanial wondered how the queen got past the guards on the stairs, then suspected illusion magic. More important was the timing of this visit. "I certainly didn't have privacy during my intimate little dinner with the king, did I?" she asked with some irony.

Ananda laughed softly. "Privacy? With the entire troupe of players watching the only two members of the audience, and one of them is busy staring at the other, caressing her neck? Watched also by the servants who had to stand there all evening with their wine and plates of uneaten food and unused cushions?"

Atanial had hopped onto her bed. She leaned back against her pillows and crossed her arms. "So I take it I passed some kind of test, and you are here for—?"

Ananda's voice was sad. "There was no test. I would have come anyway, if you had been here alone. Whatever happened. But my message would have been warnings. I am going away,

Atanial."

Atanial's nerves prickled with the cold chill of the unexpected. "Going away, as in—"

"Transferring to a place of safety. What no one except the prince knows is that his mother, Feraeth Jervaes, and I have been friends for many years."

Atanial whistled softly. "Sit down. Tell me more, please."

Ananda perched on the edge of the bed. "You know that the morvende do not have what we would call a government. But they do have leaders whose wisdom inclines others to listen. One such is Tarael of the Eleyad geliath on the northern continent. He has seen in dreams that Norsunder will move against the world soon."

Norsunder. Atanial had never quite gotten a grip on the whole concept of a place beyond space and time, controlled by inimical minds who seemed to have lived for thousands of years. She'd defined it to Sasha as a kind of hell, one mostly created by, run by and joined by humans who really, really wanted power. Including, she was told, the power to live forever. "Soon? As in days? Weeks?"

"Time is...time is different, for the morvende. It's useless to ask that question, because they cannot answer with any precision. But it could be this year, or next. Or in five. Probably not as long as ten, though, Feraeth told me, judging from some troubling events in the world elsewhere. I waited, and waited, but I think..."

Ananda paused, her profile briefly turned toward the window. The sunlight slanting in touched her frizzy hair into a halo of gold.

"I think there is no more I can do here, that what must be done will be done, but easier without me. I will go away. I first wanted to offer you the chance to go with me. The world is changing, and only the young will be strong enough to survive what is regretfully going to come."

Atanial impulsively launched herself across the tumbled bedding and hugged Ananda. "You are a sweetheart. I really appreciate that, more than you probably will ever know. But while my daughter is in danger and while Math is...missing, my place is here. That might change, and if I only get this one chance, so be it. But I have to stay and turn my hand to whatever I can."

Ananda smiled and stood, her face in silhouette against the bright window. "I thought it might be so. I did wish to ask. The illusion spell waits for two to leave, if you are reconsidering. But it will be impossible to repeat it. Once I am gone, poor Perran will search every stone of this castle, and he'll increase the wards."

"'Poor' Perran? I thought Perran and Zhavic turned into Evil Sorcerers."

Atanial's tone was half-joking, but Ananda did not smile. "They would never turn to dark magic or to Norsunder. There is a terrible rift between our kingdom's mages. Some withdrew completely and live behind wards. The Eban boy is trained by these. Perran and Zhavic felt they had to swear allegiance to Canardan because he was the king. This was to better protect the kingdom, for they feared if they didn't, he might bring in truly evil mages."

Atanial vaguely remembered Perran. He'd seemed odd back then. Now she pegged him as the kind of guy who'd be a star at Apple Computers, designing brilliant software by day, and on weekends entirely taken up with playing *World of Warcraft.*

"I think I see."

"Everything is confused," the queen said seriously. "I would say that Zhavic, having thrown in with the king, has gradually shifted allegiance, but he is still dedicated to the kingdom. Despite Canardan's earnest wish, even his orders, none of the mages really exert themselves to harm the others. There's always some magical reason why the 'traitor' mages cannot be extirpated, as the war commander often demands. Magister Glathan's death was—"

"I know. Randart's example of how to do it properly. All right, I think I see my duty. I think. Anyway, with Sasha out there in the world, I must stay. But again, thank you."

Ananda lifted a hand. "The gift is not mine, only the thought. I will leave you with terrible trouble, I know, but I was never capable of addressing it. However, I beseech you to trust Canardan's son, though it appears there is much against him. He's also Feraeth's son, and she is convinced he walks the knife-edge between seeming and truth, but to a purpose, and his purpose is good."

"I will remember that." Atanial wondered if she could believe it.

"Fare you well," Ananda said softly, and she left as silently as she had come.

Atanial lay back down, staring at the ceiling. The next day there might be a hue and cry, but more likely Canardan would suppress news of the queen's disappearance as much as he could. She would vanish from history as quietly as she'd lived.

Atanial let her breath trickle slowly out. So what about her own history? So far, she hadn't done all that well. But she was here again, and so she had a second chance.

Plan, then? For now, be a model "guest", make friends with everyone in sight, be visible, friendly, keep talking to people in hopes they would talk to her and about her, so that Randart, at least, would have difficulty making her "disappear". Learn whatever she could.

And wait to meet this Prince Jehan on whom so much seemed to depend.

The senior barracks of the Ellir Academy was located at the far end of the castle, just before the tower above the very top of Market Street. Across from Market Street was the famous brewery, and the barracks was away from all the masters and guards. It was the place every cadet yearned to live in. By the time you'd attained that pinnacle, though, you had also become aware that there was hierarchy not only in the academy, but among the seniors.

So it was Damedran Randart, the academy commander's son, whose particular group got all the beds down the window side that overlooked the top of Market Street, the brewery and the harbor beyond. The rules stated that beds were first come first served, but those not part of Damedran's inner circle who had arrived for the senior year weeks before Damedran had either discovered a taste for the dusty view overlooking the practice courts inside the academy, or they suffered a lot of accidents that the masters didn't seem to notice.

And so, when Damedran came back from seeing his father, he found his friends sitting at the open windows, idly watching Market Street below.

He paused in the doorway, his splendid shoulders set off in the brown tunic (his being tailored, not taken off the piles down in Supply), his long, glossy black hair worn loose instead of clipped back according to regs, but who was going to complain?

He waited impatiently, wondering why they were all staring out at Market Street when he was back, and they'd all been begging him to find out the final word about the games. "Market Street on fire?"

Gratifying, how they whirled around, a couple of them even

snapping to attention. He wasn't a king yet, and they were already thinking of him like one. Good. Maybe Uncle Dannath would stop jawing at him, *Think like a king!*

Red, his chief lieutenant, dashed back the pale red hair that made the origin of his nickname obvious. "The sheep managed to waylay a pickpocket or thief."

Damedran's huge cousin Wolfie said in his deep growl, "Least, we're pretty sure it was the sheep." He raised a huge paw to his unruly black hair, which he wore neatly clipped back. Wolfie did not stand on privilege, he was mainly interested in fights out behind the stable. "Sheep-white hair. Not many o' those in uniform brown."

"None of 'em wear their hair long," Red said. "Has to be the sheep. Only I thought he rode off to Sartor?"

"He rode in this morning." Damedran was uninterested in Prince Jehan, except when he was in trouble. "I'm amazed he managed to waylay a single thief. It must have taken at least thirty of his followers." As the others laughed, he strode into the barracks, nodded at two of the boys, who leaped up and sped to the doors at either end, shutting them and setting their backs to the wood.

The room now being secure he got right to the subject that interested them all the most. "My father said it's the king's own order. There won't be any yacht runs."

"Whyyyyyyyy?" That was Bowsprit Lanarg, who was the best of all the seniors at skiff running.

Damedran saw disappointment to varying degrees in all their faces, except for Wolfie's. Wolfie just liked fighting. End of subject. Damedran himself hated anything to do with the ocean. Too much work, and anyway, kings didn't go out on the water.

But he had to sound like he cared. "It's because of the

pirate Zathdar. They think he's got the old princess's daughter, and so my uncle has been ordered to take the fleet and wipe 'em out."

"Even Prince Math's girl?"

Damedran snorted a laugh. "Orders are to take her, but hey, if she gets in the way of someone's sword, problem ended—" As soon as the words were out he saw they were a mistake.

Not all his followers knew the secret plans. Definitely not Ban Kender, who was his only genuine aristocrat follower. Ban's family had been deposed when Locan Jora took over the western portion of the kingdom. *Handle him like a thoroughbred plains runner*, his father had told him in private. *That whole family, they're romantic. To them we're heroic though outnumbered, fighting for ancient rights. See you don't disabuse 'em of that notion.*

"They'd kill her?" Ban said, sure enough. And the rest (except for Wolfie, who never changed expression) reflected his dismay. "She sounded as gallant as any ballad heroine."

The others muttered in agreement.

They'd all heard the gossip about the mysterious appearance of Princess Atanial's daughter at the ancient tower, followed a day or two later by the princess herself, at the home of the ex-palace steward.

Damedran said quickly, offhand, "You heard about her fighting skill, but you didn't hear about her screaming orders at the criminals who brought her out of the other world. Last thing anyone heard was her yelling about them forgetting to bow, and where was her coach-and-six, and did anyone take her father's jewels?"

Damedran watched Ban, relieved at his faint expression of disgust. The others muttered about swagger—idiots—who did she think she was, anyway? Damedran didn't listen to any of them. Ban's opinion was important, maybe almost as important as his own. Weird, when Ban never strutted.

"We don't need that kind of trouble," Ban said at last. "Not right now."

Damedran nodded, and the others exchanged looks. They weren't supposed to talk about the secret plans to retake Jora, but they all knew. That was one of the good things about being in with the war commander's nephew.

Damedran was amazed that his lie actually worked. Then he got another idea. "No, we sure don't. Cowards, those Zhavalieshins. Skipping out and leaving us with the Siamis trouble, and now that things are settled, dancing back and expecting us all to bow down to them."

The boys expressed loud disgust. Then Bowsprit, who always had one eye on the weather and the other on the sea whenever he could, hooked a thumb toward the window. "Why is the sheep's yacht warping out?"

"He can't be going anywhere." Damedran snorted. "My uncle made it clear enough even to him he has to stay put. He's supposed to preside at the games."

As he spoke, he and the others moved to the windows. All minor boat traffic beyond the royal pier had cleared the way so Prince Jehan's beautiful yacht could be rowed out a ways from the dock.

They didn't have to warp far. The tide was right, the wind was shifting, judging from the lower layer of clouds coming in under the high wispy ones. In silence they watched the exquisitely cut curved mainsail drop and sheet home. It filled, the craft gathered speed, then the sail was brailed up again. The anchor dropped, and the yacht sat alone out in the roads, just east of the fleet ships.

"Well, he certainly won't get to sit on it to watch us compete in the harbor," Damedran said, and Bowsprit groaned. "Maybe Uncle Dannath ordered him to anchor out in the trade roads in case the pirate tries to grab him on shore."

Wolfie said, "Or maybe the sheep is so afraid of the pirate, he gave the orders before the water games were cancelled."

Hoots of derision met this suggestion.

Damedran waved a dismissive hand. "Or maybe my uncle is commandeering it for his pirate hunt. The *important* thing is, the games are now confined to ground, and we're going to win, right?"

The boys cheered. Damedran regarded them in satisfaction. The plans were all set, his father had said. Beginning with his win in every competition this year, the songs about them all winter, and on the rising tide of his reputation, his leading all the young aristocrats in galloping over the hills to liberate Locan Jora in spring. He'd be the hero who reunited the country...while Prince Jehan did what? Probably sat around watching some old geezer paint daisies.

With this prospect in mind, he laughed, triumphant, happy, burning with anticipation. As the bell clanged for the midday break's end, and the beginning of afternoon practice, he led the way out at a run.

The others stampeded after. Or most of them did.

Ban followed more slowly. He was thinking hard until he noticed Bowsprit also lingering, his pointy nose pressed against the window. After one last glance out at that beautiful yacht, Bowsprit said, "How I'd love to crew it, just once. I don't care what stupid orders the sheep gives."

Ban grimaced. Truth was, he hated that "sheep" business. It didn't seem respectful. But his father had said, *If our regaining your mother's family lands from those ruinous Jorans means putting up with Merindar boot heels all over custom for a time, then we put up.*

Bowsprit poked his arm. "And you wouldn't care if it was a fish scow. What's wrong?"

"I just now remembered. The other night, when I had leave, it was the night my mother's friend's son arrived in town. He's a patrol leader. Wounded at that old castle the mages talk about. Samdan was invalided home. Got there right before supper, and at the time I was annoyed that he interrupted. I was afraid we wouldn't eat and I'd have to report back hungry—" Ban noticed Bowsprit's impatience at all that explanation, and got to the point. "This fellow was there when Prince Math's daughter came to the old castle. I really wasn't listening, but I heard some of it. How the pirate wounded him, how she was easily as hot with a blade. They thought she was a fellow at first, because she's tall and really fast."

"You mean, she wasn't a coward?"

Ban closed his eyes. "No. She did faint, or almost faint, but that was after the fight. She did some kind of healer's spell on one of the pirate's people, who got a cut on the arm, and there was poison on the knife."

"How about the coach-and-six?" Bowsprit asked.

"Well, that might have been later. But she sure didn't do it at the castle. Samdan said she came out into the court, picked up a blade, and she and the pirate whacked their way through the prince's patrol. Then she healed the boy, who my sister says was probably Devli Eban. She didn't try to kill anyone, either. Just like the pirate. Then they were gone by magic transfer."

"Who's Devli Eban?"

"Son of the palace steward during Prince Math's days. He was a mage student with my sister, though he's out now. Price on his head and everything, for being resistance."

"Oh." They reached the door, and Bowsprit paused. They could hear the thunder of the others' boots diminishing down the stairs below. No one else was around. They were all racing to the practice courts. "So your cousin's friend's father, or whatever, was wounded. Maybe he didn't hear everything."

"Said he was two spear-lengths from them."

Both considered in silence, each remembering times when Damedran's version of the truth hadn't quite matched with what they'd understood. But did it do you any good to point such things out? Not when the liar is the son of the academy commander, and the nephew of the kingdom's war commander. And, rumor had it—but never when Damedran was around—that if anything happened to Prince Jehan, the king was looking his way for a possible heir.

Bowsprit knocked Ban in the arm again. "Let's go."

In silence they followed the others, each thinking without coming to any conclusions. Sometimes it was better not to say what you thought, and other times it was useless even to think.

Jehan paused as the two sober-faced boys passed him on their way to the quarter-staff court.

He was certain they were two of Damedran Randart's followers, though he only recognized tall, dark-haired Ban Kender. But he'd been watching the games, and how the academy had been changing under the Randarts' command, for years.

He waited until they'd rounded the stone archway between command and the barracks, and followed, but instead of turning toward the courts, he continued across the parade ground to the stable, his expression so thoughtful that Owl, who was dressed in stable homespun and lurking around on the watch, pursed his lips.

They were long practiced at deception. Jehan inspecting the high-bred horses reserved for those in command, and the scrappy redhead, who looked like so many others in this part of the world so close to Sarendan where red hair was quite common, busily swept out the stalls.

When they knew they wouldn't be overheard, Owl said, "She's all right. Other than mad as fire."

Jehan nodded. "I know. What troubles me more at the moment is Lesi Valleg, who I discovered is on the sick list. The official report is that she tripped, but Elkin tells me one of Damedran's boys got her drunk while on duty and stretched a cord across the bottom two stairs when she ran down."

Owl winced. "What for? I thought he'd outgrown the bullying."

"He stopped doing it for fun. This one might be to a purpose. Its happening right before the games is too suspicious to be accident. So the question is, what purpose?" Jehan shook his head. "Never mind that. What about Devlaen Eban?"

"He's on his way back to his cousin's new hideout, with the mages who wouldn't swear the allegiance oath. Promises to relay the messages to the mages, asking them to shadow Perran and Zhavic."

"And Elva?"

Owl said, "Devlaen told her the news about their mother being held prisoner. That sobered her enough to get her to agree to keep her mouth shut. I think she will. She's stubborn but honest. I left her in line at the hiring office, as she turned down my offer to join our crew. Her parting words to me were that she wanted to get to sea and forget all of us."

Jehan shook his head. "I really stumbled there."

"Maybe." Owl pinched his nose. "But not as badly as I did."

"We can't slip like that again."

They watched past one another's shoulders as they talked, but now they looked around to make extra certain. The stable was empty.

Jehan said, "Back to the games. Damedran's going to sweep all the categories, that much we can predict. What I wonder is if that connects with the rumored order for more weaponry from abroad? The war games ordered for autumn, including a castle siege, expensive as that is. And the requisitions for increased supplies for the guard in spring. Separately, these orders seem a little odd, but not extraordinarily so. Together, they add up to very odd indeed. Has Randart set the time for his invasion at last?"

Owl watched him as he moved dust around on the ground. He'd known Jehan for years, and was used to living life at a run. This was the prince's method of thinking aloud.

Jehan turned his way, his chin lifting. He'd reached a decision. "We have to intercept that weapons shipment. Get Aslo down to the harbor master's to underbid the others for the ships being hired to deliver the weapons. I don't care how much he has to scant his profit. I'll make up the shortfall. It's to be a sober merchant ship hired into that fleet."

Owl grinned. Their success depended on being able to pick the right battleground, and with one of their own ships sailing with the weapons consignment and relaying the position, they'd be able to do just that.

"I'll send a message to Tharlif to signal for a good-sized fleet to intercept that shipment. It won't stop an invasion if Randart really plans one, but at least it will hold him up."

Owl nodded. "You want me back on board the *Zathdar?*"

"No, let Robin take command. She's ready. You need to stay on that yacht. The most important piece of the puzzle is on it right now. The fewer who know who Sasharia is the better, and no one but us must know where she is." He ran his hand over the flanks of a dappled gray mare, and absently held out his fingers to be lipped. "Tell the *Jumping Bug* and *Mulekick* to make targets for Randart to chase, one off Aloca and one here. I want him busy all over the seas, chasing us and not other independents. Keep the navy busy and scattered as long as possible."

"And you?"

Jehan sighed. "I'm going to have to face the fire."

Owl grinned. "Orders for Kazdi to pass on to the Randarts?"

"Oh, let me see. This time it ought to be a painter. She's even more beautiful than my balladeer, and I promised to see her rendition of Lasva Sky Child being crowned queen of Colend. But I *swear* to be back by the start of the games."

Jehan left to be seen out in the practice field staring at clouds instead of watching the boys practice staff fighting. He waited until he'd spotted War Commander Randart scowling contemptuously down at him from the command tower, and drifted away.

Chapter Twenty

I couldn't see anything, and all I could smell was dust, old wool and mold. Presently the cart stopped jolting, and the sensations changed to a kind of wallowing.

Angry as the situation made me, the moment I realized I was being lowered into a boat I stopped kicking. I didn't want to end up being dropped into the drink, and if I nailed Owl in the beezer, he might not be any speed demon about fishing me back out. Ending my life at the bottom of the harbor did not fit into my evolving career plans.

I will say the pirate—that is, the prince—well, anyway, his guys were careful, despite my having gotten in a couple of solid kicks early on in the abduction. The journey in the rowboat was accomplished in complete silence. I had no idea who was doing the oar work. Likewise the horrifying lift via boom up onto the deck was also silent.

Then people picked me up again and put me on a bunk.

But did they untie me? No. I was left in that sweltering cocoon for what seemed about ten centuries.

First I lay there thinking. Remembering. Lingering over every affront, until gradually the justified anger cooled into question, which in turn begat more questions, until I fell into a nasty sort of hot, smothered sleep.

I woke with the welcome sensation of the bonds easing.

With an inarticulate roar of rage, I fought my way out of the quilt—to discover I was alone, in a cabin I did not recognize. For a moment I blinked against the light of a lantern as I gulped in sweet, cool, fresh air. Someone had thoughtfully opened beautifully made leaded glass windows. Actual windows, not just scuttles.

Even the smell of brine seemed sweet compared to the old mold of that quilt.

Someone had set the lantern on a hook inside the door, which was carved out of redwood in a theme of galloping horses.

I rolled off the bunk, lunged to the door, found it locked.

I lunged back and in another surge of rage gathered up that quilt and stuffed it out one of the windows. It took some effort, but finally I heard the satisfying splash, and for a short time I stood there on the redwood decking of the small but elegant cabin, breathing hard and watching the quilt float on the night-black sea.

Gradually the bubble holding it up diminished and the quilting soaked up enough water to sink. The last I saw of it was a pale blue corner and it was gone.

As if released from its ghostly grip, I turned around. The cabin was obviously designed and made for someone with extreme wealth. All the wood was carved, the themes being running horses, entwined leaves, artsy lilies, the lines enhanced with inlaid threads of gold.

The way the cabin was shaped indicated that once again, I was in the bow. A tiny table had been fitted into the pointy end, within reach of the bunks angled inward on either side. On this little table someone had set a small porcelain tray with a silver pot all bedewed with moisture. A glass sat next to it.

My tongue felt like a sponge left out in the Gobi Desert, and

I pounced, drinking down water until I was breathless. I continued my survey more slowly, looking for possible means of escape.

Built-in drawers with gold handles had been fitted below each bunk, the handles fashioned in the shape of two lilies with entwined stems. Above the bunk on one side was a built-in shelf containing handmade books and old scrolls tied with ribbon. Over the opposite bunk was a hand-drawn and colored map of the world, every river cobalt blue, paler blue for small lakes, different shades of green representing the predominant trees in forests, different browns for types of land. Cities indicated by highly stylized drawings of small or large towns, walled cities with walls, open ones with main roads done in gold.

It was a breathtaking work of art. I clambered up on the bunk to examine the map more closely. It was so beautiful I almost missed the sound of the cabin door opening behind me.

I whirled around as Jehan ducked slightly and entered, carrying a tray. "Like the map?"

When I was sixteen I might have yelled, *No!* Or tried to tear it up. My adult version of the correct etiquette for an abductee was to say, as rudely as possible, "From whom did you steal it?"

"My father." He flicked down a larger table from the wall, a table so cunningly worked into the bulkhead I'd missed it. He set the tray carefully down as he added, "He stole it from his relatives when he was kicked out of Remalna after a family fight and sent here to the military school under strict orders to never return. You'll find Remalna northwest of where the Mardgar drains into the Sartoran Sea. Where the gold crown is drawn in."

I couldn't help turning and saw the tiny kingdom, far smaller than Khanerenth. Indeed there was a crown, a typical piece of Merindar arrogance.

"Go ahead." He leaned against the opposite bulkhead. I noticed he was dressed in dark colors, a linen shirt dyed dark blue, black sash and trousers. "Get 'em out."

"Get what out?"

"All the insults you've piled up. You've got to have thought up some good ones. Let's hear them."

"And, what, you can laugh from your oh-so-superior position?" I snapped, eying the tray. My appetite had woken like a cage of roaring lions. I considered for about one second the moral satisfaction of flinging that tray at him, but figured he'd just duck, like the total and complete stinker he was, and there'd be all that lovely food wasted.

Because it was lovely—a tomato soup with what smelled like fresh basil, some kind of incredibly savory cheese making it creamy, and bits of the very good rice this world grows. Next to it fresh bread, with pats of the honey-butter popular all over the kingdom. A spray of purple grapes, a perfectly sliced peach and a silver urn containing hot chocolate joined a crystal decanter full of wine in making a feast for a king.

I glared at Zathdar. No, Jehan. Those were Zathdar's blue eyes watching me, but the long, fine white hair was unfamiliar. A diamond glinted in one ear. The laces in his shirt were braided silk, with tiny gold leaves fastening the ends.

I was staring. And the cabin seemed suddenly quite small. So I turned my attention back to the food.

"Go ahead," he invited.

"There are too many dishes," I said, scowling.

"Well, I haven't eaten all day, either. If it helps, feel free to fling my share out the window after Owl's mother's quilt."

Unwillingly I had to laugh. "All right. You win. That much,

anyway. Sit down."

The table exactly fitted the space between the two bunks, on which we sat opposite one another.

I'd only had that single bite in the Gold Inn so I set to with enthusiasm. Two goblets of wine plus the meal later, I sat back, trying to decide if I had enough appetite to assay the chocolate.

Neither of us had spoken, though I was very aware of him sitting an arm's reach away, the play of his hands on the goblet, pouring wine, picking up bread and cheese, homely tasks all, but executed with grace. He ate neatly, with far better manners than I suspected I displayed. But I'd been catching meals on the run for years, usually with a book in one hand.

I frowned at my goblet. Was what I felt the same as my mother had felt all those years ago, when this man's father no doubt ate intimate dinners with her while my own father was busy tending to kingly business for my ailing grandfather?

I looked up. Jehan regarded me steadily over his cup of wine.

I said, crossly, "I suppose you dye your eyelashes and brows?"

"No. Darker shade than my father's, as it happens," he replied in an easy tone, as though he fielded this nosy question every day. "For some reason most half-morvende have dark brows and lashes. The ones with white lashes come from families who have lived over a thousand years underground. Some of the more recent family lines have color here." He indicated a thin stripe at the top of his head. "Almost always black. Sometimes red or yellow or brown. A lot of 'em get rid of it by magic," he added. "If it comes in stripes."

A short pause ensued, during which I was hyper-aware of the soft plash of water against the hull of the vessel, of the flicker of the flame in the lantern, and its golden reflection made manifold by the glass sectioning inside the burnished copper frame. I breathed in the rich fragrance of the chocolate and set my goblet down.

A phosphorescent tingle sparked along my nerves. I gripped my hands in my lap.

"I apologize for the, ah, summary invitation aboard my yacht," Jehan continued, in the same conversational tone. "I'll end it when I can."

I looked up, the flare of anger back. "You mean when you will."

"No one outside of a dozen people know who I am." He lifted a shoulder in a slight, apologetic shrug. "Except the Ebans, now. And you."

"What did you do to Elva?"

"Nothing. Owl tried to recruit her. She refused. Last he saw, she was trying to find another ship to sign onto."

"Devli?"

"On his way to his mage tutors, wherever they're hiding."

I twisted my fingers. "That might even be true. But if it is, why am I not asked to keep silent, and set free to go on my way?"

"Because..." He looked away, out the window into the darkness, then back at me. "Because too many people see you as a tool necessary to grip control of the kingdom."

"Including you?"

He looked away again. Then back. "Will you listen to my side of things?" His eyes narrowed. "But you won't believe me, will you?" He moved suddenly, not toward me—though I braced for a moment—but away, to the little alcove at the point of the cabin. The bulkhead below the tiny table had been adapted into a kind of desk that reminded me of a rolltop, with a lot of little drawers.

He opened one and drew out a packet of heavy linen paper.

"You want to read my correspondence with your father?" He held out the letters.

"How do I know those are real?" I felt not so much angry as sick and miserable. "I wouldn't recognize his handwriting. I wouldn't even know his style. I was ten, the last time I saw him."

He dropped the letters back into the drawer and leaned there with hands on the desk, the silken shirt laces swinging, their golden leaves winking with tiny reflected flames in the light of the lantern. I was staring again.

He turned his head slightly, his white hair drifting over his shoulder. His gaze met mine, and fireworks lit off right behind my ribs. *I hate chemistry.* I jerked my head away, half expecting my eyes to make popping sounds like cartoon tentacles. Argh! I scowled at the carved racing horses in the wood panels.

"Why won't you listen? Do you really think I'd go to all this trouble if I was my father's tool?"

I said to the chocolate pot, "Why didn't you answer me when I asked why I'm here, but you let the Ebans go free?" A quick glance, to see the effect of my words. "You are good at deflecting awkward questions, aren't you?"

I could feel him regarding me steadily, trying to read my reactions. "They don't hold the key to the kingdom. You do."

My father.

Jehan said quickly, "You know where Prince Math is." He got up and put his hand on the latch to the cabin door. "I should mention that your mother followed you through the World Gate. And unfortunately my father has her. No, don't say it." He raised his hand as I drew in a deep breath. "Whatever you believe me capable of, I can promise you this. If my father gets his hands on you, you can absolutely count on him using your lives against one another in order to get what he wants. Chocolate? Yes? No?"

"Lost my appetite," I said wearily.

He took the tray and left. Locking the door behind him.

Pretty soon I heard through the open windows the noises of the booms being used to lower a small boat. I peered down at an angle as a silhouette descended.

I recognized Jehan by the way he moved. He had confined that moon-pale hair in some sort of knitted sailor cap. That and the dark clothing made him unremarkable, one of many people plying little boats to and fro on the dark waters between the boats all lit by strings of lanterns.

Unremarkable if your eyes hadn't memorized the contours of his arms, the line from shoulder to slim hip, the way the light emphasized the angles in his face. The arch of his brow. The shape of his lips.

I watched until he and his boat blended into the crown of lights made by the market street and the torchlit castle above, and then I dropped onto the bunk and put my head in my hands.

Yeah, that was definitely one of my worst moments.

Up in the Ellir Academy commander's suite, War Commander Randart longed for sleep. He was getting too old for all-night rides and all-day inspections, distractions, orders and logistics.

He glared at his nephew, gabbling away to Orthan as if he had never heard of sleep, and finished the rest of his ale. At least that was good. He'd have to make certain a few barrels of

Old Gold were included in the commander's stores when he took ship.

"...and they were watching him arrest some cutpurse. I never heard of him doing that before. Must have been his followers who actually did the work."

Orthan laughed.

"Red says, maybe he was trying to teach the thief some poetry and the thief surrendered only to get away."

Orthan guffawed louder, making the war commander's head hurt. "What's that? They didn't tell me Jehan took the cutpurse arrested today."

Orthan and Damedran turned twin expressions of surprise his way. "He didn't. I told you that earlier," Orthan exclaimed, and his brow began to lower. "Two of our fellows did—"

The war commander ignored his brother's long-suffering *You don't listen to me.* They'd been through that too many times. Dannath only listened when Orthan's gibble-gabble was to a purpose. He got to his feet. "All I know is, if he's not here at the start of the games tomorrow, I'll strangle him myself." He pointed at his nephew. "You! Go get some rest. You have one order, to win tomorrow."

"Oh, I'll win," Damedran predicted, stretching as he swung to his feet. "I can thrash anyone I know on the list, one handed." He snapped a fist into the opposite palm, muscles bunching. "I got Captain Traneg to show me the roster before I came up here. Some locals have signed up, but we haven't seen any locals win for years."

"People can sign on until the trumpets tomorrow," Orthan warned, knowing his son would ignore him, but it was better to endorse his brother's order when Dannath was looking so irritable. "You never know, but some day a good one might show up, like the old days, before Siamis came. You do your best when you're rested."

Damedran snorted. "The back of my hand to locals. I don't see why you don't close the games to them anyway. Yes, I know that's how we recruited in the past, but maybe it's time to change all that. Better cadets from the better families."

"Shut up and go to bed," the war commander ordered.

When he used that voice, it was best to obey. Damedran and his uncle slammed through opposite doors, leaving Orthan to finish the ale alone and then douse the light.

Chapter Twenty-One

After a sleepless night during which Jehan's brain insisted on reviewing, with remorseless repetition, every single mistake he'd made in deed or speech with Sasharia, he got up, drank the hottest, strongest coffee the innkeeper could brew, then left the humble dockside inn where he'd thought to get overdue rest. He stopped only at the bathhouse and paid to use their cleaning frame. No time for a real bath, and anyway it was going to be far too hot, he thought, staring at the knife-edged shafts of yellow early morning sunlight painting the wooden wall dividing the men's side from the women's.

The sun was climbing into midsummer brilliance when he crossed up an old pathway behind the ruins of a castle long forgotten, and now used mainly for its stone. There, in the shade of a web-clogged alcove he paused to change out of the plain clothes and hat, pulling on his brown velvet.

He rolled up his old outfit, tucked it under his arm, and started up the back trail used by locals who hired on as stable and maintenance support staff at the guard barracks and academy. A few steps up past some flowering shrubs, his shoulder blades prickled. Unseen eyes? He stepped to the side, hand going to his sword, then dropping when he saw four cadet-aged young fellows walking behind him single file.

Three walked and one sauntered, a tall fellow with black

hair and pale brown eyes of a distinctive shade—flecked with gold—that evoked flame. His features were sharp, his gaze sharper; memory stirred from somewhere way back years ago, on the other side of the world.

"Do I know you?" he asked.

The tall one grinned, but did not speak.

"Not really," another one murmured, and when Jehan looked his way his breath caught. He was about to exclaim, "Senrid?" when he realized that this fellow was not Senrid Montredaun-An, king of Marloven Hess—and head of the academy to which Jehan had gone to learn war skills so long ago.

The resemblance stubbornly persisted, though Senrid never wore this sort of thoughtful, almost scholarly expression, nor had he grown as tall. Most tellingly, this fellow's eyes were brown, an ordinary light brown, and King Senrid's were grayish blue.

"I'm David," the fellow said, pronouncing it not Sartoran DAUF-ed, but Marloven-style, DAY-vid. David gestured at the three others. "We're here to play in your games."

Jehan took in the two unfamiliar ones. First, a tallish, thin fellow with a dreamy expression, wide-set brown eyes and an unkempt mat of curly light brown hair that brought Prince Math instantly and forcibly to mind. The last was a mere boy, scarcely cadet age from the looks of him. He seemed an everyday small boy, dressed in homespun shirt and riding trousers, brown hair clipped back from a high brow, though Jehan almost immediately began observing subtle anomalies, beginning with his stillness, and the steady, observant hazel gaze that seemed far older than you ever saw in any child's face.

"And the rest of you are?" He suspected he would not get a real answer.

Nor did he. "Competitors," David said, and then, with an air of absent courtesy, "You have no objection to a little roustabout, perhaps?"

"What's that supposed to mean?" Jehan recognized that they knew who he was. Where *had* he seen that tall one before? Now it seemed important.

"Nothing untoward," David soothed. "Shall we meet after the day's entertainment?"

"I suspect"—Jehan eyed the tall one again—"that I will want very much to do that. Where have I seen you before?"

"Here and there." The tall one grinned briefly, no more than a flash of teeth. His voice was lower than you'd expect from someone that lean. Low, husky—and again familiar.

Sweat trickled down Jehan's forehead. The morning air had gone from warm to hot, and the sun was still low. "Go on. Sign up. Do whatever it is you're going to do." *Things could hardly get worse.*

The tall one laughed softly as they passed on by.

The small one was last. As he drew near Jehan he said in Sartoran, "Stay your path."

He dashed after his companions and they vanished around the mossy old wall of the ruined castle, reappearing halfway up the trail at a dead run.

Jehan veered between amusement and annoyance at some urchin advising him how to get to his own academy. As if he was likely to stray off the—

Path. In Sartoran. He listened to the words again, thinking in Sartoran instead of just mentally translating the words.

Stay. Your. Path.

In Sartoran, the connotation was closer to *You're doing the right thing.*

Now, that was strange. He paused to peer upward against the rising sun as the four mystery visitors vanished over the lip of the hill toward the public path. He forgot about the heat, his headache, even his hunger, and began to lope up the trail toward the back way into the old, abandoned storage rooms where he usually left his change of clothes. Maybe the day that had promised a long stretch of annoyance might yield some surprises after all.

Chapter Twenty-Two

Lesi Valleg wept for joy, shaking her head impatiently so her vision would not blur. She stood with a cluster of seniors at the sideline of the archery butts, and watched the little boy in homespun lift his bow, pull back and aim in the same fluid motion so he was one line from thumb to the back elbow, and when he let fly his arm snapped out so his arms were a straight line, thumb to thumb. And then down, as smooth and unthinking as the folding wings of a swan.

It was effortless, graceful, expert—and the best shot of the day, despite his age, despite the distance and oh, oh, oh, despite Damedran leaning against the wall on the other side of the butts, his bruised face expressionless.

"See that? Arm all the way back," she muttered, wiping her eyes. "It really does make a difference." And the other seniors standing near her, instead of rolling their eyes or sneering or yawning as they always had in the past, agreed with mutters of wonder.

Once Prince Jehan had told her that this was the way he'd been taught to shoot by that academy on the other side of the continent. But that fact had only earned scoffing. Every cadet knew he was a cloud-brain. And everyone knew the Marlovens were mere horse riders, they didn't train on water as well as land.

If you want to shoot you need first to learn form. Aim will then come, she remembered her old teacher saying. It wouldn't do to remind everyone. She'd be accused of swagger. And anyway, that boy had carried off the silver cup. She didn't *need* to remind them.

She followed the crowd, hoping she could talk to him. She wanted to tell him it was a pleasure to watch him. It would have been a pleasure to shoot against him, no matter who won, if only her arm hadn't been broken.

But the trumpet blew the signal to change events, and most of the competitors, locals as well as cadets, swarmed to the tables to get some water before lining up for the last and favorite event of the land games: the relay race, which took all afternoon.

"You don't have to go," Ban said to Damedran as they followed more slowly. He regretted his earlier triumph when Damedran was summarily thumped in the last grappling match, though he'd enjoyed it thoroughly (and privately) at the time.

Damedran turned his puffy face Ban's way, then flashed up the back of his hand.

Despite the insult Ban was not angry. Not when he saw the spasm of pain that tightened Damedran's features.

Ban, Bowsprit and a couple of others exchanged wry looks. Nothing felt quite real any more; life was no longer predictable. One thing was clear, despite his drubbing Damedran was going to carry on anyway.

The trumpet pealed, and everyone looked up.

"Teams gather here," bawled the captain in charge of the relay.

Damedran limped slowly to the edge of the field from which the sprinters would take off on the first leg of the relay. Paying no attention to the chatter around him, he said, "I'll ride. Can't run or canoe." He gave them a painful grimace that was supposed to be a smile.

Ban saw Wolfie peering intently to one side, his mouth twisted in the smirk that meant either he'd been fighting or was going to fight. And there was Red moseying along, looking skyward, as he passed by the various teams assembling. He slowed near the strangers who had so unaccountably appeared and taken all the prizes. Red stopped as the unfamiliar four talked briefly and quietly among themselves, bent to pick something from one boot, then he straightened up and sauntered with a bit more speed to Wolfie, and muttered behind his hand.

Wolfie beckoned to a couple of their other followers, and Ban suspected what was probably going to happen. He knew his guess was right when Wolfie stepped up to Damedran and said, "The little one is doing the ride." He chuckled the way he always did before somebody ended up getting scragged. "Guess they won't win the relay."

Damedran shook his head.

Ban said in disgust, "You're going to drop on the littlest one."

Wolfie, Red and the other two turned his way, their faces ranging from guilty to defiant to angry.

Damedran said, surprising them all, "That's not an...an...a fair scrag. Dropping on a little boy, that's just rabbiting."

"Fair?" Wolfie repeated derisively. For him, a scrag was a scrag. Any excuse served to have one, because he always won.

"Fair?" Red repeated, as if he'd never heard the word.

"But you dropped Lesi Valleg," Ban observed. It had been a guess. He saw from Damedran's quick grimace that he'd been right.

"That was different," Damedran muttered, trying not to look yet again to where the tall, thin girl with the sling-bound arm stood, her straight brows low, watching him with unsmiling intensity. "We couldn't win against her. I wanted, I needed, wins in everything." He dropped his head back, uttering a strangled laugh.

"It isn't different," Ban said.

Damedran's mouth tightened. He opened his hand. "She wouldn't have won anyway. Not against that little brat."

"Who *are* they?" asked Calan Pradiesh, Red's cousin from the coast.

"I don't know." Damedran shifted with painful care to observe the newcomers, who stood in line, the tall one grinning at something the short one said, the fair-haired one looking pensive, the one with the curly hair watching two raptors riding the thermals high up under the flat carpet of tiny puff clouds that promised rain. "But he used moves I've never seen." He fingered his shoulder, winced again. "Or felt."

They all reflected on the grappling. The lazy way the tall one moved to block, to deflect, and his whip-fast, brutal attacks. All without breaking a sweat.

"They won't win," Wolfie reminded them, rubbing his hands.

Ban studied the small boy who stood there so still and poised as he contemplated the stands where the commanders sat with the prince. Neither of the Randarts smiled, and all the seniors knew they were angry. But they could do nothing. The competition was open, had been for years.

Nobody cared what Prince Jehan thought.

Ban said suddenly, privately, to Bowsprit, "I think..." He shook his head.

Bowsprit turned his thin, pointy nose toward Wolfie's huge, muscular form, and then to the small, slender boy who was probably about nine, if that. "I think so too."

"First-leg runners, line up here," called the captain. "Second-leg canoe, follow Captain Semmeg, third-leg mountain climbers, follow Captain Torvic, and the horse riders for the last leg, you go with Captain Lesstrad to your posts. We've got animals up there waiting for you." The trumpet played the signal, and a roar went up as the relay racers separated.

Ban took off behind Captain Torvic, along with the five other members of cadet teams, two members of the royal fleet, and the blond foreigner with the pensive face, the one who had won every single sword match.

Ban loped in the fellow's direction, questions forming in his mind, but the other cadets were there first. As usual the youngest came right out with nosy questions of the sort Ban might have ventured only after a couple of ales.

"Where you from?" piped a ten-year-old.

"Oh, here and there, you might say," was the answer, with a faint trace of accent. "Never really settled in one place."

"Where'd you learn your sword work?"

The fellow smiled. "Various teachers. They tend to be hard on mistakes, so, you know, we learn to make as few as possible."

"How hard?" asked a fourteen-year-old girl with the squint-eyed distrust of the middle teens.

"Let's say...they broke us of bad habits."

Everyone, even the ten-year-old, heard the humorous ambiguity behind "broke".

"Belay the chatter and hurry up there," called Captain Torvic.

That ended the talk until they reached the site for their leg of the relay. While they waited, the newcomer prowled around looking down at the road, up at the cliffs, at the distant sea, at the sky, and though Ban watched him steadily, he never turned Ban's way.

The newcomer with the frizzy hair was first to their post, and the blond one took off. One of their own group was next, crimson faced with effort, and Ban sprinted up the mountain, hoping he would not see Wolfie or Red, but afraid he knew where they were.

When he reached the last leg, gasping with effort, the little boy was gone, and the blond fellow sat on the grass, smiling at the sky. Ban almost said something, but shook his head and started back down the trail to the academy.

It was a long, hot, gloomy walk. He took the horse trail anyway, but didn't see anyone.

When he reached the academy, it was to find out that the newcomers had won. The small boy rode bareback into the center of the parade ground on a high-spirited charger, his hands not even on the reins.

Prince Jehan was the first to applaud, and then the others joined, but not with any spirit. The river-rush of voices all talking and exclaiming was almost louder than the clapping.

Bowsprit and Ban, having hoped the boy would escape being scragged by Wolfie, Red and a few of the boys, said nothing at all as they followed the glum senior cadets to the parade ground for the distribution of the prizes.

Up in the stands, Dannath Randart was so angry he felt his blood boiling in a drumbeat through his head. But he schooled himself to sit without moving, fists on his knees, as he stared down at the shambles of his plan.

Plans could be remade. He knew that. He glowered at his

nephew, who limped from the horse picket across to the senior line. Why did the idiot have to ride in the relay when he could barely sit his horse, just to lose yet again? Now Randart had to consider ways to wrench some kind of victory from the distasteful, no, the *shameful* exhibition.

The blame would go squarely on the shoulders of the staggeringly stupid white-haired fatwit sitting to his right, who was now getting up and flicking dust from his faultless velvet, in order to go down to the field to hand out the prizes.

Randart glared at Jehan. "Those newcomers. I want them." And at the shocked look on Orthan's face, he forced a semblance of civility into his tone. "I believe the king would want to hear about their training. Please, your highness, request them to honor us for a celebratory glass up in the command tower."

Jehan, as always, was oblivious to the sudden change of tone—

Jehan. Prisoners. Market Street—cadets—

Randart put out a hand, remembering again what had bothered him when he woke up. He'd been bothered enough to go down to the lockup and ask a few questions, despite the loaded schedule. "You arrested a cutpurse in Market Street yesterday?"

Jehan's thin brows lifted. "I did?"

"Damedran saw you. That is, the boys saw you from the senior barracks. But the only thief in the lockup is the pickpocket brought in by the pier patrol on the morning rotation."

Jehan sighed, looking apologetic. "Well. I did try. But my miscreant got away."

So he *didn't* have any of his followers in the king's guard with him. "Why didn't you call up the guard? There's always a patrol within earshot."

"I thought they were off duty," Jehan said vaguely. "I did not like to disturb them."

Randart sat back in disgust. He marshaled himself enough to say with forced politeness, "I believe they are waiting on their prizes, your highness. Forgive me for detaining you."

Jehan bowed, a court bow and highly inappropriate here, but that was as usual. Everything was as usual, so why did he feel something crucial was missing from that testimony?

I'm seeing conspiracies everywhere, Randart thought. But just the same, before the prince reached the end of the platform and was about to step down into the regular stands to descend to the field, he called, "Remember, after we speak to the winners, the king requires you to remain with us. Your highness."

Once again a court bow, hand gracefully at his heart, and Jehan ran lightly down the steps to the field, where the captains had the cadets in field order, the younger boys and girls standing in more or less straight lines. While the seniors looked around for Wolfie and Red and their two cronies, Randart said to his brother, "I want the prince followed. Say it's for his safety. But put someone discreet on it."

Startled, Orthan leaned over to speak to the aide on duty, who hustled along the back of the platform to the hidden doorway leading down to the guardroom.

The brothers turned their attention back to the field, where Jehan stood next to the four small cadets who so carefully held the prizes. Both forgot the prince when they saw why the ceremonies had not begun. It was not Jehan getting himself lost counting butterflies, it was because the recipients were nowhere in sight.

Randart gripped the edge of his seat. "The little one was

just there, riding that horse. Where did he go? Find them. I want them. Whatever excuse it takes. I want to know who they are, why they were here."

Orthan got up. After a glance at his brother's face, he hustled after his own underling.

On the field, Jehan spoke a few graceful words that few listened to, gave the signal for the captains to dismiss the contestants. The cadets surged toward the mess hall, everyone voicing his or her opinion, or putting questions to the air. Comments and questions mirrored in the watchers in the stands, who filed out the other way and back down the long zigzagging steps into the harbor city below.

As Jehan traversed the halls between the guard barracks and the academy, the morvende part of his hearing, developed for generations to sift human sound from wind and water rushing along stone tunnels and caverns, registered footsteps matching his pace.

He paused at the guard room to get a drink of water after the long, hot afternoon in the sun, nodded pleasantly when the guards on duty leaped to their feet and saluted, and waved them lazily back to their seats. No one entered after him.

He left. Moseyed slowly to the mess hall, hot as it was and smelling of fish simmered in herbs and tomato. Below that he detected the distinct odor of summer-afternoon adolescent sweat. Jehan stepped into the kitchen, nipped a biscuit from one of the trays being pulled from the oven and exited through the opposite door as he tossed the hot biscuit from hand to hand.

Still there, same distance back.

Down to the cadet stable, which was built into the oldest part of the castle. There he asked about some of his favorite mounts and ordered Clover to be saddled up. "I want to ride back along the relay trails," he said clearly. "I hope our mysterious visitors did not get lost somewhere along the way."

While the duty cadets and the shadow busied themselves with horse saddling, Jehan slipped through the tack room into the old storage room, which smelled of mossy stone. He slid the bolt, then keyed the entrance to a passageway that Prince Math had shown him when he was a boy, the single time they had been here together.

When he emerged at the other end, he was dressed again in the blue outfit, a fisherman's stocking cap on his head hiding his hair, his brown velvet hanging in a net bag over his shoulder. He made his way through the rotting barrels that hid the door to the passage, slipped into the alley behind the old row of shops, and from there he strolled into Market Street as the low sun slanted ochre shafts between buildings.

Jehan didn't trouble to look around. The shadow would be riding as fast as he could for the relay trail, which was sure to keep him or her busy for a while. Jehan suspected that David and his three friends, who had indicated they would speak to him after the competition, would find him if they wanted him.

He was right. A crowd of sailors strolled by, talking and laughing; out of their number appeared two figures who flanked Jehan. The tall black-haired one grinned. "Nice sidestep."

He meant it as a compliment. They were aware of the shadow, and how Jehan had slipped the shadow's vigilance. Prickles of invisible ice cooled his neck and the backs of his arms, as the thin one flicked a hand toward one of the more modest tents.

Inside they found David holding a table, to which a harried young woman brought a loaded tray of chicken pies, cornbread and cold, frosty ale.

Almost immediately the small boy drifted in, unnoticed by

anyone else in the tent—the conversations at the other tables being mostly about the fleet being made up for the pirate hunt, and who'd hired on where, and what it was doing to trade.

The boy was wearing an outsized shirt. He slid in next to David, then said with a quiet air almost of apology, "I had to use the other for bindings."

Jehan realized then what he'd known instinctively, that these four somehow spoke mind to mind. He knew now from where he recognized the tall one, and possibly the one with the hair. They'd competed in the midsummer games years before, always well, but previously they'd never quite stood out.

Jehan sat back. "So your roustabout was intended as a general humiliation, or for fun?"

David looked surprised, and the fiery-eyed one grinned. "For instruction."

David put down his fork. "Tell me you didn't see what we were doing."

Jehan shrugged a shoulder. "So you are giving me lessons in curriculum design why?"

The mock surprise and fake air of helpfulness vanished. "Because you will need to train 'em better," David said. "And if I might suggest an added course of instruction, hill warfare against occupation."

Again the ice, burning with warning.

"Norsunder," Jehan breathed. "What? When?" He knew now who they were, but not why they were here.

Before he could speak again, the tall one flicked up a scarred hand. "Don't say anything." He flicked one ear. "They do actually have wards against certain names."

Jehan studied the four faces. "But—the stories about you— whose side are you on, anyway?"

"What's a side?" the smallest one asked.

"The easiest would be anything or anyone that fights against Norsunder taking land, people, life, liberty. Will and spirit," Jehan said deliberately.

"That would be our side," said the boy, his gaze steady. Meeting it felt strangely like falling and falling through the air.

"Not what I've heard about you." Jehan looked away, steadying himself with his hands flat on the table.

The one with the hair looked down, the tall one flashed his sharp-edged grin. David said, "Is everything said about you—action, motivation—true?"

"No."

The small one murmured, "Some of what's said about us is true. But we bring no intent to harm here."

Jehan believed that because he knew what they were capable of.

The tall one, meanwhile, had gone on eating. He looked up. "Damedran. Bad bridle training. You take the reins." He gestured, meaning qualified approval, and returned to his meal.

Jehan let out a soundless laugh. He couldn't quite point out that he had no reins to hold, not with Randart hunting him in phantom form and now, possibly in real, all because of that hasty abduction. It was only a matter of time before he slipped and Randart penetrated the tenuous disguise. When seen in the perspective of world politics—the sinister powers hunting the blood of these four and the infamous figures who had trained them—his problems seemed small.

"Everyone is going to have to pitch it together," the one with the hair spoke for the first time. "Everyone. To the best of their ability. War is coming, we cannot avoid it, but we can resist if everyone works together."

David turned his head sharply; Jehan heard a cadenced march above the general noise of the tent.

A search party of guards halted outside the tent. The patrons fell silent and the harried girl ran to the canvas door, lifted it, exclaiming in question and alarm.

Jehan turned back to his companions. They were gone, the bottom of the tent reverberating as if just dropped.

He was alone at the table. Even their food was gone, leaving him to hunch over his meal. He felt the hot, weary, exasperated gaze of the search captain sweep past him, and then came the sounds of the searchers marching farther up the row of tents.

Jehan sat there thinking, while he had this precious time to think. War, imminent. *I'd better have Tharlif stockpile those weapons she took off Randart's fleet.*

He slipped out to make his way to the boat as the sun vanished at last and shadows merged.

It was time to go try to make amends with Sasharia. And despite his headache, his regrets, the new threats to his kingdom and to the world, he looked forward to seeing her. Maybe, just maybe, he could get her to laugh.

On the other side of the castle, while riding the last leg of the relay without finding Prince Jehan, or anyone else, his shadow came across four cadets making their way slowly toward the parade ground. In amazement he recognized Wolf, nephew of the commander, and three others. All with broken bones—a wrist, an arm, a shoulder, and Wolf with a broken leg. Each wound thoughtfully splinted and bound up with neatly torn strips from a boy-sized shirt.

No one spoke as he helped them back to the academy.

Chapter Twenty-Three

The last of the day's light was a deep blue glow on the western horizon behind him when Jehan reached the yacht. He'd left orders for a single lantern at the stern rather than running lights, so he was surprised to see lanterns swinging and winking as silhouettes crossed back and forth, the sort of movement you expected to see during work aboard a ship.

What work? The sails were furled, the yacht riding at single anchor on the out-flowing tide. He smothered his lantern and waited, oars at rest, until his eyes adjusted enough to determine that the yacht was not being attacked. He'd first seen climbing figures. Now the crew was at the falls and tackle, bringing up the second boat.

There could only be one reason it had been let down. He uncovered his lantern, once again shielding it from the shore side, and pulled hard on his oars, occasionally peering over his shoulder until he could make out a shivering figure with long dripping braids huddled in a blanket on deck as the other crew members finished stowing the second boat.

"*Dolphin*," he called.

"*Dolphin* ho. Falls ready," came Owl's wry voice.

Jehan climbed up the side and crossed to the captain's deck. As he passed Sasharia, she lifted her chin, her face pale and defiant when she recognized him.

"I would have tried it too," he said.

She laughed, and his breath caught. "You. W-would. Have. G-gotten. Away." Her teeth chattered so hard she almost couldn't speak.

A step nearer, and he saw her blue lips. Angry, he turned his head. "Where is something hot—"

"Right away. Gave the orders when we got back." Owl worked in tandem with the other crew, pulling up Jehan's boat.

"Here I am," came the accented voice of Kaelande, the cook, and a heartbeat later he appeared with a tray of hot coffee, which he set on the capstan. "Dinner," he added after an inscrutable glance at them all, "will be ready anon." He vanished back down to his galley, a tall, stocky man who had been trained in Alsais's royal palace, the most exclusive cooking school in the entire southern hemisphere.

Owl turned a slant-browed, assessing look Jehan's way, and then toward Sasharia. "Looks to me like we could all use it."

Sasharia took her mug, her eyes closing as she cherished its warmth. She carried it toward the guest cabin in the forecastle, and Owl followed Jehan down into the main cabin. They sank down onto the fine-carved chairs bolted to the deck, and Owl sighed. "I didn't think she'd try a swim for shore from out here."

"I didn't either. We were wrong. But that's one more tot in the day's total." Jehan tried to shut out the image of Sasha's tall, strong body in that wet clothing. His life was complicated enough, and he knew she didn't want any part of him. But there she was, somehow larger than life in all the ways that were good, with a sudden smile like the sun on the world's first day.

He pressed his thumbs into his eyelids, trying to shutter

away Sasha's image. "Randart will probably have a search team out here by morning, soon as he can figure an excuse."

"He's onto us?"

"I think he suspects. And I'm coming to believe, despite his former friendliness, that he would like any excuse to help me suffer a fatal accident. But that's not our biggest problem. Not nearly."

Owl grimaced. "If there's something worse, I'd rather get a meal in me first."

"We'll all do that."

Owl jerked his thumb toward the front of the ship in question.

Jehan said, "Invite her. Then I don't have to explain twice."

Owl waited, but Jehan's gaze had gone diffuse the way it did when he was evolving plans, and so he left.

I stood in the cabin while my core temperature gradually achieved something resembling human levels, rather than penguin, and stared into the coffee.

I hate coffee. That is, I love the smell but find it bitter to drink unless I doctor it with honey and milk. Lots and lots of milk. But I wasn't going to complain about it now. First of all because I needed the warmth, and second because they very definitely had the high moral ground.

Human nature, or maybe it's my own nature, has mule-kick stubbornness beat hollow. If they'd yelled at me for my stupid act, I would have been planning another try. But they'd been nice about it, so I felt guilty. Guilty for simply trying my best to get away, on my own, until I figured out what was right? No, guilty because they'd gone to a terrible amount of trouble to search me out in the ocean, their faces worried sick when they found me about two nanoseconds before my numb body was about to give up.

I felt guilty and cold and waterlogged. All my gear was soaked as well, for the gear bag was not waterproof, and I'd thrown away the horrible basket-weave. Owl had put me through the cleaning frame as soon as I got on board, so the salt sting was gone, but that did not dry anything.

For a short time I stood there staring haplessly down at the soggy firebird coverlet and my other outfit. I let them drop to the deck with a squelch.

A knock a moment later. "Will you join us for dinner?" That was Owl. I knew Owl's voice very well by now. First he'd been on the other side of that hot quilt the day before. Today he'd been calling to me, calling to me, as they sought for me in the boat despite the darkness, as I was about to sink...

"No clothes." My lips were numb, my jaw shuddering. "W-wet."

No answer.

I was pressing the cup against my face when the knock came again. "Jehan offers these with his compliments."

I fumbled with still-numb fingers at the cabin door. It opened. Owl handed me folded cloth. "He apologizes for the colors, but says they went through the cleaning frame. If you give me yours, I'll put 'em through the frame and spread 'em near the galley fire."

I silently handed him the cloth things from the gear bag, then shut the door and shucked my tunic and trousers. My undies were wet too, but no help for those. At least they were clean.

I turned to the clothes. *Jehan's* clothes. The idea whopped me right behind the ribs. I held up a fine linen shirt, the lacing another of those long braided silk things with a tiny gold leaf at the end. Under that, some black riding trousers. Last, a long velvet tunic somewhat like a battle tunic, except obviously not made to be fought in. Brown, with the cup stitched on in real silver—the royal colors. Hence the apology.

I was too numb to care. The shirt was roomy and only slightly large, but the pants, tailored to a very different body, were way tight where it counted most. My wet underwear threatened to make the wedgie of the century, so I took the trousers off again, and slipped on the tunic. Its hem fell below my knees, except for the slits on the sides, but the shirt was long enough to cover me to mid-thigh. Hardly immodest, even here, when during summer many rolled their deck trousers to their knees, especially when working with water.

Still. I felt off-balance, intensely aware of a sense of intimacy in the wearing of Jehan's clothes. The cleaning frame had removed any trace of him, so they smelled like clean cloth, but that curious electricity lingered, the sensory evidence of attraction. I ran my hand down the tunic, which was cut to fit a man—the shoulders hanging over my upper arms, the front reshaped by me. The slim line of the tunic hugged my hips, which are built on the Valkyrie model. If there was a mirror in that cabin, I had not found it. Not that I'd really searched, for earlier in the day I'd only had escape on my mind.

No help for it. I looked the way I looked.

I grabbed up my wet clothes and marched out.

The yacht currently had only four crew members besides Owl: the cook, his wife and two men, one young, one older. Only one of those was in my line of sight, on watch at the helm. He gazed out to sea.

Owl and Jehan stood near the smooth, elegantly curved stern rail. When the cabin door shut behind me they turned their heads and watched me walk up the half a dozen shallow steps to the deck, the lantern light from the binnacle shining on their faces.

Is that stare universal among het males? Their gazes swept down my body, stopped twice—once north of the equator and once south—then dropped down to my feet and away. Both faces wearing inadvertent grins, a mix of appreciative and slightly embarrassed grins civilized guys show when they get caught staring.

Here's the girl part of that particular embarrassment. If one likes one of the guys, it's not annoying, it makes one feel outlined in light. Well, I do, anyway.

"The pants were too tight," I said curtly, and as soon as the words were out I knew they made everything ten times worse.

Owl turned away, one arm gripping the other arm. He was trying very hard not to laugh. I *felt* the riveted gaze of the fellow at the helm.

"You look better in that tunic than I do," Jchan said, assuming courtly manners, but his tone was genuine. Even enthusiastic. "Come into the cabin. Supper is ready."

It was a relief to follow him down the broad stairs into the stern cabin. As he stepped with his characteristic quick stride I couldn't stop myself from sneaking a peek at him from behind, that long, slim line from shoulder to— *Stop that!*

I turned my attention to the captain's cabin.

Wow, talk about a sybaritic delight. Whoever had designed this yacht didn't have a rough sailor's life in mind. There were two of everything in the fine wood carvings, shining rich gold in the light of leaded glass lanterns set in graceful golden holders. Two roses, the leaves suggestive of entwined bodies. Two lilies, same. Two dolphins leaping and sporting in repeated motif all round the bunk frame. And what a bunk. Built directly under the broad, slanting stern windows, it enabled one—or two—to lie there and look directly out at the wake glowing in the reflected golden light, foaming away and away under the glimmering stars. I leaned to look—

And felt that neon sensation again.

I whirled around, and crossed my arms when I caught Owl and Jehan staring. Not just staring but checking out my butt in that snug tunic.

Owl looked up at the ceiling as though his future lay written there. Jehan grinned, a laugh barely suppressed in the slightly husky undertone to his voice as he said, "Please sit. Tell me about your day."

Since I'd been doing my own butt-checking a minute previous, I didn't say anything. Just plunked down and thumped my elbows onto the carved table. The chairs were lyre backed, cushioned and comfortable.

"Let me see," I said cordially. "What part would that be? The nice long morning when Owl nearly suffocated me? Or would that be later, when I was still suffocating? Or, maybe after you left, when everyone was busy, the sun was sinking. I thought, great time to dive overboard. Straight into an out-flowing tide. Oops."

"What did you plan if the tide had worked for you?" Jehan poured out some wine into three goblets. "I ask because I've made a couple of ship dives myself."

"Yours being successful, of course."

He grinned over his goblet at me. "I've had more experience with remembering the flow of tides."

"Well, I didn't think I could make it all the way to shore. My idea was to reach another boat. Any boat. I could see them, or rather their running lights, or whatever they are called here. Pretend, if they pulled me out, that I'd fallen overboard on a pleasure cruise, no one noticed because of all the noise, and would someone set me ashore?"

"Except those between us and the harbor are all Randart's fleet." Jehan swept his hand all around us. "Gathering to search for the wicked pirate Zathdar."

"Oh." I sipped the wine, which was perfect, not too sweet, not too tart, a Shakespearean sonnet of subtle flavors. I took another sip, this time pausing long enough to savor it. "Wow, that's good." My annoyance melted away. "All right, so that concludes Sasharia's stupidity for the day. What about you? How did the games go, was it boring and predictable?"

"No. It was neither." Jehan began with meeting the mystery guys on the walk up to the castle. He ended his report when David and the others vanished through the back of the tent just as the searchers came through the front.

"So I made my way straight to the boat and here I am." He said to Owl, "That tall one. I know I've seen him before."

Owl hunched over his wine. "Really good with his hands? Lean? Eyes a strange shade of pale brown, almost orange in the right light?"

"That's the one."

"Didn't use a name, as I recall. Initials. MV? I think they were MV. Robin was the same age. She said she and the other sprats used to try to guess what they stood for. I remember him during that tangle with the Chwahir and those pirates out of Ghanthur, our very first cruise. Knew nothing about boats when he came aboard us, but he could fight. Don't you remember?"

Jehan leaned tiredly back in his chair, staring out at the sea. "We've had so many brushes with the Chwahir...Ghanthur...not to mention crew coming and going. That goes way back. Why, it must have been when I met you."

Owl grinned. "Just about. Yes."

They exchanged one of those looks people use when they are thinking of Past History, but before anyone could say anything the Colendi cook appeared, and with a flourish set out the dishes, delicate poached fish with fresh herbs and a dash of wine sauce, steamed carrots with a dash of another herb, and roasted little potatoes, so savory and tasty I could have eaten a plate of them.

Kaelande served more wine. His style of serving was like what I'd been taught, I noticed idly, in the more hotsy-totsy dinner houses I'd worked at, back in L.A. The same even pouring, the flick of the wrist when bringing the bottle up so there were no splashes.

I was beginning to feel a slight buzz, so I shook my head. I really did not know who was friend and who enemy, or how both could manage to be embodied in the same person. I didn't need a wine-glow to further befuddle me.

Jehan said, "That was splendid, Kaelande." He sighed. "I ate well at the tent, but that rowing seems to have woken my appetite."

"You were a few meals behind," Owl commented. "So, what now?"

Good question, I thought. *And that goes for me, too.*

Jehan frowned into his wine. "Those questions Randart asked me. I am trusting to the overwhelming number of tasks that launching a fleet entails to keep him from thinking much about what those boys saw from the barracks window. You had better vanish, all of you—"

"Wait!" I slapped my hands flat on the table. "What exactly does that mean? I'm a prisoner?"

Kaelande flicked me a look from under straight brows.

Jehan pressed his thumbs into his eyelids under his brow ridge. "You are. Not. A prisoner. But—"

Zel, Kaelande's wife, appeared in the door, her short, wispy reddish curls flying. "Biski says the fleet's getting signals."

Jehan was out of his chair fast, pausing only to pluck his spyglass from a holder. By the time I made it out the door behind Owl and Kaelande, Jehan's white hair had already vanished behind the long, elegant curve of the main sail, what we on Earth would call a Bermuda sail. He reappeared in the top next to the younger of the two men whose names I hadn't heard.

They exchanged a few quick words, snapped their glasses out, training them west on the glimmering lights barely visible to us at sea level.

Then Jehan slid down a backstay and landed lightly near us. "They're flanking us. Boats. It's got to be Randart, and he's got some excuse."

"We run?" Owl asked, but almost immediately he sniffed, looked into the direction of the breeze and shook his head.

"We fight?" Kaelande asked, and Zel rubbed her knuckles against her lips. She was a bit older than me, small, weathered, the yacht's bosun. Everyone worked the sails when needed, and obviously fought when needed as well.

Jehan sighed. "I would rather avoid loss of life. He despises the first-blood rule. If he commences a fight, it's going to be to the finish. He won't want any witnesses to tell my father the truth."

Owl grimaced. "So you think he's sprung us at last?"

"Possible. Not for certain. If he's suspicious, he will be looking for the mystery thief the boys will have described. That means the fisher's hat and the forest green tunic. The cadets saw our encounter from the barracks window, and I said I'd tried to catch a thief. Randart brought that up at the games."

Attention zapped my way.

Jehan said to me, "Well? If you want to fall into his hands, here is your chance."

"No. The only thing I am very sure of is this. I do not, and never will, trust Dannath Randart. Especially now that I know he caused Magister Glathan's death."

Jehan let out his breath in relief. "Get out of those clothes. I have to be in livery."

"Hers are wet," Owl said. "And the green will have to go over the side. If any of us wear it, we might be taken as the thief."

Zel measured me with her eyes, and slowly shook her head.

"She's a size one in the juniors, and I'm a size twelve in the Tall department." I pointed to Zel, then myself. "I can't borrow hers."

Kaelande dusted his fingers together. "But you are close to my size. Very close."

Jehan snapped his fingers. "I'll have that Zhavalieshin banner on my own bed. I don't care how wet it is, it won't look wet. The rest of whatever it is you have in that bag is innocuous enough, right?"

My heartbeat had gone into sprint mode. "Mementos collected when I was little."

Owl said to Jehan, "What's the excuse for you being here?"

"Too hot to sleep on land?"

"Stupid," two voices said at once, and Owl shook his head.

Zel sighed dramatically. "Oh, come along, I always wanted to be the girl. Can't I be the girl?"

"When's the last time there was a real girl?" Owl asked the sky.

Jehan laughed. "It seems a thousand years ago. Zel, do whatever you can to become the girl. But you have to be a painter. I told him I was visiting a painter...something with Lasva Sky Child. I don't know if he'll remember that."

Zel turned to her husband and said cryptically, but in a triumphant voice, "Told you they'd some day be useful."

"They?" came from three directions.

"Painted fans from Colend. How I met him." She patted her husband on his shoulder, sped by and vanished down the companionway to the lower deck.

Jehan faced me. "Sasha. Do you mind being a cook?"

I shrugged, feeling about five steps behind. I couldn't find the words to say I knew zip about cooking.

But he took my hapless shrug as agreement.

"Let us get ready to be taken by surprise," Jehan said.

Chapter Twenty-Four

War Commander Randart stood with one boot propped on the rail of the lead boat's bow, elbow steadied on his knee, his glass trained on the lonely craft until its elegant lines emerged from the darkness and resolved into the familiar *Dolphin*.

"That's his yacht. Close in," he said with the first evidence of satisfaction he'd shown since his arrival. His personal guard, kept on short sleep and shorter meal breaks, put their backs into their rowing, the outer boats circling outward to surround the yacht as ordered.

Not that anyone expected anything like a good fight. Not on a yacht crewed by half a dozen, if that. And captained by a prince who chased rare butterflies—ones with good figures.

The commander went back to watching through his glass. He would learn a lot by how they reacted when they discovered they were being...met.

Mentally veering between suspicion and disbelief, he'd figured that a trained military scramble after the lookout spotted the boats would at least be cause for investigation. The Prince Jehan he knew—he assumed he knew—would never remember to give that kind of order.

However, that possibility diminished with every silent lift of the oars. He could distinctly make out a couple of sailors standing at the helm, drinking from elegant goblets as they chatted. No one else in view, though there was a jerking at the single upper sail, no doubt deployed to keep the yacht pointed up into the wind instead of rolling. Randart applied his glass to the masthead. He saw starlight glinting on red hair, the silhouette a scrawny male. Sailor, nothing military. He certainly wasn't alert.

A movement below caught Randart's attention and he brought down his glass. One of the two at the helm shook an empty wine bottle, and actually peered into it. Then he lurched drunkenly around, and started. Was *that* the lookout instead? Probably. The one up on the mast was apparently asleep.

Randart smacked his glass against his thigh as the now-tiny figures ran about on the deck of the yacht in a manner no proper captain would ever tolerate, as, gradually, lights glowed to life in the open scuttles along the side, revealing a figure or two bobbing about to no apparent purpose.

No white heads in view.

His boat hooked onto the yacht, his guards not even touching their weapons. Damedran sat in the sternsheets scowling. Randart turned his way, gave him a sharp flick of the hand in command, and his nephew rose, wincing. He was probably sore, but mere physical discomfort did not matter in command. He was also tired, but so were they all.

The important thing was, if Jehan turned out to be a traitor, it had to be Damedran to defeat him.

Randart climbed up, followed by Damedran, whose breath wheezed with his effort. The war commander stepped over the rail just as the idiot emerged from the main cabin, his clothes awry, his arm around a petite red-haired woman whose clothes were also awry.

Disgust wrung Randarts innards, followed by anger. He clamped down on a reminder of the orders he'd given this

261

brainless fool not two watches ago. But then one couldn't order a prince. Everyone here knew it.

He must not misstep. He could not be in the wrong in the eyes of the men. The cost was not lives. All except Damedran were expendable. The cost was the kingdom.

"Commander Randart?" the idiot said with his usual vagueness. "Did you want a fan too?"

Randart fought against the headache he had refused to acknowledge. The pang increased to a hammer. "Fan?" he repeated, striving to keep his voice even. "What are you blather—that is, I fear I do not understand. Honor me with an explanation, your highness?"

Prince Jehan waved a hand around, then indicated the woman at his side. "Artist, paints fans. Needed one, it's so hot. Decided to buy one for my stepmother. Aren't we going back to Vadnais now that the games are done? I want to take a present to Queen Ananda."

There was Randart's cue. "I am going to sea. The king wanted you to stay put. Remember, your highness? I did tell you the king's wishes. Directly after the games."

"Of course. I remember. But we're in the harbor. Not going anywhere. I thought I might pick out a nice fan, return to shore on the morning tide. Be ready for my father's summons. Have gift for Queen Ananda. Everything in order."

It actually indicated a thought process.

Randart turned his head, summoned his personal aide with a glance, and flicked his gaze fore and aft. The man sketched a salute, beckoned to his handpicked searchers, and they began strolling the length of the yacht, not quite making their search obvious.

Jehan lifted a hand. "Come! Have a drink. Hungry?"

Randart remembered that he had not eaten since morning. And the Fool, for all his lack of brains, did supposedly have good taste in food, wine and comforts. "Yes. As it happens, I am. Damedran?" He turned to his nephew.

Damedran stood there on the deck glowering. He ached from skull to heels. His gut was indeed empty because why? Because by the time he'd limped his way into the mcss hall after the day's disaster otherwise known as the games, thcre'd been the summons to come up to the command tower and repeat everything the seniors had said about Prince Jehan's attempted arrest of the cutpurse the day before.

He hadn't remembered anything but the barest fact that it had happened, and so, by the time they'd sent someone to fetch Ban—being the most serious and trustworthy of the seniors in his group—and by the time he'd stood by while his uncle and father had asked Ban about a million stupid questions about what he'd seen (and from above! Why not ask people who'd actually been there?) it was already late. Then came the astonishing news that Wolfie, Red and the other two were all in the lazaretto. Wolfie, the strongest boy in the entire academy, had a broken leg. Given to him when he'd tried to jump a nine-year-old.

Damedran had been trying to reconcile those broken bones with his own experience when he became aware of his uncle ranting on about the fact that Prince Jehan was missing, as was the royal boat from the dock.

Come on, his uncle had said. *If it's necessary to act, you are going to need to be there.*

Well, here they were. So what kind of "act" was expected of someone who probably couldn't even grip a sword? Damedran tried to flex his stiff hands.

For all his uncle complained about the sheep's stupidity,

Damedran had discovered during a private challenge a couple of years ago that the training the idiot had gotten out west was very effective even for idiots. Damedran knew he wasn't going to win any duel, no matter what his uncle wanted. He could barely walk.

"Come," a voice said directly above Damedran, as a wine goblet was pressed into his hand. "Come sit down. You've had a rough day. I know. I've been through much the same."

Damedran looked up uncomprehending into Prince Jehan's face.

"I was hoping to talk to you," the sheep went on, not sounding like a sheep at all, though it was exactly the same calm, vague voice. "We really need some changes to the training, and who better to help me figure those out than you?"

"Who worse," Damedran said. Or he tried to say it. His voice was too hoarse.

"Now, now. One thing I learned in Marloven Hess was, you plan better after a thumping than if you win. And I had enough thumpings to prove it. Let's get some food and drink into you, first. Come into the cabin."

Damedran heard his uncle's voice, his forced joviality as he asked to be introduced to the crew, and followed the sheep down into the cabin, gulping wine as he did so. Life had turned into a dream. No, a nightmare. A place where suddenly nothing made sense.

First thing Jehan had said was, "Hide that hair!" before he sped away to make ready, and Zel had taken him at his word.

The floppy hat had vanished unnoticed, and my braids were frizzing like the Bride of Frankenstein, after the time in the quilt, followed by my salt-water conditioning treatment.

First I changed out of Jehan's clothes and into her husband's cooking outfit. At least Kaelande's clothes were roomy, as he was a stocky man. Over them I wore his apron. While I sat on an upturned bucket, Zel's small fingers undid all my braids with lightning speed. She twisted my hair (which would make the most flagrant neo-pre-Raphaelite maiden look bald) into a knot, skewered it with a sail-making tool of some kind, then yanked Jehan's knit sailor cap over it all. It hurt my scalp enough to make my head throb, but it held.

Jehan appeared at the galley door. I straightened up—carefully, as my topknot brushed the ceiling—and his face changed expression. It was the most serious I'd ever seen him.

"What? What?" Zel and I exclaimed together.

"You look just like Mathias." And before anyone could speak, Jehan yanked open one of the cupboards, pulled out a wooden container, lifted the lid. He grabbed a handful of flour and threw it in my face.

I gasped, coughing.

"They're here," Owl's voice had carried softly from the deck.

"Don't touch it," Jehan flung over his shoulder at me. To Kaelande, "She's drunk. Make it look real." He grabbed Zel's hand and the two of them scrambled up the companionway and ducked down low, almost crawling into the cabin as I stood there blinking ground wheat off my eyelashes.

And while the Randarts were busy hooking on, their boats thudding against the *Dolphin*'s hull, their boots loud as they clambered up, Kaelande explained in a running whisper what everything was in the galley, and where the food was stored, his hands gesturing so fast I was retaining maybe one thing in six.

Meanwhile he splashed wine lightly down my—his—summer shirt of blue cotton and more on the apron. He filled two goblets, pushed one into my hand. "Drink! We need wine breath."

We each took a good swallow, then stood at either side of the galley door and peered up through the hatch.

The war commander tromped past, followed by half a dozen hulking guards. Though I'd never seen any of the Randarts close up before, I recognized them immediately: huge guys, buff as all get-out, bony faces with tough-guy cheekbones. Thick black hair. The commander's was streaked with gray in a way that any Hollywood hairdresser would charge a thousand bucks to arrange. As for his expression, his armed-to-the-teeth, I'm-in-command-here walk, sinister? *That* I remembered.

Damedran looked like a high-school-aged edition of his uncle, with long and glossy hair. But he wasn't moving like his uncle, at least not now. I knew what had happened to him, but it was quite shocking to see his blackened eye, bruised jaw, one swollen ear and his slow, painful step. He might strut all over the academy like Mr. I'm-Too-Sexy-For-My-War-Tunic, but right now he looked like he longed for a week's R and R—a thousand miles away.

A touch on my shoulder. "Let's get some listerblossom into that one," Kaelande murmured, and spoke the soft words that made fire flare up on the little galley stove.

He set a kettle over that to boil and pointed at a cupboard to my right.

Everything was beautifully fitted together like the most complicated puzzle box ever invented. The cupboard door slid up revealing a row of tiny boxes, each neatly labeled with the name of an herb. He touched the listerblossom, and indicated the tea strainer.

Light from the lantern hanging over the companionway ladder was blocked. We turned around to face Randart himself.

He was tall, husky, and absolutely exuded menace, at least

standing there in the galley door, a naked knife stuck through his sash, a sword at his side and his eyes narrow slits of suspicion.

It seemed to me he gave Kaelande the briefest of glances and focused all his attention on me.

I heard the sound of the water change to a boil. Yes! It gave me something to do, and maybe even within my limited cooking ability. With shaking fingers, I tried to pinch my listerblossom into the tea strainer—the yacht lurched—I dropped some of the listerblossom. Kaelande's fingers twitched as if to take over, but he reached for his wine instead, and I took the hint, swooped up my goblet, took a swig.

With burning eyes, I finished measuring out the tea and poured the water.

Randart watched all this without speaking.

From behind came Jehan's voice. "Do I smell healer tea?"

I thought of my American accent, faked a pitiful cough as I cudgeled my brain for any kind of accent. Kaelande was from Colend—this was a prince's yacht—special chef—special accent? But I have no idea how to reproduce that lovely singsong characteristic of the Colendi, which was about as opposite of my plain L.A. accent as you could get.

Well, when in doubt, there is always Pepé Le Pew-style fake French.

Using that, I drawled, "Ze healer brew, it is for ze young mastaire."

Jehan's expression did not alter a whit. "Ah, excellent thought, Lasva."

Lasva, one of the most common names from Sartor to Colend.

Jehan took the tea. "We would like dinner. Is it possible?

You seem to have begun your off-duty libations a trifle early. Please serve in the cabin. Kaelande, will you stay on as galley aid?"

Kaelande bowed, and after a moment I bowed too, the forgotten goblet tipping in my hand. The last of the wine sloshed onto the deck. Kaelande and I reached for the cloth on the little hook over the cleaning bucket, and our heads bumped together. Kaelande laughed, kissed my shoulder, which made me whoop with surprise.

Randart turned away, rolling his eyes in disgust. From the companionway came his voice, "I don't suppose you have a reason for keeping on hire a drunken cook?"

"Ah, but she is an artist. In all ways, the kitchen and in—"

Randart retorted in a voice of acute revulsion, "Spare me. I'm surprised your entire crew is not made up of women. Pardon, your highness, *artists*."

"Do not think I have not tried to achieve that very thing! But they get bored, they move on to something else. I cannot seem to get them to stay."

"My sympathies," Randart's voice diminished, "I find are entirely with the women. So you've had that cook for a while? Didn't your father mention he'd hired a man, a Colendi?"

Their voices were mere mumbles now, drowned by the lapping of the sea against the hull, and the creaking wood.

While I listened, Kaelande swiped up the rest of the flour as well as the wine, and dunked the cloth into the bucket. The snap and flare of magic restored the cleaning cloth, which he hung up to dry. Then he gestured me into the corner, out of the way while he swiftly retrieved ingredients from this or that cupboard, his hands moving so fast they were almost a blur to my tired eyes.

"Can you cook?" he whispered.

"Mac cheese, tuna melts and PBJs," I muttered. "Uh, all those require boxes, cans, microwaves. You may as well call it magic."

"You'll have to serve. I think he remembers me." Kaelande drew a wicked knife from a nifty holder fitted above his cutting board and began chopping onions and olives. "What you are going to make is a Colendi dish called the Duchess Changes Her Mind—" He named it in Colendi, explaining that the words held two meanings. (Since it was Colendi, I wouldn't have been surprised if it had six meanings. Think French style of the *Ancien Regime*, except with the age and sophistication of the Imperial Chinese Court.)

Then he opened the spice-and-herb cupboard again, and carefully removed a single sprig of a pungent spice.

As he began mincing it with swift chops, the fresh scent threw me back in memory to my childhood.

It's so strange, how smell can be even more powerful at evoking memory than all the other senses. Even sight. Though we always think first of sight.

But I no sooner sniffed that herb than I was right back at the palace in Vadnais, a little kid again, looking up at Canary's big grin, his dashing long hair and heroic stature. Canary...my mother laughing at something he said...

My mother. A prisoner in Vadnais.

My mother's voice, *The thing about Canary was, he always had to be the rescuer, the solver, the good guy. He might even have believed what he said—*

Good guy. Canary.

There was some important thought here, but I was distracted by Kaelande, who started explaining how to cook his dish, which was a kind of very, very light crepe, into which wine-and-oil sautéed onions, tomatoes and olives were

269

wrapped. Over it some of that crumbly, delicious cheese was
sprinkled.

"Now. You must cook this together," he murmured, dashing
wine and the spice over the olives and onions in a shallow pan.
He added the tomatoes last, murmured something, gestured,
and the flame lowered. He set the shallow pan over it, and I
wedged my way in to his left. We stood there shoulder to
shoulder, and for a moment I considered that, how this guy and
I were definitely inside each other's personal space, but there
was no sense of a boundary crossed. He didn't seem to feel
anything either. No furtive looks, his touch was neutral. Yet I
supposed from the galley door we looked like a lovey-dovey pair,
so close together. Now, if Jehan had been in here—

Just the idea of being pressed up against him in this tiny
galley sent heat from my cheeks to my chitlins.

Concentrate! I began to sauté the mixture, frowning down
at the gently sizzling ingredients as I sniffed the scent.

Canary. What was happening to Mom? *Canary wouldn't
throw her into a dungeon. That wouldn't be the action of a
supposed good guy—*

That inward tug again, something important, some
connection I was missing. Canary, my mother. That wasn't it,
though it was related.

Boots clattered back and forth across the deck a few inches
above my head. I stirred the ingredients, glaring down at them
while Kaelande fashioned perfect crepes with what seemed like
preternatural speed, his arm jostling mine, his breath a soft
whistle on a plaintive series of three or four notes. No one
appeared in the galley door. Every so often Kaelande wiped
something on my apron, and even splashed me once or twice,
and I remembered I was drunk. I flicked a few drops to my face
for artistic verisimilitude, catching a brief grin from Kaelande.

I turned my thoughts inward, considering Canary and my mom, what she'd told me over the years. All the little incidents added up to this: he tried to get her on his side.

Closer, closer. Okay, there was some insight here, instinct insisted.

So keep thinking. Canary was attractive. He was attracted to Mom. He hadn't been faking it. Her so-called free-love hippie days had taught her the difference. He liked her, was attracted...needed to be the good guy...

Why is this important? Argh! I stirred vigorously. Instinct was poinking and prodding at me now. But why? I wished I had not drunk that wine.

All right, think it through again. Canary, pretending to be the good guy. Canary, attracted to my mother. Wanting her on his side, and so he used her attraction. Heck, he used his own attraction. He used his looks, his charm, said what people wanted to hear, did everything he could to try to get people to buy into his plans, and see him as the good guy... *Almost there—*

Canary and Mom. And here I was with his son. Who was doing his best to get me to buy into his plans. Meanwhile lying to everyone. Even his pirates didn't know the truth about him.

So the question now is, how much is he lying to me?

That was it. I grimaced down at the golden onions in my shallow pan. That was a nasty one. *So face it.* How much is Jehan Jervaes Merindar using my own attraction—and his to me—to seduce me if not into his bed, into his plans?

"It looks like it's done," Kaelande whispered.

I started. I'd been standing there with the wooden spatula in the air, and hastily gave the mixture a guilty stir. Luckily the flame had been too low for it to burn.

He took the pan, dashed an even portion of the mixture onto each crepe, wrapped them with nimble fingers, laid out the crepes on plates (lined up along a narrow board that folded down, so he could do six at once), poured in the filling, rolled the crepes, added a spray of the tiny grapes. "Can you serve?"

I grinned. "I can't cook, but boy howdy can I serve." As his eyes widened, I stashed the plates up my arm in classic waitress carry, hooked four wine goblets with the fingers of the other hand, and with my thumb grabbed up the square wine bottle.

He saluted wryly and I eased my way up and onto the deck, steadying myself for a moment against the rail. I was acutely aware of myself standing there in the clothing of a man I didn't know before yesterday. Here I was, Sasharia Zhavalieshin, pretending to be a cook, and all to support the false role of someone who might be an enemy.

How long was I going to go along with his changing stories, I wondered, leaning my hip against the carving of laughing dolphins running along the rail.

Until he kisses me? And then what?

I cannot tell you how much I hated the thought that he had it all planned, that the dangerous evening would end with the hero prince grabbing the dashing princess for love's triumphant kiss—

He wouldn't. Would he?

I glared down at the plates on my arm and remembered what I was supposed to be doing. At my current rate of travel the food would be congealed into a nasty mess before I even reached the cabin.

The deck was full of big men moving about with either covert or overt purpose, none paying me the least heed after a disinterested glance. Dannath Randart vanished into the cabin

I'd used, but my stuff was gone, the gear bag over the side (the green tunic inside it as ballast), the mementos and coins stashed in Zel's things.

I descended the few broad steps into the cabin. Jehan and Damedran sat with their heads together at the table, Jehan writing things down as they talked in quick, low voices.

Damedran's wary body language, his reluctant agreements to Jehan's softly murmured questions, were easing as he sipped at the mug of listerblossom.

Zel lounged on the bed like an odalisque, playing with half-circles of myriad colors. A step toward her and the half-circles resolved into open fans, laid like rare flowers against the splendid barbarity of my Zhavalieshin coverlet. Some of the fans were made of lace and thin streamers of ribbon, others a kind of rice paper, gilt in exquisite patterns, and painted. Subtle fragrances arose, carried on the gentle breeze from the open stern windows.

She glanced up at me, then over her shoulder, pursing her lips.

I set the wine bottle on the table, the glasses next to it.

Jehan was saying, oh so persuasively, "...completely rethink the infighting—"

"But Master Grescheg wins every competition with Obrin and those fellows from Alsais—"

"Competition. Perhaps there is a difference between hand-to-hand grappling for a medal and fighting in the street? Think about today. That tall fellow broke competition rules, didn't he?"

"He did. I didn't call 'em on it because it seemed cowardice—"

"We all saw that, and it testifies to your credit. But consider this. Would you have him at your back in the street? Or if Norsunder rode over the border in force?"

"Norsunder?" Damedran looked doubtful.

I'd backed up to listen, the plates still stacked on my arm.

"It could happen. You won't remember the Siamis days, it was just before you were born. Did anyone tell you about how frightened people were? The talk of Detlev, Siamis's uncle? We don't know much about him, except that those who held his leash are far worse. And if they find a way to cross into the world..."

"Yes," Damedran cut in, his brow a scowl line. "I would want them at my back in any kind of fight. The grappling, and the archery. Nobody could beat that little runt. Not even our best master."

The voices had risen slightly, one with the slightly nasal intonations of late adolescence, gruff with dislike and distrust, the other more tenor, controlled, with that faint humor.

He's trying to win Damedran. What role was he playing now?

"And you saw how he shot. The Marloven bow drill is tedious, that I grant, however the form is unbeaten throughout the world, and you saw the evidence today..."

Under how many layers was the truth buried? I stared down at Zel's fans, each a treasure. She must have seen my admiration in my face, for she smiled proudly. Then a glance past me. Her smile vanished. She lay back in a languishing pose.

Boot heels rang on the deck, and the voices stopped. Focus shifted as Dannath Randart filled the doorway to the cabin. He took us all in with a single glance, frowning when he spied the paper before Jehan. He sat, abruptly reaching for it. His hand stopped partway, and Jehan offered it to him with a courteous air.

Randart glanced at it for about five seconds, as I approached the table.

Randart slewed around, watching as I dealt the plates in my very best serving manner. The narrow-eyed suspicion tightening his eyes eased a fraction more each time I snuck a peek at him. By the time I finished playing sommelier with the wine, complete down to the pouring flick of the wrist, he had clearly filed me in the "servant" category, and thereafter ignored me.

The silence stretched into tension, which made distinct the soft slapping of the water against the hull, the creak of wood, the click and ting of silver utensils on porcelain plates. The three ate, the boy and the prince waiting for the war commander to speak.

The power of the moment lay with him, though it was not his ship, but the men up on the deck obeyed him and only him.

Right now the Randarts are the only ones here not faking a role.

Finally Randart leaned forward and tapped the paper. "What's this?"

Jehan said, "My suggestions for new training. Old training to be adapted to new. We all think our own experience best. Why not try what I learned out west? Combine it with what we have here in the east."

"We can't do worse, Uncle. I saw that today," Damedran put in, surly and defensive.

Dannath Randart's slack-lidded eyes flicked from nephew to royal heir and back again. Impossible to tell whether the silence meant surrender or threat. Maybe he didn't know himself. He opened his palm toward Damedran. "Very well. Do what you like. I have to take ship tomorrow. I have pirates to find and destroy." He picked up his fork, then shot a glowering assessment at Zel. Ahah, he was reassessing her status. Would she be invited to eat? There was that extra plate, congealing fast.

She lay curled up on the bed, the two gold-framed lanterns making a fiery aureole of her wispy ringlets. She uncoiled her feet and stood, drifting in a deliberately provocative, swaying walk, to lean against Jehan's chair, one of her hands playing with one of her fans, twirling it, swirling it idly.

"Sit down and eat, my dear," Jehan invited, pointing to the fourth plate. "It's getting cold. And you know how Lasva threatens to go back to Colend if we do not treat her food with respect."

"I'm not hungry now," Zel said in a crooning voice. She smiled up at me. "The Colendi are forgiving, I know. I will paint you a fan, Lasva."

"Yiss. Iz gud," I sounded more like a TV Russian spy than a TV Frenchwoman, I realized too late.

Randart's face crimped in disgust. He said nothing, though. Just dug in, rapidly finishing his crepe.

No one spoke as they finished the meal. For a time the only sounds were those of the ship and of the rising wind, the water. Once I moved into view to pour more wine. Jehan mouthed the words *thank you*, though he kept his gaze unswervingly on his guests. At his side Zel leaned, one finger twining in his hair in a way that made my insides squeeze, so I looked away. The uncle ignored me as if the wine poured itself.

When his plate was clean he stood. "I have ordered the mages to make you another gold message box, your highness. Do try not to lose it. I'll return now, and send a message to your father. If you discover anything you wish to tell me before morning, I can be found in the command tower before we depart on the morning tide."

He marched out, his boots thumping up the stairs to the deck, where he gave an abrupt command.

That caused the force of brown tunics to line up and climb down into the boats, a kind of reverse-play of their arrival. I wondered if *they'd* gotten any dinner before the summons to make this trip. From the mutters of some of them and the black looks sent their commander's way, it didn't seem likely.

The crew doused the yacht's deck lights. The ship faded to darkness, except for the golden glow in the cabin, and faint light from the hatchway and the galley beyond.

Jehan moved to the rail to watch them begin to toil their long way back to the harbor through an increasingly choppy sea. Zel and her husband joined him on one side, the two of them holding hands, whispering and occasionally laughing, the relieved laughter of danger passed by. Owl drifted up on Kaelande's other side.

The other two crew were at their posts, one on the mast, one at the helm.

Since Jehan had no one at his left I joined him, peering out to sea as I absently pulled off the knit cap, and yanked free that horrible thing binding my hair so tightly. As there were no lights, I figured we had to be invisible from the boats by now. Even starlight was gone, covered by thick clouds.

The husband and wife moved off, talking in low voices. The last I heard was Zel offering to help dunk the dishes and tidy the galley.

Owl vanished down the hatchway, yawning.

Randart's lights were nearly diminished behind the rising waves when a long purple branch of lightning split the sky, and rain struck with breathtaking suddenness, on us, on the sea, and on the departing rowboats.

We were drenched in moments, but behind us lay warmth, food, shelter. The commander and his force had a very long row ahead of them.

"Perfect end to a disastrous day," Jehan said.

Lightning flared again, reflecting in his eyes so they shone like sapphire and burnished his hair to silver. He smiled straight into my eyes, and laughed.

I smiled back as my hair streamed into the wind—forgetting Mom, and Canary, and roles, and lies, and all the distresses of the day. For that moment I was proud and triumphant and caught by Jehan's gaze, so brilliant in the flare of lightning, and I laughed too.

I laughed until his hands caught me by the shoulders, and rain glittered on his eyelashes as soft lips met mine, warm and tasting of sweet wine, and then my thoughts unribboned, my muscles unlaced, and I couldn't think at all, at all.

About the Author

To learn more about Sherwood Smith, please visit www.sherwoodsmith.net. Send an email to Sherwood at Sherwood@sff.net or join her LiveJournal group to join in the fun with other readers at

http://community.livejournal.com/athanarel/profile.

GREAT
cheap
fun

Discover eBooks!

THE FASTEST WAY TO GET THE HOTTEST NAMES

Get your favorite authors on your favorite reader, long before they're
out in print! Ebooks from Samhain go wherever you go, and work with
whatever you carry—Palm, PDF, Mobi, and more.

Samhain
Publishing
Ltd

WWW.SAMHAINPUBLISHING.COM

LaVergne, TN USA
23 December 2010
210021LV00001B/149/P

9 781605 041704